THE
PORKCHOPPERS
Ross Thomas

"Thomas has written . . . [an] exposé of the high-level
maneuvering (all the way to the White House) that is so
much a part of American politics—and the operation of
a big labor union is nothing if not politics. . . . Thomas
sounds like a man who has been around."

—*New York Times Book Review*

THE
PORKCHOPPERS

Ross Thomas

PERENNIAL LIBRARY

HARPER & ROW, Publishers

New York, Cambridge, Philadelphia, San Francisco
London, Mexico City, São Paulo, Singapore, Sydney

For Warren Bayless

A hardcover edition of this book was published by William Morrow &
Company, Inc. It is here reprinted by arrangement with William Morrow
& Company, Inc.

First PERENNIAL LIBRARY edition published 1984.

Library of Congress Cataloging in Publication Data

Thomas, Ross, 1926-
  The porkchoppers.

  Reprint. Originally published: New York: Morrow, 1972.
  "Perennial Library."
  I. Title.
PS3570.H58P6 1984   813'.54   84-47675
ISBN 0-06-080727-X (pbk.)

84 85 86 87 88 10 9 8 7 6 5 4 3 2 1

PORKCHOPPER *n* [*pork chops,* labor-union slang for economic benefits + *-er*]: a labor-union officer regarded by fellow unionists as motivated chiefly by self-interest.

—*Webster's Third New International Dictionary*

THE
PORKCHOPPERS

1

They were old hundred-dollar bills, a little limp now, even a little greasy, and one of them had a rip in it that somebody had neatly mended with a strip of Scotch tape. There had been seventy-five of them to begin with, but by the time they reached Truman Goff only fifty were left—fifty one-hundred-dollar bills, $5,000, and exactly the price that Truman Goff had decided to charge that year.

It had taken three weeks for the $5,000 to reach Goff. This was due only in part to the chronic whimsy of the Post Office. The major delay was caused by the five other persons who had dipped into the original $7,500 sum, each taking out two or three and even ten of the bills for himself before resealing what were left and mailing them off to the next address along with the white, three-by-five-inch card that bore the name that was printed with pencil in what most newspapers like to describe as crude block letters.

First stop for the $7,500 and the penciled name had been the fifth-story, one-room office of a fifty-two-year-old private detective in downtown Minneapolis who specialized in what he always described to clients as electronic surveillance. The detective's name was Karl Syftestad and most of his clients were middle-aged husbands who thought, or just hoped, that Syftestad could slip around and get something on their wives that would hold up in divorce court.

In good years, Syftestad's agency in the Benser Building netted him about $9,000 that he dutifully reported to the state and federal tax people. He usually managed to

1

make another, unreported nine or ten thousand for arranging what he regarded as introductions.

For $300 he could introduce you to someone who would sell you a new Cadillac or Continental for only $3,500, if you weren't too concerned about the validity of its Texas title. For beatings, Syftestad charged $500 and always assured customers that the prospective victim "will sure as shit know he's had a good stompin." The beatings were administered by a Minneapolis fireman during his off-duty hours. Syftestad and the fireman divided the $500 fee equally.

The letter containing the $7,500 was delivered to Syftestad at 11 A.M. on August 14, a Monday. The only other mail was a junk piece from a wholesale camera dealer in St. Louis that Syftestad read carefully before tossing into his wastebasket. He read all his mail carefully because he didn't get much.

There wasn't anything to read in the brown, oblong, manila envelope that contained the $7,500 other than the name penciled on the white card. Syftestad recognized the name and he felt that he should somehow give it its due so he pursed his lips and whistled a couple of notes off-key. Then he counted the money.

It was the seventh time in four years that Syftestad had received a letter like the one that now lay on his desk. The first one that came had contained only $5,000—and a penciled name. It had arrived two days after Syftestad had received a phone call from a man who identified himself as Bill, Just Bill.

"You're gonna like what I'm gonna tell you," the man who claimed that his name was Just Bill had said.

"What am I gonna like?"

"We're gonna let you make a couple of bills every now and then for doing nothing."

"What's doing nothing?"

"Doing nothing's doing nothing. You'll get an envelope with some money in it. All you gotta do is take out your two bills, find another envelope, and send what's left along to an address I'm gonna give you. You'll have to buy your own stamps."

"That's all?" Syftestad had asked.

"That's all. That's absolutely all. Like I said, it's for doing nothing."

"Yeah, well, I don't know——"

"Syftestad."

"Yeah?"

"We like you. We really do. We don't wanta see anything happen to you and the reason we chose you is because we think you know how easy it is for something to happen to somebody. Am I getting through?"

"Yeah," Syftestad had said. "Kind of."

"Well, that's fine then. It's only just sort of playing post office. That's all it is really."

"You're sure that's all?"

"Why should I lie to you?"

"Why shouldn't you? Everybody else does."

The man who called himself Bill had chuckled in a sad, tinny, humorless sort of way, as though he wanted to demonstrate that he knew how to do it. "Well, there's no funny business on our part and I'm sure that there's not gonna be any funny business on your part, if you follow me and I think that you do."

"Uh-huh. I follow you."

"Okay then, that's fine. Now you got something to write with?"

"I got something."

Over the telephone the man who called himself Bill slowly had given Syftestad a name and address in East St. Louis, Illinois. It was a simple address and the name was even simpler, but Bill told Syftestad to read it back twice. When he was satisfied that Syftestad had everything right, Bill had said, "Just one more thing."

"What?"

"Don't lose it."

Then Bill had hung up and Syftestad never heard from him again——except indirectly through the letters that contained the money and the penciled names. The first letter had contained $6,000. The next three rose to $6,500, then to $7,000 where they had remained until the seventh and last letter, which contained $7,500.

Because Syftestad was an ignorant man, the penciled names that the previous six letters contained had meant nothing to him. If he had been an assiduously careful reader of *The Minneapolis Tribune,* he might have seen, but probably not remembered, one or two or even three of the names during the course of a year, but they would have been buried in short, dull stories from AP or UPI about something fairly high-minded and therefore uninteresting that had happened in Los Angeles or New York or Chicago or Washington.

But Syftestad didn't read newspapers much anymore, except for an occasional glance at the sports pages. He got whatever news he thought he needed from television, which was where most people got theirs, and the six names that had come across his desk during the past four years were not the kind that made network newscasts.

So Syftestad was content with his ignorance because he was smart enough to believe that he knew why a stranger would entrust him to send large sums of money to an address in East St. Louis. I sure as hell wouldn't want to see my name written down on one of those little white cards, Syftestad thought, whenever he thought about it at all, which wasn't often, because there wasn't enough money in it to think about it often and besides, it was kind of unpleasant, and Syftestad didn't like to think about anything unpleasant if he could help it, which he usually could.

But the name that was written on the card that now lay before him on his desk meant something because it belonged to a man who hired people to see that it occasionally got on the network newscasts. The people that he hired to do this were fairly successful because the position that the man held was sufficiently important to command some national interest. Not much perhaps, but some.

Syftestad poked the card with his right forefinger. The name on the card meant money, if he could figure the angle. For a moment or two Syftestad grew mildly enthusiastic about the possibilities. The enthusiasm waned when he remembered the man who had called himself Bill over the telephone. You're not smart enough to figure an angle against people like that, he told himself. You're just smart enough to play post office. So he sighed, took two one-hundred-dollar bills from the pile in front of him, folded

4

them and put them in his trouser pocket, found an envelope, and used a ball-point pen to print the name and address of the man in East St. Louis, Illinois, the name and address that had been given to him four years ago.

As he dropped the envelope down the mail chute, Karl Syftestad told himself that he would start reading the paper more carefully during the next few weeks. It might be real interesting, he decided, like reading about something that you had something to do with.

2

Three days later, on August 17, a Thursday, the envelope that the Minneapolis private detective had dropped in the mail chute was delivered to a corner bar at the intersection of Margate Avenue and Winder Street in East St. Louis, Illinois, which meant that the letter had found its way to the heart of a professionally tough neighborhood in what people who are usually up on such things regard as a professionally tough town.

The corner bar was called just that, The Corner Bar, by its owner and proprietor, Julius C. Eames, who was black, a little over 214 pounds, and who had won the place eight years before in a crap game over in Joplin, Missouri, by making a four the hard way. Eames hadn't gambled much since, because he was convinced that he had used up whatever luck the Lord had allotted him that night in Joplin when he had walked out of the game with the bar and $5,469 in cash. Now he contented himself with selling a fair amount of Dixie Belle gin, Smirnoff vodka, Thunderbird wine, and Falstaff beer. He also sold quite a bit of Seagram's Seven, but not much Scotch.

The Corner Bar earned him a living, but not what

could be called a good one, so he supplemented his income by helping his customers out with small loans. He lent them $50 on Friday and they paid him back $60 a week later. Eames usually had about $1,500 out on loan and there weren't many defaulters, partly because most of his customers genuinely appreciated the service and partly because all of them knew about the stickup.

The stickup had happened four years before, just after Eames had received a phone call from the man who called himself Just Bill and who had wanted Eames to provide much the same service that Syftestad had agreed to provide in Minneapolis. Eames had refused, a little curtly. Three days later a tall, slender brown youth had walked into The Corner Bar, aimed a .22 Iver Johnson target revolver at Eames, and demanded money. Eames had nodded thoughtfully and then started around the bar, heading for the slender youth who shot him three times before Eames reached him, took away the .22, and broke the youth's neck with the edge of his left hand.

When Eames got out of the hospital nine days later he was something of a neighborhood hero. He also received another call from the man called Bill.

"We sorta liked the way you handled that kid we sent around to see you," Bill had said. "The way we heard it, you done a real neat job."

"Say you sent him?"

"That's right. Of course, he was just a kid. We coulda sent around somebody a little older. With a bigger gun. You know what I mean."

"Uh-huh," Eames had said. "I do exactly. Maybe you better tell me again just what it is you want me to do."

So Bill had told him and now Eames, for the seventh time, was concentrating mightily as he sat in the back booth of The Corner Bar and laboriously printed out the name of a man who lived in Buffalo, New York. Eames didn't bother to read the name that was penciled on the white card.

The man who lived in Buffalo had been born there thirty-six years before and now ran an Italian restaurant that he had inherited from his father, Frank Martelli, who had died in 1959 while sitting peacefully in his living room. The undertaker hadn't been able to do much with Frank Martelli, because of the way the shotgun pellets had taken away most of his head, so the casket had been closed at the funeral. The younger Martelli, who was called Frank Junior by everyone although his real name was Enrico, took over the restaurant after his father died and because he kept his mouth shut, his father's former business associates let him alone most of the time.

When Frank Junior got the letter from Eames on August 21, a Monday, he took five of the one-hundred-dollar bills, stuffed them away in a pocket, and quickly placed the remaining sixty-six bills in a brown envelope that he had already addressed to a box number in Jack, Oklahoma. Frank Junior recognized the name that was penciled on the white card and crossed himself. Since the death of his father, he had turned to his religion, becoming almost devout but not so much so that he ever told anyone about the penciled name on the white card, not even his priest.

The post office in Jack, Oklahoma, was in the general store that old man Wimple had owned and run for forty-two years. When the letter from Buffalo, New York, arrived he put it in that new fella's box. That new fella was using the name Bryan Simpson and he had lived with his wife on a 160-acre farm about nine miles out of Jack for six years now, running a few head of white-faced cattle, but not growing anything except blackjack oaks as far as most folks could see. Everyone around Jack thought that Simpson's wife had money because he was sure a shiftless sort and drank a lot to boot. He also looked a little Indian, which—in that part of Oklahoma—was only something to comment on, but nothing to get upset and bothered about.

Simpson didn't open the letter until he got back to his farm. He counted the money first and put six of the bills aside for himself. He glanced at the white card and grinned when he recognized the name. It was sure going to be something to watch on TV, he thought. After he addressed the envelope and sealed its contents of sixty one-hundred-dollar bills and the white card with the penciled name, he went to the closet and took out a small gray cashbox and unlocked it.

He put the six one-hundred-dollar bills in with the rest of the money in the box, which was what was left from the $126,000 that he had taken from the L Street Branch of the Riggs National Bank all by himself one summer afternoon in Washington a little over six years ago. He then got in his Chevrolet pickup and drove 81 miles to Ft. Smith where he mailed the letter.

From Ft. Smith, Arkansas, the money and the white card flew to Los Angeles where they were delivered on August 29, a Tuesday, to Miss Joan Littlestone who lived in an apartment in the 900 block on Hilldale a block or so down from Sunset. Miss Littlestone was known to be bright, pleasant, and scrupulously fair with customers and employees alike. She supervised six girls and was highly respected in the trade in which she had been engaged, in one capacity or another, for thirty-seven of her fifty-three years. When the man called Just Bill had telephoned her, she had readily agreed to do what he wanted her to do because it was her nature to do what men wanted her to do, no matter how bizarre. The fee of $1,000 per forwarding seemed ridiculously high to her, but she hadn't questioned it. She had learned long ago that some men liked to pay more than they should; that, in fact, some men liked to be cheated and, as always, Miss Littlestone tried to be accommodating whenever she could and when the risk was low. Or at least not too high.

She took ten of the bills for herself and then carefully printed the name and address of the man who lived in Baltimore on the envelope. She glanced at the card that came with the money, but only the first name that was penciled on it stayed in her memory. Surnames hadn't proved too useful, or reliable, in Miss Littlewood's business and she seldom bothered with them.

It took six days for the letter to travel from Los Angeles to Baltimore by air because of a minor mix-up at O'Hare field in Chicago. The letter was waiting for Truman Goff when he arrived at his three-bedroom tract house in West Baltimore after putting in a full day at his job as produce manager of a Safeway store in the inner

8

core of the city where the pilferage rate kept rising at a steady, almost predictable rate.

Goff drove an Oldsmobile Toronado, which was rather fancy for a supermarket produce manager, but not so much so that anyone would wonder where he had got the money. They would ascribe its ownership to self-indulgence and assume that it wasn't paid for anymore than theirs were paid for and like theirs, probably wouldn't be until it wore out and Truman Goff would have to see what he could trade it in for.

When Goff got home that Monday evening in early September his ten-year-old daughter, Miranda, was watching television as usual. It was nearly nine o'clock because the Safeway where he worked stayed open until eight.

Goff said how are you to his daughter who replied, hi, Daddy, and he went on into the kitchen and said, what's new, to his wife as he opened the refrigerator and took out a can of National beer.

"Not much," his wife said. "You got a letter. It came in the mail today."

"Who from?"

"I don't open your mail."

"I just thought it might be on the outside. A return address."

"I didn't see any."

"Well, where is it?"

"Where the mail always is. On the dining table. When you want to eat?"

"When I finish my beer," Goff said. "What're we gonna have?"

"Those pork chops you brought home Saturday. I didn't put 'em in the freezer so we'd better eat 'em. Pork don't keep."

"Yeah, I know," Goff said, and carrying his beer went from the kitchen into the dining area and picked up the manila envelope. He thought he knew what it was, but he wasn't sure. It could be a come-on for dirty pictures, he thought. They sometimes send the stuff out in plain envelopes like that, hand-addressed and all.

Goff put the envelope in his pocket and went into what

9

his wife called the spare bedroom and what he called the den. It held a studio couch that could be made into a double bed, a maple kneehole desk, his wife's sewing machine, a small chest of drawers, and a four-shelf bookcase that was filled mostly with paperback westerns except for a big Bible and a three-year-old copy of *Who's Who*.

After putting his can of beer down on the desk, Goff opened the letter by ripping the flap with his forefinger. He didn't smile when he saw the money inside. He counted the fifty one-hundred-dollar bills quickly onto the desk, then folded them once and buttoned them away in his left hip pocket. He looked at the card and then up at the ceiling, mouthing the name silently until he was sure he had it right. He tore the card into tiny pieces and went down the hall to the bath where he flushed the pieces down the toilet.

When he came out of the bath, his wife called to him from the kitchen. "You ready now?"

"In a minute," he called back.

"It's gonna get cold."

"In a minute, goddamnit," he yelled and went back into the den, took the copy of *Who's Who* from the bookcase, turned to the C's, and read all about the man that he was going to kill.

3

Donald Cubbin looked as if he should be president of something, possibly of the United States or, if his hangover wasn't too bad, of the world. Instead, he was president of an industrial labor union whose headquarters was in

Washington and whose membership was up around 990,000, depending on who did the counting.

Cubbin's union was smaller than the auto workers and the teamsters, but a little larger than the steelworkers and the machinists, and since the first two were no longer in the AFL-CIO just then, it meant that he was president of the largest union in the establishment house of labor.

Cubbin had been president of his union since the early fifties, falling into the job after the death of the Good Old Man who was its first president and virtual founder. The union's executive board, meeting in special session, had appointed the secretary-treasurer to serve as president until the next biennial election. As secretary-treasurer, Cubbin had spent nearly sixteen years carrying the Good Old Man's bag. After he was appointed president, he quickly learned to like it and soon discovered that there were a number of persons around who were anxious and eager to carry his bag, and this he particularly liked. So he had held on to the job for nearly nineteen years, enjoying its perquisites that included a salary that had climbed steadily to its present level of $65,000 a year, a fat, noncontributory pension scheme, a virtually nonaccountable expense allowance, a chauffeured Cadillac as big as a cabinet member's, and large, permanent suites in the Madison in Washington, the Hilton in Pittsburgh, the Warwick in New York, the Sheraton-Blackstone in Chicago, and the Beverly-Wilshire in Los Angeles.

Over the years Cubbin had faced only two serious challenges from persons who wanted his job. The first occurred in 1955 when a popular, fast-talking vice-president from Youngstown, Ohio, thought that he had detected a groundswell and promptly announced his candidacy. The Youngstown vice-president had received some encouragement, but more important, some money from another international union that occasionally dabbled in intramural politics. The fast-talking vice-president and Cubbin fought a noisy, almost clean campaign from which Cubbin emerged with a respectable two-to-one margin and a permanent grudge against the president of the union that had meddled in what Cubbin had felt to be a sacrosanctly internal matter.

11

Cubbin was a little older in 1961—he was fifty-one by then—when for the second time he detected signs of opposition. This time they came from a man that he himself had hired, the union's director of organization who, after getting his degree at Brown in economics, took a job as a sweeper in a Gary, Indiana, plant (an experience he still had nightmares about) and who possessed, along with his degree, the conviction that he was destined to be the forerunner of a new and vigorous breed of union leadership, the kind that would be on an equal intellectual footing with management.

Cubbin could have fired him, of course. But he didn't. Instead he placed a call to the White House. A week later the director of organization was awakened at six-thirty by a call from Bobby Kennedy who told him that the President needed him to be an assistant secretary of state. Not too many people were saying no to the Kennedys in 1961, certainly not the director of organization for Cubbin's union who was then only thirty-six and terribly excited about being chosen to scout for the New Frontier. Later, when Cubbin had had a few drinks, he liked to tell cronies about how he had buried his opposition in Foggy Bottom. He did an excellent mimicry of both Bobby Kennedy and the director of organization.

Most actors are good mimics and Donald Cubbin probably should have been an actor. His father had been one. So had his mother until their touring company collapsed in Youngstown in 1910. Cubbin's father took the first job he could get, which was in a steel mill. It was only temporary, until the child was born, but the child, Donald, arrived six months later along with new debts and somehow Bryant Cubbin never did get out of the steel mill, not until he died of pneumonia during a layoff in 1932 when his son was twenty-one years old.

Donald Cubbin was in Pittsburgh when his father died. There weren't any jobs in Pittsburgh in 1932, or any place else, so Donald Cubbin was attending business school during the day and acting in amateur theatricals at night. When his father died, Cubbin had a lead part in Sidney Howard's eight-year-old play *They Knew What They Wanted*. He played Joe, the roving Wobbly.

The amateurs charged 15 cents admission and their audiences were small, partly because 15 cents was a lot of money in 1932 and partly because most of the amateur actors were awful, although they somehow had enough judgment to select fairly well-written plays.

In the small audience that night was Bernie Ling, a twenty-seven-year-old, third-string publicity man for Warner Brothers who was in Pittsburgh to see what kind of free space he could get for a new and terrible film that could lose his studio a lot of money. Ling had only contempt for motion pictures, but he liked plays. They had real people saying real words and Ling could lose himself in the story while still noting with pleasure the nuances of gesture and diction and what he liked to refer to as stage presence.

When the twenty-one-year-old Donald Cubbin strode out onto the stage, Ling stirred in his seat a little. It was not Cubbin's looks that made him stir. There was a surplus of good-looking youngsters in Hollywood. There always would be. But still, the kid was all right, about six foot tall, not too heavy, maybe 160 or 170, with a hell of a good head of hair, black, straight and thick, and features that a tough chin ransomed from prettiness. He would age well, Ling thought, and then decided that there was still something else, some other quality that had struck him. Not the voice, although it was good, almost too good, a deep, hard baritone equipped with what seemed to be natural projection that rolled it out over the audience. Somebody had taught him that, Ling decided before settling back to watch the play and search for the word that would describe just what it was that the kid had. By the end of the second act Ling thought he knew what it was. Dignity. The kid had dignity, the kind that is usually the small reward of those who at age forty or fifty, having scraped at the bottoms of their souls, survive the revulsion and are never thereafter much dismayed by the awfulness of others.

Whatever it was, Ling thought it was salable so he left the play before the third act was over and took a taxi to the all-night Postal Telegraph office and sent a telegram to his uncle who was a producer at Warner Brothers.

13

"SPOTTED POSSIBLE YOUNG MALE LEAD PITTSBURGH STOP STRONGLY URGE SCREENTEST BERNIE," the telegram read after Ling and the Postal Telegraph man argued for a while about whether "screentest" was one word or two. They finally agreed that it was one word after Ling gave the man two tickets to the rotten picture that was opening at a downtown theater the following day.

Donald Cubbin didn't meet Bernie Ling until two days later, after he had returned from his father's funeral in Youngstown, bringing his mother back with him because she had no other place to go. Between them, Cubbin and his mother had $21.35. He moved her into the room next to his at the boardinghouse and then took the streetcar to the business school where he told Asa Pettigrew, its owner, director, and founder, that he was quitting.

"Can't you hang on for three weeks until you get your certificate?" Pettigrew asked.

"No, I can't hang on. I have to get a job."

"I can't refund any of your tuition, you know."

"I know."

Considerably mollified, Pettigrew said, "Well, I got a call this morning."

"About what?"

"About a job. They want a male secretary who can do bookkeeping. It's not a regular company and it might be only temporary and the reason they want a male is that they do a lot of swearing and dirty talking."

"Where is it?" Cubbin said.

"I don't know if you want to get mixed up with this bunch. They're some kind of labor union. Probably reds."

"I need a job, Mr. Pettigrew."

"Might not last long."

"It's better than nothing."

"They'll probably be run out of town and you along with them."

"I'll have to take that chance."

"They're dirty talking. They said so themselves."

"Fine."

"Pays twelve-fifty a week."

"Good."

14

Pettigrew handed Cubbin a slip of paper. "You call this man here. Tell him I recommended you."

"Thanks, Mr. Pettigrew."

Pettigrew shrugged. "I told 'em they could get a girl for ten bucks who'd put up with their dirty talking, but they said they wanted a man, but that they didn't want any nance. You know what a nance is, don't you?"

Cubbin nodded. "I've got a pretty good idea."

He got the job, of course. The Good Old Man himself hired Cubbin in the shabby, one-room office that was located in the heart of what they later called Pittsburgh's golden triangle. "Let's see what you can do, son," he said.

Cubbin nodded, sat down in a chair, and took out his pencil and a stenographer's notebook.

"Dear Sir and Brother," the Good Old Man began. He was not so old then, not quite forty-five in 1932, but already he dictated his letter as if delivering a short speech to an audience of a thousand or more, reaching his roaring peroration in the next to last paragraph and ending each letter with a heartfelt and whispered "Fraternally yours."

Cubbin took it all down in Pitman at around eighty words per minute and typed it up on the office L. C. Smith at a steady sixty-five words per minute. After the Good Old Man read it, he looked up at Cubbin and smiled, "I don't have much education, son, but I'm not stupid. I put a couple of little grammatical errors in on purpose. You took 'em out. Why?"

"They weren't bad enough to leave in," Cubbin said.

The Good Old Man nodded. "That's a pretty fair answer," he said after a while. "You say you can also keep a simple set of books?"

"Yes, I can do that."

"All right, you're hired. Be here tomorrow at eight. You know anything about unions?"

"No."

"Good. You can learn about 'em my way."

When Cubbin got back to his boardinghouse to tell his

15

mother that he had landed a job, he found a tall, thin young man waiting for him on the front porch. The tall, thin young man introduced himself as "Bernie Ling of Warner Brothers."

Cubbin heard the Warner Brothers but discounted it as part of some kind of a sales pitch. "I'm sorry," he said, starting to brush by Ling, "but I can't afford one right now."

"I'm not selling," Ling said. "I'm making you an offer."

"Of what?"

"A screen test. In L.A."

"Bullshit," Cubbin said and started past Ling again.

"Here," Ling said, taking a telegram from his pocket. "Read this."

The telegram was from Ling's producer uncle, a man who enjoyed some partly manufactured notoriety for his unwillingness to squander words. The telegram read, "BUS FARE ONLY LOVE FISHER."

"I don't get it," Cubbin said.

"Fisher. That's Arnold Fisher, a producer. My uncle. At Warner Brothers. I'm with their publicity department. I saw you the other night in the play. I wired my uncle and they're willing to pay your bus fare to L.A, for a test. No shit."

"You saw me?" Cubbin said, thinking a message to his father: Why did you have to go and die and be out of a job?

"I think you might make it out there," Ling said. "I mean really make it."

Cubbin slowly handed back the telegram. "Sorry, but it's just not possible right now."

"Christ, all you have to do is get on a bus."

There was a moment for Cubbin when it was all possible, better than possible, it had all happened, the bus ride, the screen test, the instant fame, and the gigantic salary. He had it all for one impossibly fine moment until he remembered his mother, the new widow, waiting alone upstairs, waiting for the only person she knew in Pittsburgh to come home and tell her how she was going to live for the rest of her life. I'll send for you, Mother, he thought, but told Bernie Ling, "My father's just died and I can't leave my mother."

"Oh, well, that's tough. I'm sorry."

"Maybe later when things get straightened out."

"Sure," Ling said. "Here's my card. When you get things settled drop me a line and we'll try to work something out."

"You say you really think there's a chance?"

"I never wire my uncle unless I think there's a damn good one."

"Well, I hardly know how to thank you—"

"Forget it. No, hell, don't forget it. Drop me a line instead."

"Sure," Cubbin said, "I'll do that. As soon as everything's settled."

But he didn't and six months later Ling left Hollywood for a job with a newly formed New York advertising agency where after a time he grew rich enough to help back a few plays that had depressingly short runs.

As for Donald Cubbin, there wasn't a day in his life that he didn't remember his front-porch conversation with Bernie Ling and the decision that he had made. And there wasn't a day in his life that he didn't regret it.

The six-place, twin-jet Lear 24 bearing Donald Cubbin and his entourage of four had just left Hamilton, Ontario, and was pointing itself toward O'Hare International in Chicago when Fred Mure, having waited until his boss had finished reading the entertainment section of the newspaper, which was the first section he always read, leaned across to tap Cubbin on the shoulder.

"Yeah?"

"Chicago in an hour. Not bad, huh?"

God, he's an idiot, Cubbin thought. But he nodded and said, Not bad, before surrounding himself with the paper again. It was his second trip to Chicago in less than a month and he would make at least three more trips there before the month was over because he knew that they were going to try to steal it from him, and the best place for them to make their try was in Chicago. It was a town,

17

Cubbin thought, where they were very good at stealing almost anything and where, over the years, they had made a fine craft out of stealing what they would try to steal from him, which was, of course, an election.

4

Not too many persons other than those who retained his services knew exactly what it was that Walter Penry did for a living. His wife had some notion, but she spent most of her time by their pool in Bel-Air while Penry spent most of his time traveling, or in Washington, where the headquarters for Walter Penry and Associates, Inc., was located.

Penry had about ten associates but his two principal ones were Peter Majury and Ted Lawson and they knew what he did. At least most of the time. Majury was a planner and manipulator and haunted the corridors of Washington dressed invariably, winter and summer, spring and fall, in a long, belted trench coat that looked as though it had been bought cheap at an Afrika Korps surplus sale. Majury spoke in a tone that was just louder than a whisper and spiced with a slight accent that somebody had once described as Slav Sinister, but which was actually German, the legacy of his parents, both Swabians, who emigrated to New Braunfels, Texas, in the thirties and never bothered to learn English. When he wanted to, Majury could also speak with a grating Texas twang.

Ted Lawson, the other principal associate, was a big, slab-sided man who seemed to gangle as he walked. He was usually all bluff heartiness and employed a loud bray for a laugh because he had decided that that was what people expected from a man of his size who had a bright, beefy complexion and a mouth that nature had turned up merrily at the corners. If one could make a choice about such things, Lawson would have chosen to be a loner, but there wasn't any money in that so he had become what he was, a man who could fix things for people who needed things fixed. It didn't matter much what needed doing, Lawson knew somebody who could do it.

What Walter Penry and Associates, Inc., actually specialized in was skulduggery, the kind that stayed just within the law. Walter Penry knew what the law was because he had been given a degree in the subject by the University of Iowa in 1943 although he had never practiced because he had joined the FBI instead, thus avoiding the discomfort of military service while honorably serving his country at a reasonable salary.

Penry had resigned amicably enough from the FBI in 1954 with what he always referred to as a spotless record. The reason that he resigned, at least the reason he gave the FBI, was to go into business for himself, but that was only partly true. The real reason was to conduct a bit of industrial espionage for a cosmetic firm that would, in two months' time, net him twice what his annual salary was as a special agent working out of Los Angeles.

Using the money that he made from his first industrial espionage assignment as capital, Penry founded his firm with headquarters in Washington and a branch office in Los Angeles, although the branch office at that time consisted of nothing more than his wife and his home telephone. His home now had an unlisted number but his wife still answered it with, "Walter Penry and Associates."

Penry knew what kind of business he was after from the first. There were many unpleasant tasks that various organizations needed done and Penry let it be known that he was willing to do them. He had once spent an entire February afternoon in Dallas firing the top management of an electronics firm while its president and founder and major stockholder, who was something of a coward, basked on Sapphire Beach in St. Thomas.

Penry also worked the periphery of politics, for hire to

either party, specializing in deep background investigations that would produce information intended to have jolting political repercussions. Thus far his more noteworthy efforts had prevented three prospective cabinet members, two Democrats and a Republican, from being sworn in. Another time he had come up with information, twenty years old but still damaging, that had kept a Supreme Court justice off the bench.

But of all Penry's clients his favorite was the immensely fat old man who sat across the table from him now, picking disconsolately at a dish of white chicken meat and cottage cheese. The fat old man was Penry's favorite client for several reasons, not the least of them being that he was the one who paid him his second largest retainer, but the principal one being that Penry considered the old man to be as smart and as realistic as he himself was. Had Penry but known it, the old man considered him to be a bit simple, but the old man thought of nearly everyone that way.

The old man had been born on January 1, 1900, and he often proclaimed that he would live to see her out, referring, of course, to the end of the century. He was enormously fat, carrying nearly three hundred pounds, all of it lard, on a five-foot-eleven-inch frame. The old man had been born on a hardscrabble wheat farm just outside of Hutchinson, Kansas, and his earliest memories were of talk about money, and its lack, its use, its purpose, and its nature. His father was not only a farmer, he was also a money nut, at various times a Greenbacker, a Populist, a single taxer, a free-silver partisan, and a devoted follower of "Coin" Harvey, an Arkansas economic prophet of doubtful merit who had died broke. Nevertheless, the father had given his son the name of the prophet and he fat old man had gone through life as Coin Kensington.

Although his formal education had ended with the eighth grade, Kensington still thought of himself as a student and listed that as his occupation whenever some form required it. His first job had been with a small cooperative grain elevator where he had mastered double entry bookkeeping in less than a week, going on at sixteen to become a teller in the Merchants and Farmers

20

Bank in Hutchinson. The bank had had to wait until he was twenty-one before it could make him cashier.

By 1923 he was the bank's president, the youngest in the state, possibly the youngest in the country. After not quite a year of it he decided that he had learned all he could about Kansas banking so he resigned. Two months later he was in London, standing underneath the sign of three golden acorns on a grimy street in The City. He took a deep breath, pushed open a forbidding door, and announced to the first person he saw that, "I'm Coin Kensington from Kansas and I'm here to learn about money."

After an hour's conversation and a close study of five letters of recommendation that Kensington had brought along from some Chicago and New York bankers that he had dealt with, the senior partner in the London merchant bank offered Kensington a job—at fifteen shillings a week.

"But that's only three-fifty a week."

"It's something more than that, Mr. Kensington."

"What?"

"It's your first lesson."

Three years later the merchant bank sent Kensington to New York to look after its considerable investments. "The day before I left for New York," Kensington liked to say when telling the story, "the three senior partners had me in. Well, one of them said, 'It won't last, of course,' and I said, 'No.' 'Another two years,' another one of them said, 'three possibly.' 'Yes, three,' the first one said. Then they had one of their nice little silences and after a while one of them said, 'Do keep a sharp eye on things, Kensington,' and another one of them said, 'Mmmmm,' which really meant, 'You'd goddam better,' so all I said was, 'Of course,' and because that's all I said they seemed delighted.

"Well, I'd learned about money by then. I don't mean to brag, but I'd learned what it *is*—and there ain't maybe two dozen men in the world who know that. So for the next three years I made them money in the New York market, I mean a lot of money. Then in July of twenty-nine I sent 'em a coded cable that had just three words, 'Get out now.' Well, they did and that made 'em a whole bunch more money. Then in late August I sent them another coded cable, this time four words: 'Maximum short position advised.' Well, they wouldn't. Now those fellas were about as smart a bunch of moneymen as you're likely to run across, but when it comes to selling short you got to be just a little bit inhuman like a pirate, if you're going to make any real money, because you're betting on catastrophe and when you do that you're betting against the hopes of millions, which again ain't natural, and let me tell you it takes brassgutted nerve. Well, these fellas over in London didn't have that much nerve, although they had a right smart amount, so I sent them a nice little letter of resignation and used every dime I had to sell short on my own. Well, you know what happened. By December of twenty-nine I was a millionaire and not just on paper either and I still wasn't quite thirty years old."

Kensington went on prospering through the next four decades, becoming enormously rich. He contributed sporadically and almost indiscriminately to various Democratic and Republican candidates who caught his fancy, set up a foundation "to ease my conscience," he told the press, and, in an unofficial capacity, he ran various errands for half a dozen Presidents.

Now Kensington had taken on yet another Presidential chore, not because be relished it, but to pay off some old political debts and, as he put it, "to sort of help keep a lid on things, at least for a while yet."

The fat old man scraped up the last of the cottage cheese and poked it into his mouth. He spotted a few morsels that he had missed and mashed them up through the tines of his fork and licked them off. He put the fork down a little sadly and looked across the table at Walter Penry, whom he considered to be a bit simple.

"So it doesn't look too good for Cubbin?"

"No. Not too good."

"Drinking too much?"

"Not so much that. They've got a couple of guys who keep him on pretty short rations. Or try to."

"Been too long in his job, huh?"

"Partly. The big pitch is that he lost touch with the rank and file."

Kensington snorted. "That all?"

"There's more, but they're saving it, at least that's what Peter tells me."

"He's that funny little fella of yours, ain't he? The one with the accent?"

"Yes."

"He any good?"

"I think so."

The old man looked down at his scraped plate. He abruptly shoved his chair back, muttered "to hell with it" as though to himself, and waddled across the living room of the hotel suite to its small kitchen. He opened the refrigerator, took out a container of Sara Lee Brownies, and carried it back to the table where he ripped off the top, carved out a four-inch-square chunk, and crammed it into his mouth, smiling at the comfort it gave him.

"That's not on your diet, is it?" Penry said.

"No, it ain't," the old man said in a defensive tone. "You want some?"

"No, thanks."

Kensington looked relieved. "About the only pleasure a mean old man like me has left, eating. Can't drink because of my heart. Stopped smoking when I was twenty-four because it was a damn-fool habit. As for women, well, I just don't think about that much anymore. Tell a damn lie, I just don't do anything about it."

Penry watched while the old man ate the rest of the cake and then carefully scraped up the crumbs and icing and ate that too. The foil container looked as if it had been washed. He won't last another year, Penry thought.

When Kensington was through with the cake, he jerked his thumb over his shoulder at the window of the hotel suite. "They claim to be pretty worried over there."

"I can imagine," Penry said. If he had gone to the window, he could have looked out over Lafayette Park and beyond it to the White House.

"It's not because they love old Don Cubbin either."

23

"No."

"They're worried about that other guy, Hanks."

"Samuel Morse Hanks. Sammy Hanks."

"Yeah, Sammy Hanks. He's the dingdong daddy from Dumas or tries to be, don't he?" Kensington said.

"It's the image he's cultivated over the years."

"You still say that?"

"What?"

"Image."

"Why, yes, I suppose I do."

"Didn't think anybody said that anymore."

Penry made a note in what he thought of as his mental tickler file to make sure that he never used "image" again, at least not around Old Man Kensington.

"Well, what's wrong with Hanks, don't they pay him enough?"

"As secretary-treasurer he makes fifty-five a year, ten less than Cubbin. His expense account is just as good or better."

"So it's not money then?"

"No."

"Too bad," the old man said and began nodding his big head that was almost completely bald except for a fringe of cropped white hair around his ears and neck. He looks like a new baby, Penry thought for the fourth or fifth time that day. Like a new, smart, fat, sassy, red-faced baby.

The old man went on nodding for several moments, not conscious that he was doing it, but only of the thoughts that streaked through his mind. He could hold several thoughts in his mind at once and sometimes he wondered whether others could. Just now he was thinking about Sammy Hanks and what kind of a man he was and about whether Walter Penry was capable of successfully carrying out the assignment that he was about to be given, and just how long it would be before he could get rid of Penry so that he could get the remaining container of Sara Lee Golden Cake with the fudge icing out of the refrigerator.

"How old a man is Hanks, forty-three, forty-four?" Kensington said.

"Thirty-nine."

24

"Ah."

"How 'ah'?"

"Well, he's young enough to get his personal concern for the future of the union so mixed up with his personal ambition that he can't tell 'em apart. He's a pisscutter, huh?"

"He tries to be."

"Well, Cubbin does that pretty well with that voice of his when he's a mind to."

"It goes over better when you're on the attack."

"How long's Hanks been secretary-treasurer?"

"Six years."

"Wasn't he sort of a protégé of Cubbin's at one time?"

"Yes."

The old man nodded. "At least we got us a familiar pattern. The president's out acting big shot and shooting his mouth off on 'Meet the Press' while the secretary-treasurer's out meeting with the locals, doing favors, building up his political capital until wham, the president's out of a job and the secretary-treasurer's got it. It's happened before often enough."

"I know."

"Their contract runs out when, October thirty-first?"

"Yes."

"And the election's October fifteenth?"

"Yes."

"So whoever's president is going to be doing the final negotiating when it comes to nutcracking time. What's Cubbin got his mind set on?"

"Well, he already got thirty percent over the next three years from fabricating and processing."

"That's fabricating and processing. What about the basics?"

"He figures he can get twenty-one percent from the basics without a strike. Maybe twenty-four percent with one."

"It ain't worth it then."

"No."

"And Hanks wants to go for thirty percent?"

"More."

25

"So he'll pull 'em out."

"It looks that way. He says there's no reason why they shouldn't beat or match the auto workers."

Kensington sighed. "Well, Hanks has got a point, but those people over in the White House ain't interested in it. They don't want any strike and they sure as hell don't want any thirty-percent wage increase because they think it'll hurt the economy which, translated, means it'll hurt their own chances of getting reelected."

"So?"

"So over there in the White House they've decided that they'd like to see Don Cubbin reelected president of his union. Can you fix that?"

"It'll cost."

"Yeah, well, anticipating just that we had a little meeting in Philadelphia last week. Some of the boys were there from Chicago and Gary and Los Angeles and New York and Denver and all and they agreed to get up a little kitty to help Cubbin out, although it'd be best if he don't find out too much about it."

"He won't."

"So how much you gonna need to get him reelected? Just roughly."

"Three quarters of a million."

"That all?"

"His own people will come up with another quarter of a million."

"So that's how much it takes nowadays, huh, about a million?"

"About that. We've heard that Hanks is going to try to get by on five hundred thousand."

The old man grew interested. "Where's he getting his?"

"From banks, the ones that he's kept those big, low-interest union deposits in. They're grateful. So are the outfits that he's loaned money to from the pension fund. He's tapping them hard, too, we hear."

"What's he call that committee of his?"

"Hanks?"

"Yes."

"The Rank and File Committee."

"Well, just how much can he count on from the rank and file? In other words, how much will the membership cough up to get themselves a new president?"

"Not much. Maybe fifty thousand."

Kensington shook his head slowly. "Trade-union democracy will never cease to amaze me. Or amuse me, maybe I should say. How much you want for your fee?"

"A hundred thousand."

"Including expenses?"

"It's going to be a short campaign and they'll be low so I'll donate them to the cause."

"And you won't have any trouble working yourself into the thing?"

Penry smiled for the first time and Kensington wished that he hadn't. It was an animal's smile, the rogue kind who has left the pack and gone off on his own. "I owe Cubbin a few favors. I'll just let him know that I'd like to pay them back."

"What do you think his chances are?"

"Without our help?"

"That way first."

"Six-to-four against."

"And with?"

"Better than even for reelection, but it'll be close."

Old Man Kensington rose slowly and with effort, wheezing a little. "Well, I'll take care of the money; you take care of the election."

"All right."

"About this fellow Hanks."

"What about him?"

"What's his problem?"

"I'm not sure I—"

The old man made an impatient gesture, flicking his left hand down and out. The fellow was simple, after all. "Cubbin's a drunk. What's wrong with Hanks?"

"I see. Well, not much really, although there is one thing."

"What?"

"They say he's just a bit crazy," Penry said, smiling again, but the old man didn't see it because he had already turned away, heading for the refrigerator.

27

5

A little over five blocks away that September afternoon in Washington, in another hotel, a cheaper one at the corner of Fourteenth and K, Samuel Morse Hanks was having a fit.

It was really more of a tantrum than a fit, but he was lying on the floor, face down, pounding his fists into the carpet and screaming something that sounded like "cawg." He screamed it over and over while the spit trickled down his chin. Four men sat around in chairs and watched him with expressions that registered a little interest, if not much concern.

The bed and bureau had been removed from the hotel room and now it contained a scarred wooden desk that looked rented and was, a couch, eight or nine folding gray metal chairs with padded seats, two telephones, one of them with an outside line, and a green metal filing cabinet whose drawers were doubly secured by a built-in combination lock and a metal bar that ran through their handles and that was fastened at the top with a padlock that looked tricky.

The room was one of twelve on the hotel's third floor that had been rented as its campaign headquarters by the Rank and File Committee whose candidate for union president now lay on the floor, pounding the carpet with his fists, and screeching the word that sounded like "cawg" again and again.

Finally, one of the four men stubbed out his cigarette, rose, and walked over to where Sammy Hanks lay screaming. He nudged Hanks in the shoulder with the toe of his shoe. "All right, Sammy," he said, "you've had your fun."

The screams stopped. "For Christ's sake, get up and go wash your face," the man said. "You've slobbered all over it."

Sammy Hanks pushed himself up to a kneeling position, hiccupped once, and then rose to his feet. Saliva glistened on his jutting chin that at one in the afternoon already looked as though it needed a shave. Hanks glared at the four men, three of them white and one black. "You know what you bastards are?" he said.

The black man, the one who had shown the least concern while Hanks lay screaming on the floor, smiled lazily and said, "What are we, Sammy?"

"You're fuckin pathetic, that's what," he said, snarling the words so that their tone nicely matched his scowl. Before any of the men could reply, he turned quickly and darted into the bathroom, making sure to slam the door. The four men looked at each other, exchanging glances of exasperated commiseration. The one who had nudged Hanks with a toe sat back down and lit another cigarette.

The four men were near enough in age and size and demeanor almost to have been cut from the same pattern. They were all in their late thirties or early forties, bigger than average, all of them over six feet, carrying a little too much fat, with shrewd eyes set in seamed faces that weren't aging well, especially the black's, whose face looked as if it had been hastily chiseled out of some dark, porous stone.

Although the four men did not look pathetic, they did look wary, as if they had made some dubious bet that there was no way to hedge. They were, in fact, the porkchoppers in charge of the palace revolt, the highly paid professionals who would be out of a job if they lost. So if they had nothing to say to one another now, it was because it had all been said before when they had first decided to put their jobs and careers on the line, knowing all about Sammy Hanks and his tantrums and his mercurial moods that could jitter from hard, bright cheerfulness to raging despair and back again in less than fifteen minutes.

The black man had said it all when they were discussing Sammy Hanks's candidacy six months before. "Okay," the black had said, "so he's a manic-depressive, but he's our manic-depressive and he's sure as shit the only one who's got a chance of beating Cubbin."

After that, there really hadn't been much more to say although each of them, alone and a little afraid with his dark night thoughts, had wondered about the gamble he had made and whether he was really willing to risk his $30,000-a-year job that had provided the house and the pool and the GGG suits and the boat and the cars and all the rest of the crap that was supposed to be the answer to everything, but which had turned out to be just something else that you had to take out insurance on.

The four men not only looked something alike, but they thought, or rationalized, alike and each of them, by much the same method, had convinced himself that he had made the right decision. You could always get another house or car or boat or even a wife, if it came to that. But if you were a man of limited education but quick intelligence, and afflicted with gut-twisting ambition, then you realized that they only invite you once to where the quick boys play and if you don't accept that invitation, they seldom send another.

While the four men sat around in the hotel room and looked at the carpet and the desk and at everything else except each other, Sammy Hanks held the end of a bath towel under the cold water tap and wondered why it was that most hotels never supplied any goddamned facecloths or washcloths or whatever you called them. We called them wash rags when I was a kid, he thought, and that should tell anyone all they'd ever need to know about me.

He used the wet end of the towel to wash the spittle from his face and the other end to dry himself with. As he looked in the mirror he thought what he had always thought since he was six or seven years old, You're the ugliest goddamned person in the world.

30

He may well have been among the top ten contenders.

Whenever he and the strikingly handsome Donald Cubbin appeared on the same public platform, someone always made a crack about beauty and the beast.

For one thing, Hank's head was too large for his short, slight body. The head would have been nicely proportionate if it had rested on the neck and shoulders of someone who was at least six-and-a-half-feet tall. It would have looked in proper proportion then, but it still would have been ugly.

Hanks also had bad skin. It had started when he was six, a virulent, precocious kind of acne that had persisted through adolescence and on into maturity, the despair of an endless series of dermatologists. A full beard could have been an answer, except that when he tried to grow one it grew in a crazy-quilt pattern that made him look even worse.

Another personal tragedy was his nose, an enormous pink pickle that dived down toward his chin that seemed to be jumping up to meet it, especially when he talked. It was the acne-splotched face of an aging Punch whose mud-colored eyes were set much too far apart and which were guarded over by thick, black eyebrows that looked like shoe brushes.

It was Hanks's mouth that saved him, or rather the smile that the mouth formed. The smile warmed you. It made you feel delightfully superior because only you had the gumption to like such an ugly man. More important, you wanted him to like you. Sammy Hanks knew what his smile did and he used it often.

When Hanks came out of the bathroom he crossed to the desk and settled himself behind it, no more discomfited by the exhibition he had provided a few minutes before than if one of the men in the room had mentioned that his fly was unzipped.

"All right," he said, "let's start all over. Let's have those results again."

The man who had nudged Hanks with the toe of his shoe sighed and took a sheet of paper from his inside breast pocket. His name, was Art Olkes and he was

31

Northeast Regional Director, which meant he was the union's liege lord for everything north of Pennsylvania and New Jersey.

"I'll start with the Northeast again," Olkes said.

Hanks nodded. "Fine."

"You've got forty-five percent, Cubbin's got forty-four, eleven percent undecided. Okay?"

"Okay."

"The Mid-Atlantic," Olkes said. That was everything south of Pennsylvania and New Jersey down to and including Alabama. "You've got forty-two percent, Cubbin's got forty-eight percent. Ten percent undecided."

"Okay," Hanks said. "We'll give him the South."

"Pennsylvania, Jersey, Ohio, and West Virginia, the Upper Midwest Region."

"The big one," Hanks said.

"You've got forty-three percent, Cubbin's got forty-four. Thirteen percent still undecided."

"That's not so bad," Hanks said.

"You want the West Coast now?" Olkes said.

"Yeah, give us that now."

The West Coast Region was everything west of Pueblo, Colorado. "You're leading," Olkes said, "forty-seven to forty-three with ten percent who haven't got enough sense to make up their minds." Hanks merely nodded.

"All right," Olkes said, "here's the Midwest Region again." The Midwest Region was everything west of Ohio to Pueblo. "You're behind there, like I said, forty-one to forty-eight with eleven percent don't-knows."

Sammy Hanks nodded again and looked at each of the men in turn. He smiled because he knew it would make them feel better if he did. When he spoke, he made his tone that of a reasonable man who is trying to explain a simple idea. He was all charm and he knew it.

"Then it works out like this, doesn't it? I'll take the Northeast and the West Coast and Cubbin will get the Mid-Atlantic and the Upper Midwest. If he takes the Midwest itself, he wins; if I take it, I win. The Midwest is Chicago and I'm by God not going to lose Chicago, is that clear?"

The black man stirred in his chair, crossed his legs, and

cleared his throat. Hanks glanced at him. "Do you want to talk or spit?"

"Talk," he said.

Hanks made his big head nod abruptly once more. "Go ahead."

The black was Marvin Harmes, thirty-seven, and the youngest man in the room. He was regional director of the union fief known as the midwest which mostly meant Chicago and the industrial towns that lay just outside it in Indiana.

In 1964, when many still thought that there would be a somehow happy ending to the nation's racial turmoil, Donald Cubbin had decided to appoint a black to the next high-echelon vacancy in the union. It seemed like such a good idea that he even mentioned it during a television interview. The vacancy he had in mind, however, was in the union's research or legal departments, not in the center of its power structure.

Unfortunately, three days after he made the statement, the incumbent Midwest Regional Director, an elderly Irishman, had taken drunk and rolled his Cadillac over eight times halfway between South Bend and Gary. A diligent labor reporter on the Chicago *Sun-Times* called Cubbin on his promise and so, as Cubbin later put it, "there was nothing to do but look around for a house nigger."

Marvin Harmes had been the choice, and doubtless a superior one, except that he detested Donald Cubbin and was now one of Sammy Hanks's most partisan supporters. Harmes despised Cubbin for having chosen him as regional director because he was a black. If Sammy Hanks had done the choosing, Harmes would have been supporting Cubbin. Harmes didn't have much faith in happy endings for anything.

"It was like I was saying before when you—" Harmes stopped and started over. "It was like I was saying before. I admit the Midwest looks dicey just now. Forty-eight to forty-one percent's a big lead for Cubbin, if that poll's right. But hell, we haven't even started yet. I can put fifty guys to work tomorrow, real arm twisters. And besides, we've got almost six weeks to—"

"Five weeks," Hanks said.

"Okay, five weeks. I can change a whole lot of minds in five weeks."

"You think you can?"

Harmes frowned. "Look, Sammy, I've got just as much riding on this as you do."

"I know. That's why I asked you."

"Well, I'm telling you it can be done."

Hanks turned to one of the four men who was noisily stripping a cigar of its cellophane wrapper. He was Emil Lorks, a vice-president of the union who lived in West Los Angeles in a house with a pool, two Russian wolfhounds, and his wife. As a vice-president of the steel union, Lorks drew only about $10,000 a year in per diem and expenses. His principal income, around $27,000, came from his job as business agent of a large, rich local whose base was a relatively new and gigantic fabricating plant about twenty miles east of Los Angeles. Lorks was up for reelection and he was worried about his chances.

"Well, Emil?" Hanks said.

Lorks's hair was still a pale, fine blond and he liked to wear it a little long so that it lapped over his shirt collar. He struck the cigar in his mouth, tipped his chair back, looked up at the ceiling, and patted his hair. He was stalling for time so that he could think of how to agree with Sammy Hanks without getting the nigger mad. He was a damned good nigger, but he sometimes went off half cocked. "I think," Lorks said slowly, "that we oughta do both. Now just think about it a minute. If we do both, we can't lose."

Lorks shifted his glance from the ceiling to the men in the room. Hanks was nodding. Harmes was impassive. Olkes looked vaguely impressed. The fifth man in the room was also the oldest. Like Lorks, he was a vice-president up for reelection. He was also business agent of one of the big Pittsburgh locals that paid him nearly $27,000 a year for his services. He got another $10,000 a year from the union in per diem and expenses. He lived in a seven-room apartment with his wife and nineteen-year-old son who was studying piano and didn't seem to like girls much, which worried his father whose real name had been Zbigniew Kowalczewski until he had had it legally changed to Ziggy Kowal. He knew over three hundred Polish jokes and he told at least twenty of them in every speech he made.

The four other men in the room were now looking at Ziggy Kowal. In what Lorks had said he sniffed a compromise that would satisfy everyone, keep the nigger happy, and Sammy from wiggling around on the floor again. And it wasn't a bad idea either, Kowal thought, and decided to make a little speech about it.

"Well, you guys know that there's nothing dumber than a dumb polack and the dumbest polacks in the world work in the plants around Chicago."

"We got some pretty dumb niggers up there, too," Harmes said softly.

"They ain't as dumb as us polacks. Well, I was up there a week ago as you all know and I was trying to find out how they were gonna vote. Now I don't know what your poll says about 'em, Sammy, but from what they told me they're all gonna go for Cubbin. Now that's a sizable chunk of votes and maybe we can change their minds in five weeks and maybe we can't. I'm not sure we can because they're so goddamned stubborn. But like Harmes and Lorks said, we oughta try. But I also think we oughta take out a little insurance so that's why I'm willing to go along with Sammy."

Sammy Hanks let the silence that followed grow for a few moments. Then he turned to Olkes. "Well?"

Olkes shrugged. "I guess we'd better do both, like Emil says."

The last man that Hanks needed consent from was Harmes, the one who would have to do it. "Marvin?" Hanks said.

Harmes shrugged. "It's gonna cost," he said.

"Everything costs," Hanks said. "So we're agreed. We run a real tough campaign around Chicago. But like Ziggy says we take out insurance."

"Don't fancy it up, Sammy," Harmes said. "Just say it out plain what it is you want me to do around Chicago."

The scowl came back on Hanks's face. "All right, goddamnit, I want you to steal the fuckin election."

"I just wanted to hear you say it plain," Harmes said.

6

The idlers and loafers in the lobby were always rewarded with a minor spectacle whenever Donald Cubbin took an elevator up to his hotel suite. If the spectacle lacked pomp and ceremony, it at least involved enough ritual to make onlookers aware that Somebody Important was going to take an elevator ride.

If Cubbin were just arriving in a city, the arrangements began as far away as the airport, in this case O'Hare International at Chicago. After the Lear 24 had landed and taxied to its place of temporary rest, three cars, a large blue Oldsmobile 98 and a green Cadillac Fleetwood followed by a Plymouth taxi, drew up to the plane. All three cars had special airport passes displayed on their windshields.

The Oldsmobile and the Cadillac contained loyal Cubbin supporters including a sixty-three-year-old vice-president from the Chicago-Gary area, Lloyd Garfield, who, in Donald Cubbin's borrowed opinion, wasn't worth a bucket of warm spit. Nevertheless, Garfield knew where he could lay his hands on a sizable amount of money for the campaign and Cubbin would treat him with polite contempt. Garfield would have been surprised if he had been treated any other way.

Fred Mure was first out of the plane. He was listed on the union's payroll as an organizer, but he was actually Cubbin's shadow. If they were traveling, it was Mure who got Cubbin up in the morning and saw him into bed at night. He served Cubbin as valet, bootlegger, whipping boy, retainer, occasional confidant, and, some said, bodyguard because of the .38 Chief's Special that he carried in his hip pocket. He was a handsome thirty-five-year-old man without even a high school diploma, who over the years had grown moderately wealthy by acting on the stock-market tips that came his way from those who had wanted something from Cubbin and who thought that Fred Mure could help. Sometimes he had.

Mure's public devotion to Cubbin bordered on the slavish. It occasionally transformed itself into jealousy, which amused Cubbin who found Mure a little pathetic, but useful. Cubbin sometimes tried out explanations of complicated union economic proposals on Mure because "if that dumb son of a bitch can understand it, anybody can."

After Mure helped Cubbin out of the plane, he stood back and watched while Garfield and two other Chicago supporters did the welcoming. When he was sure that Cubbin had no further need of him, he trotted over to the cab, got in, and handed the driver two bills, a ten and twenty.

"You can keep 'em both if you get me to the Sheraton in thirty minutes."

The cab driver stuck the bills in his shirt pocket. "I can try, buddy."

Mure got in the back seat, took a small notebook out of his pocket, and used a ball-point pen to write down, "Cab fare, $40, Chicago." It was another one of his jobs, to keep Cubbin's expense records, and he did it meticulously and with a commendable amount of imagination.

The two other men who got out of the Lear were Cubbin's keepers. Ostensibly, one was the campaign manager and the other was the public relations expert. Their principal task, however, was to keep Cubbin sober—or fairly so—until the campaign was over. They already had been ten days on the job and both looked haggard, having just spent most of the one-hour flight from Hamilton, Ontario, thinking up reasons why Cubbin shouldn't sample the two imperial quarts of Canadian whiskey that he

37

had bought tax free at the airport. Fred Mure had been no help. He liked to see Cubbin take a drink. "It makes him feel better," he had once said. "Makes him relax."

"It makes him drunk, you dumb son of a bitch," the campaign manager had told him.

Cubbin's principal supporters had thought of getting rid of Fred Mure until the campaign was over, of sending him to Miami Beach or better yet, to Bermuda. All expenses paid. But when he had been approached, Mure had shaken his head stubbornly and said, "Don needs me."

The only person who could get rid of Mure was Cubbin himself, but when the campaign manager had mentioned it, Cubbin had looked at him strangely and then said, "He stays," in a tone that made further argument impossible.

The campaign manager was Oscar Imber, who had taken his master's degree in economics at the University of Texas, writing his thesis on "The Use and Misuse of the Pension Fund of the International Brotherhood of Teamsters, Chauffeurs, Warehousemen and Helpers of America." The thesis had won him an immediate job offer from the teamsters' union, which had been tempting, but he had turned it down for a similar offer from Cubbin's union that promised a little less money, but far more authority. After eight years, Imber was administrator for the union's pension fund which, at last count, was up around $611,000,000. Because of the Federal Landrum-Griffin Act, which outlined the rules that unions must follow when conducting their elections, Imber had cautiously taken leave of his official job to become the Cubbin slate's campaign manager. He had done so not because of any fondness for Cubbin, but because his own job was one of the ripest plums in the union. If Cubbin lost to Hanks, Oscar Imber would barely have time to empty his desk. He at first had tried to stay neutral, but it had proved impossible when in separate, equally heated discussions with both candidates, they had let him know that they regarded those who were not for them as against them.

Imber had flipped a coin to make his choice. It had

come up heads and Cubbin. Once having made his decision, he informed Cubbin that he was taking over the managing of the campaign because "You haven't got anybody else around with enough sense to do it. If they've got any sense, they've gone over to Sammy." Cubbin was so relieved that somebody was taking charge of the campaign's details that he hadn't argued.

As he watched Cubbin climb into the Cadillac Imber spoke to the man next to him. "What time's he due on that TV thing?"

"Midnight."

"It's going to be a long day."

"They all are."

The man that Imber spoke to would have been tall if he had straightened up out of his slouch. He carried his thin body like a wire question mark that somebody had once started to straighten out but had given up on halfway through. His head jutted forward from his lean neck as if on some perpetual, private quest. His hair was black, long and touched with gray at its shaggy ends. He had bright blue eyes that seemed a little cold, a slightly hooked nose, and a thick, black moustache curving around the ends of a thin mouth that managed to look hungry.

The thin man was Charles Guyan and for the past ten years he had earned a comfortable if uncertain living by trying to get men whom he usually felt nothing but contempt for elected to public office. He had been successful three-fourths of the time and there was a steady demand for his services, which, along with inflation, now enabled him to charge $50,000 a campaign plus expenses. The $50,000 was all profit because Guyan had no overhead, not even a permanent address. When he wasn't working a campaign, he and his wife lived on their thirty-two-foot Chris-Craft and cruised the inland waterway from Florida to Virginia. Guyan felt that he had four years left before his steadily mounting disdain for his profession rendered him ineffective. In four years he would be forty and he wasn't at all sure what he would do then and he worried about it a lot.

Seated now in the back seat of the Oldsmobile 98, Charles Guyan and Oscar Imber listened patiently while the car's owner, a minor union official from Gary, gave them his version of the political climate.

"It's warming up," he said. "We're stirring up lots of interest."

"That's good," Imber said. "How does it look?"

"Oh, Don's gonna make it okay if he keeps his eye on the ball."

"John?" Imber said.

The minor union official whose name was John Horton turned his head around and away from the road he was supposed to be watching. "Yeah?"

"You want to know something?"

"Sure," Horton said, his attention back on the road and his driving again, "what?"

"You don't know what the fuck you're talking about."

It didn't bother Horton. "You just wait and see, Oscar. Old Don's gonna make it all right, if he keeps his eye on the ball."

"John's supposed to deliver his local," Imber said to Guyan. "I doubt if he could deliver a bottle of milk."

"Don't you worry about my local," Horton said over his shoulder. "You don't have to worry none about that. You'd better worry about those nigger locals, that's what you'd better worry about."

"Your local's eighty-percent black, John," Imber said.

"Uh-huh, about that, but they're all good niggers; you don't have to worry none about them."

"Just the other ones, huh?"

"Well, you don't have to worry none about mine, I'll guaran-goddamn-tee you that."

Imber slumped back in the seat. Guyan stared moodily out of the window. They rode in silence for several minutes until Imber said, "Well, you've had ten days of it. What do you think?"

"It's a throwback to the thirties."

"How?"

"I can't use commercials on TV or even radio because we're only trying to influence about nine hundred thousand votes in what . . . forty-some states?"

40

"About that."

"So the cost is prohibitive. I've got the world's most natural TV candidate, but I can't use him. If this were a regular election I'd say spend every dime you've got on TV but it's not, so I can't use it, and that leaves only one thing."

"What?"

"Print."

"So?"

"So it bothers me."

"Why? Hanks has the same problem."

Guyan sighed. "I've never run a print campaign before. Not all print. I've got a candidate who looks like he oughta be voted for and I've got an opposition candidate who looks like somebody just dug him up out of the cellar, and I can't use either of them in commercials. Jesus!"

"Well, what about printed stuff?" Imber said.

"I don't have much faith in it."

"Why?"

Guyan sighed again. "Who the hell reads anymore?"

Three blocks from the Sheraton-Blackstone Hotel Fred Mure told the cab driver to stop at a liquor store. He went in and paid six dollars for four half-pints of Ancient Age bourbon. He put two of the half-pints in his coat pockets and two in his trouser pockets. Back in the cab he told the driver, "Let's go."

"That stop's gonna make us a minute late," the driver said.

"Don't let it worry you," Mure said, taking out his notebook and writing down "HFO—$12." HFO stood for "hospitality for others."

At the Sheraton Mure jumped out of the cab and pushed through the revolving door. Waiting in the lobby was a group of five men. One of them stepped forward, but Mure waved him back. "Wait right there, Phil. He'll be here in five or six minutes."

"We just wanta see him for a minute."

"You can see him upstairs."

"Appreciate it, Fred."

41

But Mure was already heading for the bell captain's desk. The captain rose quickly when he looked up and saw Mure.

"How are you, Jimmy?" Mure said.

"Fine, Fred, and you?"

"Keeping me on the run."

"What'll you need?"

Mure looked at his watch and then pointed at the bank of elevators. "Give me number one and number two in five minutes."

"Right. How many bags?"

"Need a couple of boys."

"You've got 'em. Staying long?"

"A few days. I'll take care of you later."

"Sure, Fred."

Mure moved away from the bell captain and stationed himself in the lobby where he could keep an eye on both the elevators and the revolving door. He also let his gaze wander about the lobby, mentally classifying its occupants. No nuts, he thought. Just people.

The captain had summoned four of his bellhops who nodded as he gave them instructions. "Cubbin's due in about three minutes. You two get on the door. You two bring number one and two down and hold them. Just like always."

The four bellhops nodded and moved toward the elevators and the revolving door. Five minutes later the green Cadillac bearing Donald Cubbin pulled up at the hotel entrance. The uniformed doorman jumped for it. Cubbin was first out followed by the vice-president and the other two members of the Chicago reception committee. From the blue Oldsmobile came Oscar Imber, Charles Guyan, and John Horton, the minor union official. Before Cubbin had made it to the revolving door the bellhops had already gathered the bags from the two cars.

Cubbin was first inside the lobby, his long, double-breasted raincoat open and flapping, a cigar clenched between the white teeth of his smile, his eyes restlessly moving from side to side searching for anyone who deserved a wave or a nod or a hi-ya, pal. When he saw the group of five men he winked and jerked his head toward the elevators, not breaking his long stride.

"Number one, Don," Mure murmured as Cubbin flashed past him. The idlers and loafers in the lobby had turned to watch the entrance that had now swelled into a small procession.

"Who is it?" an idler asked a loafer.

"Lorne Greene," the loafer said, not wanting to seem stupid.

"Who's that?"

"Pa Cartwright. On TV. You know, on 'Bonanza.'"

"Oh, yeah. I thought it looked like him."

Cubbin entered the elevator swiftly, Mure just behind him. Well schooled, the bellhop who was piloting the automatic car turned the key, closing the door.

"Stop on six, Carl," Mure said.

"Right, Mr. Mure," the bellhop said.

The elevator stopped at six, but the doors didn't open. The bellhop kept his face carefully to the front of the car as Mure handed Cubbin one of the now opened half-pints of Ancient Age. Cubbin tipped the bottle up and swallowed greedily. Then he handed it back to Mure who told the bellhop, "Okay, let's go," and slipped the bottle back into his coat pocket.

Donald Cubbin closed his eyes and sighed appreciatively as he felt the whiskey go to work.

—

7

Truman Goff, who had looked up the man he was going to kill in *Who's Who,* had three weeks' vacation coming from the Safeway store in Baltimore and he arranged to take one week of it during the second week in September

43

and the other two weeks beginning October 9, a Monday.

The manager of the Safeway wasn't surprised at Goff's request because his produce manager always took his vacation at odd times and actually it made things easier because Goff was always there during the summer to fill in when others were away on vacation.

Goff's decision to take his vacation so late in the year was no surprise to his family either. For the past three years, since their daughter had turned seven, the Goffs had vacationed separately. His wife had returned in July from a three-week tour of Europe which had cost Goff $995 plust the $300 he had given her to buy stuff with. His daughter had spent six weeks of the summer at a Methodist camp in Pennsylvania, just as she had done the previous two summers while her mother had taken packaged tours to Hawaii the first year and to Mexico the second. Now whenever she and her husband watched television together, which wasn't often, and a foreign city was shown, Mrs. Goff usually said, "I been there," even if she hadn't, which irritated Goff who had never been out of the States and had no desire to go. But his wife's "I been there" still irritated him which, of course, was why she said it.

Truman Goff's wife wasn't sure where her husband got the money to pay for her tours. He said he played the horses with a scientific system, but she didn't believe it. Still, for the past three or four years he always seemed to have plenty of money and as long as he spent some of it on her she wasn't going to worry about where it came from.

When Goff came home after arranging his vacation he told his wife, "I'm gonna take a week off starting Monday."

"Where you going?"

"I don't know. Maybe Florida."

"It's still hot down there."

"I like it hot. I'll leave you the car."

"You'd better leave me some money, too."

"Yeah, well, here's four hundred. You can buy the kid some new clothes for school."

Goff handed his wife four one-hundred dollar bills. They were old, well-used bills and one of them had a rip in it that someone had neatly mended with a strip of Scotch tape.

"Well, have a good time," his wife said, putting the money away in her purse.

"Yeah, sure," Goff said and started carefully turning through *The New York Times*.

"What're you reading that for?" his wife said.

"They got a better racing section than the *Sun*," Goff said, stopping on page 13 because it contained a one-column headline that read:

Bitter Campaign
Seen in Fight for
Union's Presidency

Donald Cubbin's second wife was waiting for him when he eventually made it to his four-room, two-bath suite on the Sheraton-Blackstone's twelfth floor. Cubbin hadn't seen his wife in three days, but they greeted each other as if it had been a couple of years.

"How's my darling little girl?" Cubbin said, booming the words out as he wrapped his arms around his wife and picked her up about three or four inches off the floor before he set her back down and kissed her wetly on the mouth.

"Honey, it seems months," his wife said, smiling up at him with the handsome teeth that a Beverly Hills dentist had capped for $1,700.

"How've you been, sweetie?" Cubbin said, taking off his raincoat.

"Fine, darling, but I missed you so much."

"I missed you, too, honey."

It went on like that for a while, the terms of endearment punctuating every phrase. Fred Mure stood a little back from the couple, smiling as he watched them greet each other.

Oscar Imber and Charles Guyan had also come into the room and they tried to avoid looking at what Imber called "The Don and Sadie Show." But there was nothing

45

else to look at and after a while both men watched with a certain amount of detachment as the couple exchanged endearments and traded some more wet kisses that involved what Guyan thought of as "too much tongue work."

Cubbin's first wife had died seven years before, leaving him with their only child, a nineteen-year-old son, and a surprisingly dim memory of a vague, shy woman who had been a vague, shy girl when he had married her when she was nineteen and he was twenty-four.

Six months after his wife's death, Cubbin had married Sadie Freer who was nearly three decades younger than he. There had been nothing either shy or vague about Sadie who had first met Cubbin when the UPI bureau in Pittsburgh sent her to interview him.

The last time they had tried sex together had been seven months before. It hadn't been any good, in fact, it had been rotten, with Sadie at first doing all of Cubbin's favorite tricks and even inventing some new ones. But nothing had worked and finally Sadie told him, "You've had too much to drink, honey. Why don't we wait till tomorrow."

But somehow they had never got around to trying again and Cubbin was relieved that he no longer had to make the effort or endure what he considered to be the shame of failure. Cubbin found that if he drank enough, he didn't even dream about sex. After a month or so, Sadie had also discovered a satisfactory substitute. In the meantime their display of public affection continued, even more cloying than ever; because they were, after all, genuinely fond of each other.

After the greeting of his wife was over, Cubbin turned to Imber and Guyan. "Now I'm going to have one big drink of that Canadian whiskey I bought."

"One won't hurt you," Imber said.

"Well, that's all I'm going to have till after that interview."

"I'll fix it, Don," Fred Mure said. "Sadie?"

"Anything," she said. "A bourbon and water's fine."

"You guys?" Mure said to Imber and Guyan. They both asked for bourbon and water.

46

As Mure turned to go for the drinks, Cubbin said, "And send Audrey in here." Mure nodded that he would as he went through the doorway.

Cubbin settled himself in an upholstered, low-backed chair and looked at Guyan. "So you really think it went okay, what I said to that TV guy in Hamilton today?"

Guyan nodded as he sat down on the room's green couch. "You slanted it just right for the Canadians, I think. You won't have to change too much tonight. He'll probably ask you the same thing."

"You mean why do I think Sammy's running and whether I think I've lost touch with the rank and file?"

"That's what they've all been asking so far," Guyan said.

"Did you notice who that TV guy in Hamilton walked like?" Cubbin said.

"Walked like?" Imber said.

Cubbin rose. "Like this," he said, bending himself backward and holding his arms a little out from his sides as he pranced across the room in a pigeon-toed gait.

"Christ," Imber said. "You're right. Cary Grant."

Cubbin beamed. "The older ones like Grant and Wayne are easy. But the new ones all act like Burton and—"

Cubbin was interrupted by Fred Mure with the drinks. Mure was followed by a forty-year-old blonde who carried a slim, black attaché case. She was Audrey Denn who had been Cubbin's secretary for fifteen years. She put her attaché case down, went behind Cubbin's chair, and said, "Okay, handsome, relax."

"What've you got?" Cubbin said to Audrey Denn as he reached for the drink that Fred Mure handed him.

"Take a sip first," she said.

Cubbin took two large swallows.

"All right?" she asked.

"Fine," he said.

Audrey placed her hands on his neck, down near where the muscles started up from his shoulders. She started to massage the neck muscles skillfully. "You've got some letters to sign, I mean right away, and above five phone

47

calls that can wait till tomorrow and one that can't wait. You'd better take it pretty soon."

"Who from?" Cubbin asked.

"Walter Penry. He called from Washington and said it was important."

"Get him for me, will you?"

"Relax, goddamnit," she said and went on massaging Cubbin's neck muscles while his wife watched with a slight smile and wondered, as she always wondered, how many years it had been since Don had stopped taking Audrey to bed. Ten years at least, she thought, probably when Audrey had finally got married. Now the two of them shared the easy intimacy of former lovers who don't have to bother with pretending anymore. It must be a relief, she thought, not pretending, and then she thought about something more pleasant, about when her own married life would improve. That would be after the election, of course. Everything was going to be after the election. In the meantime—well, in the meantime she would accommodate herself as best she could. Which wasn't bad really.

"Okay," Cubbin said, "that's good. Now get Penry for me."

Audrey Denn tapped him lightly on the shoulder, like a barber telling a customer that it's all over, and said, "You can take it on my phone."

"Fine," Cubbin said and finished his drink in three swallows. "Now what else?"

"I've got a delegation from Local 127 stashed away in room C," Fred Mure said.

"One twenty-seven," Cubbin said. "That's Wheeling, West-by-God-Virginia. That's the bunch I saw downstairs. The guy in the lobby I spoke to's name is—" Cubbin looked up at the ceiling. He prided himself on his memory. "Phil. Philip Emerey. Right?"

"Right," Mure said.

"What do they want?"

"They got their local to pass a resolution backing you. They want to give it to you along with some money."

"How much?"

"I don't know, probably a coupla hundred."

48

"Christ, it cost them more'n that to fly up here."

"They didn't fly," Mure said. "They drove all night."

"No shit?" Cubbin said, surprised and pleased as always that anyone would do anything for him that involved physical discomfort and not much in the way of reward. It wasn't humility that made Cubbin feel that way. It was a nearly total lack of it. "I'd better spend a little time with them then."

"You'd also better spend some time with Lloyd Garfield and his welcoming delegation," Oscar Imber said. "They want to give you a little money, too. About twenty-five thousand dollars' worth."

Cubbin rose and shook his head impatiently. "I've already talked to them," he said. "Hell, I rode in with them from the airport and spending that long with Old Man Garfield is worth twenty-five thousand. Jesus, what an idiot!"

Oscar Imber was lying almost prone on the couch, his drink balanced on his chest, his eyes on the ceiling. "It's the biggest local contribution we've got so far, Don."

"Well, what am I supposed to do, go down on my goddamn knees to him? I never could stand the old prick." Lloyd Garfield was sixty-three, thirteen months older than Cubbin.

"Spend another five minutes with him," Imber said. "Give him as much time as you give the Wheeling delegation. That's five thousand a minute."

"You'd better, darling," Sadie Cubbin said, deciding that she'd better say something before Cubbin became petulant. "Oscar and I'll talk to Garfield while you talk to the people from Wheeling. Then maybe all you'll have to do is thank Garfield."

"See if you can get the money from him first, Oscar," Cubbin said. "I don't want to have to ask him for it and I don't want to handle it. Christ, that's all he talked about on the way in."

"I'll place that call to Walter Penry in ten minutes," Audrey Denn said. "That'll get you out of your meeting with Garfield."

"Yeah, that's good," Cubbin said and turned to look for Fred Mure. "All right, Fred, let's go."

The two men left by the door that opened on to the twelfth-floor corridor. "They're in C, so we'll go in through D and make a stop in the john," Mure said.

Cubbin only nodded and followed him. Inside the bathroom that separated rooms D and C of his four-room suite, Cubbin drank from the remainder of the open half-pint of bourbon that Mure handed him. "I can only let you have one more belt before the broadcast," Mure said.

Cubbin peered critically at himself in the bathroom mirror and patted his silver hair. "Just make sure you're around when I need you," he said.

Mure tried to look hurt and almost managed it. "Don't I always, Don?"

Cubbin stared at him for a moment. "Yeah, I guess you do at that."

8

Cubbin spent far more time with the delegation that had $200 to give him than he did with Old Man Garfield and his $25,000 committee. The $200 bunch was composed of working stiffs, he thought, who had had to lose a day's pay to make the trip from Wheeling to Chicago and would now have to show up for work the next morning all worn out from a long night's drive. Besides, they were a little in awe of Cubbin and called him President Cubbin and told him that they were backing him 100 percent and that he was the best thing that had ever happened to the union.

Old Man Garfield and his Chicago welcoming committee weren't in the least awed by Cubbin. They called him Don, talked about how lucky he was to have their support, repeatedly mentioned the sacrifices that had gone into raising the $25,000, and toward the end Old Man

Garfield had drawn Cubbin over into a corner where he delivered a nice little lecture on temperance.

Cubbin by then had drunk just enough bourbon to make him almost reckless and he was thinking about how fine it would be to tell Old Man Garfield to take his $25,000 and shove it when Audrey Denn came into the room and told him that his call to Washington was ready. Cubbin stuck out his hand to Old Man Garfield and said, "It's always an experience being with you, Lloyd, and knowing that I can count on you for advice on just about anything."

"Just you remember that little piece I gave you about you know what," Garfield said and winked hugely. Cubbin winked back. "You bet," he said.

"We'll see her through, Don," Garfield said. "Just keep the faith, baby, like the nigger congressman used to say."

Cubbin turned from Garfield, not bothering to disguise his wince, and left the task of talking to Garfield and his committee to Sadie and Oscar Imber and Charles Guyan. Followed closely by Fred Mure, Cubbin headed for room B of the suite. As he entered, Audrey Denn spoke into the phone she was holding. "I have Mr. Cubbin for you now, Mr. Penry."

Cubbin took the phone and waved a hand of dismissal. Audrey Denn nodded and headed for the door. So did Fred Mure. Cubbin covered the phone and hissed, "Not you, Fred." Into the phone he said, "How are you, Walter?"

In his Washington office on Seventeenth Street near L, Walter Penry had the desk speaker on. His office had all the trappings that W. & J. Sloane thought that a successful executive's office should have. There was a sunburst clock on the fabric-covered walls, some tweedy-looking couches and chairs, a kidney-shaped coffee table, some "English style" prints of Washington scenes, and an immense walnut desk that he had purchased secondhand from a cabinet member whose spendthrift notions on how he thought the government should decorate his office had created such a furor in the press that he had finally had to sell off his fancy fixtures and settle for General Service Administration issue. Penry had also bought the cabinet member's pale gold drapes that were real silk.

Penry was leaning well back in his burnt-orange leather executive chair, his feet cocked up on his desk. Across from him, seated in two tweedy armchairs, were the two principal associates of Walter Penry and Associates, Inc., Peter Majury and Ted Lawson. Majury wore an attentive expression on his thin face. Lawson looked as if he expected to hear something funny, but he usually looked that way.

After Cubbin and Penry exchanged pleasantries about their respective families and the weather, Penry said, "What's all this I hear about you having a little opposition this time out, Don?"

In the Chicago hotel room, Cubbin beckoned to Fred Mure. "It's not too bad," he said into the phone. "I think we'll be able to handle it all right."

Fred Mure took a half-pint of the Ancient Age from his pocket, unscrewed the cap, and handed the bottle to Cubbin who took two deep swallows. In Washington, the sound of Cubbin's breathy exhalation came clearly over the speaker and Peter Majury made a careful note about it on a yellow legal pad.

"Well, look, Don, are you going to be in Chicago tomorrow?" Penry said.

"Until Monday or Tuesday."

"The boys and I would like to get together with you tomorrow, if we could. We've been kicking around some ideas and we might even be of some use to you."

"I'd always like to see you, Walter, you know that," Cubbin said, "but I'd better tell you right now we're running a shoestring campaign and I don't think there's enough money in it to make it worth your while."

"Don?" Penry said.

"Yes."

"Did I mention money? Did I ever hint at it?"

"No, but—"

"Don?"

"Yes."

"We're friends, aren't we?"

"Sure. We're friends."

52

"Well, I just wanted to make sure you thought so because that's why I called you. Because we're friends and friends help each other out. Now you've helped me out in the past, haven't you?"

Cubbin didn't really like to think about that. Helping Walter Penry out had involved doing nothing. It had, in fact, involved not making a decision, so if anything, it had been a negative kind of help. "Well, I don't know, Walter," Cubbin said. "I haven't really done much."

This was true. One of the largest specialized manufacturing companies in the nation should have been organized by Cubbin's union years ago. It was a company that was owned 100 percent by an immensely rich, immensely eccentric recluse who was Walter Penry and Associates' principal client. He would remain their client as long as his company remained unorganized. The company had grown into a major concern during Cubbin's tenure as union president. Over the years, Cubbin had directed only token efforts toward organizing it. He had sent the union's malcontents, its failures, and its drunks to do the job and when they reported back that they had been unsuccessful, Cubbin had told them to try again. Some of the union's failures and malcontents had made a career out of not organizing that particular firm and whenever Cubbin got pressure from his board about it, he would send out some other incompetents. As in every organization, there were always plenty of them around.

The agreement between Cubbin and Penry that the eccentric recluse's company would not be organized had never been explicit. Penry wasn't even sure that it was tacit, but he had found that as long as he was pleasant, friendly and helpful to Cubbin, his client's company stayed unorganized. Being pleasant and friendly was Penry's stock in trade; being helpful was introducing Cubbin to various New York and Los Angeles actors and actresses who were told that their careers might be enhanced if they were attentive and flattering to the union man. Because Cubbin, at sixty-two, was still stagestruck, this had been an easy, even enjoyable task for most of them and some of them had even become his close acquaintances, if not his good friends.

Penry knew that if Cubbin's union made even a half-way serious attempt to organize the firm, it could be sewn up in six weeks. He also knew that if Sammy Hanks got elected president, the attempt would not be halfway serious, it would be completely so, and Walter Penry and Associates would lose its most valuable client.

The reelection of Donald Cubbin was the most important current project that Walter Penry and Associates had and Penry didn't want to think about what would happen should Cubbin lose—although he knew he would have to think about it soon and have a contingency plan ready to go just in case. It was what a realist would do and Penry prided himself on being realistic, which meant, of course, figuring out how to make a dollar from disaster.

"Don," Penry said, "why don't you keep tomorrow afternoon free? The boys and I'll fly up tomorrow morning and then we can have a good talk—at my place." By my place, Penry meant the Hilton. He almost always stayed at Hilton hotels because he had once done some work for the chain and the management was so grateful for having been extricated from a possibly embarrassing situation that Penry had been presented with a silver card that entitled him to a 30 percent discount. The Hilton chain also had gold cards that entitled the bearer to a 50 percent discount, but its management hadn't been quite grateful enough to give Penry one of those.

"Well, maybe I could drop around for a little while," Cubbin said.

"Make it around one and we'll have some lunch."

"Okay. Lunch'll be fine."

"See you tomorrow then, Don. I'm looking forward to it."

"Sure. So am I."

After Penry switched off his desk speaker he looked at Peter Majury who by now had covered one page of his yellow legal pad with scribbled notes.

"Well?" Penry said.

"Interesting, but not startling."

"What?"

"He's been nipping, but not too much," Majury said. "That means that he's secured a steady supply—probably from that Mure person who shadows him. Ancient Age, as I recall."

"Just how in the hell do you know it's Ancient Age?" Ted Lawson said.

"It's my job to know, Ted. Mure usually keeps four half-pints about his person. This enables Cubbin to have a quick one whenever the need arises and from his careful pronunciation of certain words such as 'after' and 'handle,' I'd say his intake thus far today has been nearly three-fourths of a pint."

"How much would you say he's putting away every day?" Penry said.

"It must be nearly a fifth or a quart, if my research is right."

"It usually is," Lawson said, but without any admiration.

"Can he function?" Penry said.

"It depends upon what you mean by that. At a little over a pint he can still move around, but his control has diminished. After a quart he would be completely unconscious. If he follows his usual pattern, he has a quick one or two in the morning to get going, and then tries to do everything that needs any careful attention by noon. After that he can have several large drinks and still perform the duties that require little or no concentration—such as making public appearances, delivering a speech, and so forth. Fourtunately, his duties are not too arduous."

"He hasn't done a day's work in the ten years that I've known him," Lawson said.

"It depends on what you mean by that," Penry said. "I've seen him conduct round-the-clock negotiations. I was there at the request of industry, not his, but I'd say that he was damned near masterful."

"How long ago was that?" Peter Majury said.

"Three years. About this time three years ago."

"Well, for one thing he was on stage then," Majury said. "He wasn't being the president of his union. He was *acting* the way that he thought the president of his union should act."

"He did a damned fine job," Penry said.

"He would have made a most competent actor, perhaps

55

even a great one given proper direction. But you saw him at his best three years ago. I'm afraid his drinking problem has worsened since then."

"Well, he's not going to quit the sauce," Lawson said.

"No, he's not going to do that," Penry said.

"Personally," Majury said, "I think that under the circumstances his people are handling him almost as well as he can be handled. If we enter into his campaign, my only suggestion would be to shield him from as much stress as possible."

"You mean nursemaid him?" Lawson said, making it clear that he didn't like the idea.

"No, he's got a number of those around—all of whose good intentions are subverted by the Mure person who, in effect, is Cubbin's bootlegger. No, I think we leave Cubbin alone as much as possible."

"You're getting to your point, aren't you?" Penry said.

"Yes. I think I am."

"Well?"

"Sammy Hanks."

"Yes," Penry said, "Sammy is the problem, isn't he?"

"He has those tantrums, you know."

"I've heard."

"Have you ever seen one?"

"No."

Majury looked at his shoes. "I once spent three hours with someone who had. She was a rather good observer. She gave me a graphic description. Most graphic."

"So?"

"While her description was interesting, she told me something else that was even more so."

He's going to tell it in his own time, Penry thought. In his own way. Nothing will hurry him. "What?" he said.

"She told me what it was that could make him—uh—blow. Invariably."

"Yes, I see," Penry said.

Lawson was nodding. "Now it's getting more interesting."

"She said she discovered it quite by accident," Majury said. "But that it always worked. She tested it, just to make sure."

"And what do you think we should do about it?" Penry said.

It took Majury fifteen minutes to describe what he thought should be done about it and when he was through, Lawson said, "When'd you dream all this up?" There was nothing but envious admiration in the question.

"While Walter was talking to Cubbin."

"Jesus, it's rotten," Penry said.

Majury smiled and used his right hand to smooth his long, black hair. "Yes," he said, "isn't it."

9

The television show that Cubbin was scheduled to appear on that night started at twelve in Chicago and was aimed at those insomniacs whose thirst for banality remained unquenched even after an hour and a half of Johnny Carson or Dick Cavett.

The host of the show was an ex-*Chicago Tribune* police reporter who did his homework, or had it done for him, and who liked to ask his guests depressingly personal questions that had won him the sobriquet of "Mr. Nasty Himself." At least that's how he insisted that he be introduced before each program.

The host's name was Jacob Jobbins and the official title for his program was "Jake's Night." It was an hour-and-a-half show and the number of guests varied from one to three. The attraction of the program, of course, lay in Jobbins' ability to make his guests squirm, which delighted and fascinated his audience at home who couldn't sleep anyhow and who told themselves, or anybody who was still up and willing to listen, that by God, he'd never get me up there and ask me questions like that, but who really yearned to be up there telling it all.

So the various flacks around the country tried to get

their client writers and actors and politicians and flashy criminal lawyers and singers on "Jake's Night" because Chicago was a big market and it was felt that humiliation paid off at the box office and the bookstores and the record shops.

Jobbins got many of the questions that he asked from the enemies of the people whom he planned to interview. He was always getting scrawled notes that urged him to ask so-and-so things like "why they tossed him in the clink in Santa Monica in April 1961." And often, after careful checking, Jobbins would ask about it and his guest would either freeze or try some maladroit verbal fencing until Jobbins' gentle but persistent probing broke through the guest's defenses and then the entire, often sordid story would tumble out to the delight of those who were lying in bed at home and watching it all through their toes.

If Jobbins knew how to ask questions, he also knew how to listen. In fact, he may have been one of the world's great listeners, a skillful user of the long silence and the sympathetic, understanding nod that seemed to say, "I know, I know, God, how well I know," as his guests stripped themselves of their last shred of dignity, reveling, it often seemed to Jobbins, in their self-abasement.

But immolation paid because "Jake's Night" commanded a large and loyal audience that actually bought the books and records and went to the shows that the writers and singers and actors crucified themselves to tout. As one publicity man put it, "Christ, after you see some poor slob strip himself bare you feel so sorry for him that you go out and buy his record just to cheer him up."

This would be Donald Cubbin's third time on "Jake's Night." When he had first appeared on the show three years before, Jobbins had been unable to penetrate Cubbin's formidable dignity and the show had been dull. The next time Cubbin had unbent a little and admitted that yes, he thought that Jimmy Hoffa was a thief and that the late Walter Reuther had been a damned fool to take his auto workers out of the AFL-CIO and besides that Reuther had been a smart aleck who never knew when to shut up. As for the war in Vietnam, George Meany could say whatever he wanted to say, but Cubbin thought it was senseless, tragic waste and Cubbin had said so since sixty-four and would go on saying so even if a cut in defense spending would throw his members out of work. Furthermore, Cubbin felt that if Hubert Humphrey hadn't sold his soul to be Johnson's nominee and had come out against the war when he should have, back in sixty-six or even sixty-five, he'd be the most popular man in the nation today instead of a has-been. And no, Cubbin wasn't worried about becoming an alcoholic although sure, he took a drink every now and then, but who didn't?

If Jobbins' second interview with Donald Cubbin hadn't been too revealing personally, it had at least produced enough pungent remarks to make the wire services move a seven-paragraph story on it. This time Jobbins had a little more material to work with and almost before Cubbin could seat himself, Jobbins began.

"The last time you were here, Don, you called Hubert Humphrey a has-been among other things. Now that's what a sizable portion of your membership is calling you. They say that you've lost touch with them. Why do they say that?"

"The man who wants my job says that, Jake. The members don't say it."

"I checked with a couple of Chicago bookmakers this afternoon and they're willing to lay eight to five that you won't get reelected."

"You should have bet five; you'd make yourself some money."

"Let's get back to this charge that you're losing touch with your membership. You belong to some rather exclusive clubs around the country, don't you?"

"I belong to some clubs; I don't know how exclusive they are."

"But not everyone can join them, right?"

"Not everybody would want to."

"You belong to one in Washington called the Federalists Club, don't you?"

"Yes, I belong to that."

"And hasn't it been called the most exclusive club in Washington?"

"I don't know about that."

"Well, not many of your members belong, do they?"

"No, I don't think they do."

"Could they join, if they wanted to?"

"If they were invited and if they could afford the dues. I sometimes think that I can't."

"If they were invited, you say?"

"Yes."

"Who belongs to the Federalists Club?"

"Mostly men who have an interest in politics and government, and in the arts and sciences."

"And in business?"

"Yes, certainly. Business."

"Big business, you mean."

"All right. Big business."

"And one has to be invited?"

"Yes."

"And you were invited?"

"Yes, I was invited."

"Isn't it true that you asked to be invited?"

"No, that isn't true."

"It isn't?"

"No."

"I have a copy here of a letter from you to a Mr. A. Richard Gammage. Mr. Gammage is president of Gammage International. You've heard of Mr. Gammage and Gammage International?"

"Yes."

"Yes, I suppose you would have since Gammage International owns about half of Cleveland and some thirty thousand of your members work for that concern."

"I know Mr. Gammage."

"Yes, apparently you do. In fact, you seem to know him well enough to call him by his first name."

"I call a lot of people by their first names."

"Of course, Don, we all do. Well, in this letter you call Mr. Gammage 'Dear Dick.'"

"So?"

"So I'm just going to read a paragraph. Just one. This is

a letter from you to A. Richard Gammage whom you call 'Dear Dick.' "

"Yes."

"Before I read it, I suppose it should be mentioned that Mr. Gammage is one of the principal negotiators when you conduct your industry-wide bargaining, isn't he?"

"Yes, he's one of them anyhow."

"In fact, he might be called the chief negotiator, mightn't he?"

"I said he was one of them."

"Well, he's sort of your counterpart in industry, isn't he, Don? I mean you're the principal negotiator for your union and Mr. Gammage is the principal negotiator for industry, isn't that roughly it?"

"Roughly."

"In other words, just to simplify things, it's Mr. Gammage and you who finally decided just how much your members are going to get in take-home pay?"

"That's a gross oversimplification."

"But there's an element of truth in it, right?"

"Just barely."

"Well, in this Dear Dick letter which is signed by you, you say, 'I have done some checking around and if you and Arthur could resubmit my name, I am sure it would go through this time. I certainly do not want to embarrass you and Arthur again, but from what I have been able to learn, there should be no objection to my membership this time around and you know what it would mean to me.' Does that sound like you, Don?"

"I don't remember writing it."

"No? Well, on September third, 1965, according to the records of the Federalists Club, your name was submitted for membership on the recommendation of Mr. A. Richard Gammage and Mr. Arthur Bolton. It received only one blackball at a general membership meeting and so on September fourth, 1965, a letter inviting you to join was sent by the club's membership secretary. I should add here that Mr. Arthur Bolton is the general counsel to Gammage International. I should also add that the records of the Federalists Club show that on January ninth, 1965, your name was submitted for the first time by these same two gentlemen and it received three blackballs, which was one more than enough to keep you from being invited to join. Would you like to make any comment?"

"No, I don't think it deserves any."

"Well, do you have any idea of why you were blackballed the first time?"

"Apparently someone didn't like me. Not everyone does."

"But why did you want to join a club that didn't want you?"

"There were only three members who didn't."

"So you asked Mr. Gammage and Mr. Bolton to try to get you in again?"

"Yes, I suppose I did."

"Why did you ask them?"

"Because they were members."

"Are they friends of yours?"

"Well, yes, I suppose they are."

"In other words, you negotiate the contracts for your union members' income with your friends. Isn't that all rather cozy?"

"Friendship has nothing to do with the negotiations."

"Nothing at all?"

"Nothing at all."

"I see. So when you go up for the final negotiations on your new contract, which I believe begin next month and you see Mr. Gammage and Mr. Bolton sitting across the table from you, they'll be just another couple of company men and not two close personal friends that you're indebted to for having risked embarrassing themselves by putting your name up for membership in a club that rejected you the first time."

"They'll be just a couple of men."

"You're still a member of the Federalists Club, aren't you?"

"Yes."

"You've never thought of resigning?"

"No."

"I see. What percentage of the membership of your union, Don, would you say is black?"

"I don't know what the percentage is. We don't ask our members what color they are."

"But it's a sizable percentage?"

"Yes."

"Possibly fifty percent?"

"I don't know, possibly."

"How many black members does the Federalists Club have?"

"I don't know."

"Isn't it true that it has none?"

"I don't know."

"Have you ever seen a black member in the club?"

"Well, I don't go there a lot. I never noticed."

"Isn't it true that the bylaws of the club prohibit the membership of anyone who is of African or Oriental descent, as they so delicately put it?"

"I've never read the bylaws."

"Well, that's what they say. Do you remember a man called Austin Davies?"

"No, the name doesn't ring a bell."

"Well, he's a black man. He used to be an Assistant Secretary of Commerce."

"I recall his name now, but I don't think I know him."

"Well, perhaps you remember in March of 1966, five months after you joined the Federalists Club, when several of its members approached you about supporting the membership of Austin Davies."

"Yes, I remember now that you mention it. I agreed to support him. Of course I did."

"Yes, I think you did. There were eleven members who sponsored Mr. Davies and you made the twelfth, right?"

"Yes, I believe so."

"Then what happened?"

"As I remember, Mr. Davies' membership application was rejected."

"By how many blackballs?"

"I don't know the exact number."

"But it was a large number, wasn't it?"

"I think so."

"There were fifteen blackballs, Don."

"If you say so."

"The committee of twelve who had sponsored Mr. Davies had discussed this possibility, hadn't it?"

"Yes, we'd talked about it."

"And what had you planned to do?"

"I don't think we planned to do anything except maybe resubmit Mr. Davies' name at some later time."

"You planned more than that, Don."

"I don't recall."

"You planned to resign as a body—in protest against the Federalists Club's discriminatory practices. You remember it now, don't you, Don?"

"Well, there might have been some talk of it."

"There wasn't just talk of it, you all made a solemn pact to resign in protest if Davies was blackballed. Well?"

"It might have been like that. Like you said."

"And eleven of the twelve members on the committee did actually resign, didn't they?"

"It was—well—it was a matter of individual choice, I mean—"

"Don."

"Yes."

"Why didn't you resign?"

"Well, it seemed a pretty drastic step and—uh—I thought I could do more good by staying where I was and trying to change the rules from within you know."

"Don, have the rules been changed?"

"No, not yet. At least I don't think so."

"And you're still a member?"

"Well, yes."

"You're still a member of a lily-white club made up of politicians and big-business types who refuse membership to any black. Now am I right?"

"Well, yes, but—"

"That's all, Don. We've got to break for a commercial."

In the studio waiting room Oscar Imber and Charles Guyan watched the show with a kind of horrified fascination. Over and over Guyan kept saying, "Well, it's not network, at least it's not network."

Fred Mure watched the show with them. As the two men sank deeper into their despondency, Mure said, "I don't know what you guys are pissing and moaning about. I think old Don looks pretty good in there."

10

Cubbin didn't have to ask either Charles Guyan or Oscar Imber how he had gone over. He could see it in their faces. Fred Mure, on the other hand, was beaming. "You done real good, Don," Mure said.

"Just give me a drink, stupid."

"Sure, Don," Mure said and handed Cubbin an opened half-pint bottle. Cubbin drank deeply, but didn't hand the bottle back. "Let's get the hell out of here," he said.

Mure drove back to the hotel. Cubbin sat next to him in the front seat, nipping steadily at the bourbon. His dignity had deserted him now. He huddled against the righthand door, his raincoat collar up around his ears, trying not to remember what had just happened, trying to make the whiskey make him forget.

After they had driven for five minutes in silence, Guyan said, "Well, at least it wasn't network."

"You already said that about fifteen times," Imber said.

"I should never have let you guys talk me into it," Cubbin said, anxious to blame someone else for the horror that had befallen him. "I didn't want to go on his goddamned show. The guy's a louse. Everybody knows that. Everybody."

Guyan thought about reminding Cubbin of whose idea "Jake's Night" had been, but he knew it wouldn't do any good and might even do more harm. It had been Cubbin's idea, of course. "I know how to handle Jake," Cubbin had told Guyan. "Not everybody knows how to score points on his show, but I do. You just have to keep him a little off balance and keep coming up with the unexpected."

But Guyan couldn't think of anything to say so he said what he had been saying. "Well, hell, at least it wasn't network."

"Don't give him that crap," Imber snapped. "Tell him how bad it really was. Tell him what an ass he made of himself."

Cubbin twisted around in the front seat to look at Guyan. His blue eyes were wide and almost pleading. The son of a bitch is going to cry on us, Guyan thought.

"Was it really bad?" Cubbin said, his face imploring Guyan to tell him that it wasn't.

Guyan looked out of the car window. "It was bad," he said after a while. "I know what I'd do with it."

"What?" Imber said. "Tell our leader here what you'd do with it."

"I'd use it on the blacks. That's where it's going to hurt you, with the blacks. The whites don't give a shit whether you resigned or not from some fancy club because it wouldn't let some spade in. In fact, it might even win you a few points with some of them, maybe all of them, I don't know. I don't know what whites think about blacks anymore. But the blacks aren't going to like it. That's for damn sure."

"Sammy Hanks will have a transcript of that show in the mail special delivery to every local by noon tomorrow," Imber said. "That'll be just the start. Sellout's going to be the issue. Sammy'll tell the blacks that you're ready to sell them out for membership in some snotty club. He'll tell the whites that you pal around with the bosses and how can you expect a guy who sucks up to the bosses to know anything about the needs of a working stiff. Christ, Don, you've just handed him his whole campaign on a silver platter."

"Country-club unionism," Guyan said in a musing voice.

"Huh?" Cubbin said, lifting the bottle to his lips again.

66

"Country-club unionism. That's what I'd call it." A true professional, Guyan grew mildly enthusiastic about a good idea, no matter that it could wreck his client's hopes. "Christ, I'd dig up every picture I could find of you with a golf club or a tennis racket in your hand. 'What Kind of Deal Will This Man Make for You on the Seventeenth Hole?' "

"That's not bad," Imber said.

"It wasn't a country club," Cubbin said weakly.

"It doesn't matter," Guyan said. "All Sammy had before was some vague kind of charge that you'd lost touch with the rank and file. Now he can pinpoint where you lost it."

The liquor had begun to come to Cubbin's rescue. His face had taken on a deep flush. "Look, fella, you're working for me—not Sammy Hanks. So instead of sitting there shelling out ideas about how he can beat me, why don't you come up with a few for our side? That's what I'm paying you for and I'm getting pretty goddamned sick and tired of listening to you tell me what a wonderful campaign you could do for Sammy Hanks."

"I was just trying to anticipate what he's going to do."

"Well why don't you try anticipating what I'm going to do?"

"Because you're on the defensive, Don. You're the incumbent and to get your job Sammy has to attack and you have to defend. If you know how he's going to attack, then you not only defend, but you also counterattack."

"You sound like some goddamned general."

"You're the general, Don," Guyan said. "I'm just a lieutenant colonel a little overage in grade."

"Yeah, well, Colonel, you'd better come up with something that'll make Sammy—uh—sound a retreat, that's what."

"I'll work on it."

Cubbin emptied the half-pint into his mouth. "Give me the other one," he said to Fred Mure.

"That's all there is, Don."

"Don't give me that shit, just give me the other bottle. I can still count."

Mure sighed loudly and handed Cubbin the last of the four half-pints. Imber and Guyan watched glumly as he unscrewed the cap, tipped up the bottle, and drank.

"You got any more of them around?" Imber said.

"Any more of what, these?" Cubbin said, waving the bottle a little.

"Any more skeletons in your goddamned closet is what I mean."

"Let me tell you something, sonny boy," Cubbin said, turning his deep baritone into a harsh, grating noise. "I'm the fuckin president of this fuckin union and if you want to keep your fuckin job you'd better start worrying about how long I'm gonna be president because if I'm not, you're gonna be out on your ass."

"I worry about it all the time, President Cubbin, sir," Imber said, not trying to keep any of the sarcasm out of his tone. "I worry about it so much that I make myself sick, but not half as sick as I'll be if we're slipped another little surprise like we were slipped tonight. That's why I asked about skeletons. Have you got any more of them banging around anywhere?"

Cubbin's face was flaming by now. "Just what d'you mean by that, Oscar, that I'm some kind of a freak, maybe some kind of a closet queer or something, is that what you mean?"

"I don't know what I mean, Don," Imber said. "Let's forget it; it's late."

Cubbin turned around in his seat, the scarlet fading from his face as he took another drink. "Well, there's nothing wrong with me, nothing bad anyhow. I might have made a few mistakes in my life, but hell, who hasn't? But that doesn't mean a man has to be turned inside out in public just to see whether he's fit to be president of some fuckin labor organization. Christ, I shoulda gone to the coast that time when I had the chance."

"You'da made a damn fine actor, Don," Fred Mure said as he smoothly slid the car to a stop in front of the Sheraton-Blackstone.

"Who the hell asked you?" Cubbin said.

"Well, I got my own opinion and I think you'da made a hell of a good actor, that's what I think."

"What are you just sitting there for?" Cubbin growled. "Why don't you go in and get the goddamned elevator ready?"

"Sure, Don," Mure said. "I was just going."

Cubbin continued to sit in the car while Mure went into the hotel. He tipped the bottle up, drained most of it, felt a little better, and turned to the two men in the back seat. He grinned at them. He was all good humor again. "I wonder what I'd do if I didn't have that dumb cluck to kick around?" he said and then turned back still grinning, but not expecting an answer.

By the time Cubbin reached his twelfth-floor suite he had drunk the last of the four half-pints of Ancient Age, making his total consumption for the day a drink or two over a quart.

He was still on his feet, still talking, and apparently still lucid when he strode into the suite demanding a drink.

"Come on, Don," Fred Mure said. "Let's go get your pajamas on while Sadie fixes you a drink."

Cubbin turned to his wife. "You mad at me, honey? These guys are mad at me," he said, indicating Oscar Imber and Charles Guyan.

"I'm not mad at you, darling," Sadie said and went over and put her arms around him.

Cubbin looked at Guyan and Imber over his wife's shoulder. "I want you guys up here at eight o'clock tomorrow morning. We've got a lot of work to do. Eight o'clock. We'll have breakfast."

"Sure, Don," Imber said, "eight o'clock," and thought, you'll be lucky, fella, if you've finished throwing up by ten. He looked past Cubbin and his wife, who were still involved in an embrace, to Fred Mure who stood by the door to the bedroom. Imber lifted an eyebrow and Mure nodded.

"Well, we'll let you get some sleep, Don," Imber said.

"Eight o'clock," Cubbin said. "We'll have breakfast."

"Sure, Don," Guyan said.

After the two men had gone, Fred Mure said, "Let's get those pajamas on, Don, and then we'll all have a drink."

Cubbin looked down at his wife. "You saw it, huh?"

She nodded and smiled. "I saw it."

"I fucked up, didn't I?"

"Get your pajamas on and we'll have a drink and then we can talk about it."

"Come on, Don," Fred Mure said.

Cubbin turned slowly from his wife and moved carefully toward Fred Mure. He now had to concentrate on moving his feet so that he wouldn't weave and stagger. When Mure reached for his arm, Cubbin jerked it away and snarled, "I can make it."

"Sure, Don."

When he came out of the bedroom a few minutes later, he was dressed in a scarlet-silk bathrobe, pale blue pajamas and fleece-lined black slippers. He was also walking steadily, with long, firm strides. Sadie estimated that that would last for all of five minutes.

She handed him a glass that contained three ounces of whiskey, three cubes of ice, and two ounces of water. If she was lucky, he would never finish it. Cubbin took the drink and gulped at it. "That's better," he said and looked around for some place to sit. He chose a deep armchair and lowered himself into it.

"You saw me on that shit's program, huh?" he said to his wife who was handing Fred Mure a drink.

"I saw you."

"How was I?"

"You were good, darling, but his questions were unfair."

"He's a louse. You know I've done that guy favors. Lots of favors. He didn't have any cause to—"

There was a knock at the door and Cubbin broke off. "What time is it?"

"A little after two, Don," Fred Mure said.

"Who the Christ is coming around knocking on my door at two in the morning?" He tried to get up, but Sadie said, "I'll get it."

She moved over to the door, put the chain on, opened

it a crack, said, "My God!" and closed the door long enough to take the chain off and swing it open wide. Standing there, a scuffed black leather one-suiter case in his left hand was a tall young man, around twenty-six or twenty-seven, with old sad, wise eyes that were a startlingly pale blue, a white grin that belonged to a merry six-year-old, and a tan that a Miami lifeguard might have envied.

The young man put the suitcase down, cried, "Mommie!" in a deep baritone and took Sadie in his arms and kissed her on the mouth with what began as mock passion, but which was almost beginning to turn into something more when he released her. He turned from her to the still seated Cubbin whose face was now brightened by a genuine smile of pleasure. "And dear old Dad, God's gift to the hard hats. How are you, my father? Back on the sauce, I see."

Cubbin stopped smiling his delighted smile only long enough to take a deep swallow of his drink. Goddamn, he's a good-looking bastard, Cubbin thought, and then said, "It's past two in the morning. What the hell are you doing here?"

The young man waved an arm at the hotel room. "Why, Dad, I've come home." He turned to Fred Mure who was also grinning. "And Filthy Fred Mure, our own Stepin Fetchit. How are you, Freddie?"

Mure moved quickly to the young man and stuck out his hand. "Jesus, Kelly, it's good to see you. Let me getcha a drink."

Kelly Cubbin, his father's only child, smiled at Mure and said, "Just tell me where it is, Fred. I can get it."

"Hell, no. What're you drinking, Scotch?"

"If you've got it."

"Sure," Mure said and hurried from the room to the bedroom where the bottles and glasses were kept out of the sight of visitors. Mure kept them out of sight because he felt that it wasn't dignified to have them sitting around when visitors came. "They might get the wrong idea," he told Cubbin.

"All right, let's have it," Cubbin said to his son, his words slurring a little.

71

"Have what, chief?"

"You're supposed to be in Washington. You're supposed to be on the job there. What the hell you doing in Chicago? I didn't ask you to come to Chicago."

"And I thought you'd be glad to see me. My, it is a wise child who can predict his own father."

"Hell, I'm glad to see you, Kelly. You know I'm glad to see you. But Christ, you're supposed to be in Washington, working and—"

Kelly turned his back on his father and looked at Sadie. He lifted one eyebrow questioningly and she nodded slightly. Kelly turned back to his father. He studied him for a few moments and said, "Father, dear Father, drink up because whatever I tell you tonight, I'll simply have to say all over again tomorrow."

"What the hell are you talking about?" Cubbin said.

"I mean you're soused and you won't remember tomorrow." He turned back to Sadie. "Have you got a place for me?"

"Sure, honey. Take room E, it's the last one down the hall."

"What brought this on?" Kelly said, moving his head slightly toward his father.

She shrugged. "The campaign, I suppose. He'll go along fine for three or four days and then—bang. He dives back in a bottle."

"Just because I've had a few little drinks," Cubbin said, starting to rise. "Just because I might have had a drink or two, just because I might have done that, well, it's no reason why you have to talk about me like I wasn't even here."

Kelly moved over and gently pushed his father back into the chair. "Relax, chief, you're fading."

Cubbin started to struggle out of his chair again but sank back unprotestingly at another gentle shove from his son. "I don't understand," he muttered.

Fred Mure came into the room again and handed Kelly a drink. "Thanks, Fred," Kelly said and looked down at his father. He smiled at him but the merriment had gone from the smile. It was replaced by a mixture of sad affection and amused concern. He should never have gone for it this time, Kelly thought. He should have retired and let them fight over it. He doesn't want it anymore because it bores him. I wonder how long it's bored him.

"You're looking good, sir," he said.

Cubbin peeped up at him, a little shyly. "I think I might have had a couple too many today," he said, waving his glass around.

"Well, it happens."

"Yeah, well what happened to you?"

"I was placed on administrative leave. That was after the hearing."

"What hearing?"

"About my attitude."

"What about it?"

"It wasn't quite what they had in mind."

Cubbin looked at his son, focusing his eyes on the lean, tanned face and his mind on what was being said. Both took a lot of effort. "They tied the can to you, didn't they?" Cubbin said.

"They did indeed."

"Why, Kelly?" Sadie said.

Kelly shrugged.

"Well, hell, I can fix that tomorrow," Cubbin said. "I can make one little phone call and fix that."

"No, I don't think so."

"You want your job back?" Cubbin said. "I'll get it back for you."

"I don't think Kelly wants it back, darling," Sadie said.

"You don't want it back?" Cubbin said sleepily, his words slurring badly now."

"No, I don't think so."

"Whyn't you want it back?" Cubbin said and let his chin sink toward his chest. Fred Mure moved quickly across the room and took the half-empty glass from Cubbin's fingers.

Kelly Cubbin stood looking down at his father for a few moments. Then he drained his drink and turned toward Sadie and Fred Mure. "You need any help with him?"

"No, he'll walk it by himself," Mure said.

"Then I'll see him in the morning and we can go through it again."

"Give Kelly the key to room E," Sadie said to Mure.

Mure fished in his pocket, took out a handful of room keys, selected one and handed it to Kelly.

"Thanks," Kelly said. He turned toward Sadie. "How's it look for him?"

She sighed. "I don't know. Not good."

"You mean he might win?"

She nodded. "I'm afraid he might."

"You shouldn't say that, Sadie," Mure said. "Don's gonna win okay and everything's gonna be fine."

Kelly and his stepmother exchanged glances and then Kelly smiled at Fred Mure. "Sure he will, Fred. I'll see you both in the morning. Good night."

"Good night," they said.

When Kelly had gone, Fred Mure went over to Donald Cubbin and bent down close to his ear. "Mr. Cubbin, the President will see you now," he bellowed.

Cubbin sat up with a start. "What—what—where?"

"This way, Mr. Cubbin," Mure bellowed again.

Cubbin rose easily, turned, and guided by Mure headed toward the bedroom door. He walked normally, even purposefully. Mure guided him into the room and over to the bed. "Let me take your coat, Mr. Cubbin," he yelled in Cubbin's ear.

Cubbin let Mure slip the bathrobe from his shoulders. "Just get in here, Mr. Cubbin," Mure yelled again, helping Cubbin to sit on the turned-down twin bed. Cubbin's eyes were closed now and he made no protest as Mure lifted up his feet and swung them onto the bed. Sadie watched from the doorway as Fred Mure drew the bed covers up over Cubbin.

"Better turn him on his side, Fred," she said, slipping out of her robe. "He sometimes chokes when he's on his back."

Mure rolled the unprotesting Cubbin over on his left side so that he faced the wall. Then Mure started to unknot his own tie. "Are you all right, Mr. Cubbin?" he said in a normal tone. Cubbin only sighed deeply.

Mure turned toward the other twin bed. Sadie was

already in it, the covers drawn up to her chin. "Hurry, darling," she said.

Mure stripped off the rest of his clothes and crawled in beside her. As Mure's hands touched her, Sadie thought what she always thought, that as a substitute husband, Fred was a little untutored, but he made up for that with enthusiasm. And then she stopped thinking altogether.

11

They let Donald Cubbin sleep the next morning, which was a Friday. And while Cubbin slept, his enemies and friends alike were up and at work, doing whatever they thought must be done either to reelect him to office or to assure his defeat.

In Chicago on the tenth floor of the Sheraton-Blackstone Hotel, in room 1037, Charles Guyan, the public relations man, sat before the writing table that came with the room and stared at a blank sheet of paper that he had rolled into his Lettera 32 portable. He had been staring at it for an hour, four cups of coffee ago. For fifteen minutes of that hour he had thought about how he should compose his letter of resignation. For the remaining forty-five minutes he had thought, and thought hard, about what kind of a campaign he could put together for Donald Cubbin. After scratching some figures on a sheet of paper, he began to type a memorandum that read:

FROM: GUYAN
TO: CUBBIN
SUBJECT: HOW TO WIN YOUR ELECTION
FOR ONLY $1.01 PER MEMBER OR
A MERE ONE MILLION DOLLARS.

A million dollars was the lowest figure that Guyan could come up with. If we spend that much, he thought, he might make it. If we don't, then it will be ex-President Cubbin.

In room 942 of the same hotel, Oscar Imber was on a long-distance call to a man in Philadelphia whose letterhead claimed that he was "The Keystone State's Largest Ford Dealer." Cubbin's union leased nearly a hundred Ford Galaxies from the dealer, turning them in when their speedometers reached the 5,000-mile mark. It was a profitable arrangement for the dealer and Oscar Imber was calling to remind him that if Cubbin was defeated, the arrangement would come to an end, and how much did the dealer feel he could spare for Don's campaign?

"Well, Christ, Oscar, I don't know anything about union politics, but I consider Don my friend and I'd like to do something to help him out."

'Well, you can help him out about five thousand bucks' worth."

"Jesus!"

"I was just talking to Don yesterday about this leasing contract we have with you," Imber lied. "It's on a year-to-year basis, isn't it?"

"Yeah, that's right. Year-to-year."

"Well, Don and I were thinking that after the election's over it might be advantageous to put it on a five-year basis. That would be after the election, of course."

"Yeah," the Ford dealer said. "That would be real fine. Well, what do you want me to do, send a check?"

"We'd like it in cash, Sam. We'll send somebody around to pick it up. Would tomorrow morning be okay?"

"Well, yeah, I suppose so. You wouldn't want to send me a letter or memo or something about the five-year deal, would you?"

"No, I don't think I want to do that, Sam."

"Well, hell, can I at least get a receipt?"

"Sure," Imber said, "you'll get a receipt."

After he hung up the phone, Oscar Imber added up a column of figures. Thus far that morning he had raised $19,000 for Cubbin's campaign and he was down to those whom he considered to be the nickel-and-dimers, the small suppliers who were willing to contribute a little money, but only a little, to the campaign because the union was a valuable customer and if Cubbin was re-elected, it would continue to be so. Weeks before Imber had tapped what he considered to be the flushbottoms, the ones who dealt in some way with the union's sizable financial resources. He had raised money from them, large chunks of it in a few places, but in each instance he felt, or even knew, that Sammy Hanks had been there first, throwing his weight around as secretary-treasurer of the union. Imber knew that the flushbottoms were contributing to both sides, hedging their bets, but he also had the feeling that they were contributing more to Hanks's campaign than they were to Cubbin's. They can smell a loser, Imber thought, just like they can smell money.

He sighed and started to direct-dial another number in Washington, this time the president of an office-supply company who might be willing to part with a couple of thousand. One thousand's more like it, Imber thought as he listened to the phone ring in Washington. And that'll be more than he ever gave anyone else in his life.

In Washington that morning, in his two-story red brick home in Cleveland Park three blocks west of Connecticut Avenue, Sammy Hanks was listening on the telephone while someone in Chicago read him a transcript of Cubbin's appearance on "Jake's Night."

"He said that, huh?" Hanks would say from time to time and smile delightedly. His five-year-old daughter, Marylin, came into the living room and stood watching her father gravely. "Come here, honey," Hanks said and the little girl moved over to him, climbed into his lap, and put her arms around his neck.

"No, I wasn't talking to you, Johnnie, I was talking to my kid. Keep on reading. You were where Cubbin says that he didn't resign from the club because he could work from within or some such shit. Yeah. That's it."

Hanks went on listening to the reading of the transcript, holding the phone away from his mouth so that he could use it to make funny faces at his daughter who laughed and squealed and sometimes hid her eyes behind her hands. Marylin didn't think her father was at all ugly.

Finally, Hanks said, "Well, hell, that's nearly perfect, isn't it? I mean it couldn't have been any better unless old Don had taken a pratfall or something. And you say you've already got it run off?"

He listened for a moment, made another funny face at his daughter, and said, "Okay, now I want that to go out to every local special delivery. Yeah, I know special delivery's not any faster than regular mail anymore, but it's still more impressive so let's do it. Okay? . . . Okay. Now I want you or somebody else in Chicago to write the letter that goes with it. I don't want it to come from me. I don't give a fuck what it sounds like or whether the grammar's any good as long as it sounds hurt, you got me? Now whoever writes it is all sad and hurt because Cubbin didn't help that black out and because he's sucking up to the bosses, you know what I mean? Fine. You guys are really on the ball up there. I'm surprised. . . . Well, hell, Johnnie, I'm not that surprised. You did a good job and thanks for calling. . . . Yeah, I'll talk to you later."

Hanks hung up the phone and made another face at his daughter. "You're funny, Daddy," she said and giggled when he made another one.

"Didn't you know, honey? I'm the funniest man in the world."

It was not quite 9 A.M. in Cleveland, but A. Richard Gammage was already at his desk on the twenty-seventh floor of the Gammage Building which had a view of Lake Erie and downtown Cleveland and Gammage sometimes wondered which was the more depressing, the dying city or the dying lake.

He was the third A. Richard Gammage to head his company and he sometimes felt that his major contribution had been to change the firm's name from The Gammage Manufacturing Company to Gammage International.

Gammage International manufactured various home

and industrial equipment and A. Richard Gammage had little faith in any of it and even less interest. He felt that his products were no better or worse than those manufactured by his competitors and that they would all wear out at approximately the same time. He was always faintly surprised whenever *Consumer Reports* gave any of his household products an acceptable rating.

Gammage had first come to know Donald Cubbin well on one of those committees that are always being formed by the Federal Government in Washington. Cubbin had represented Labor and Gammage had represented Industry. They had hit it off together because neither was quite sure what the real purpose of the committee was, but only that its recommendations would be steadfastly ignored.

They had lunched a few times together in Washington after that because Cubbin could be a genuinely amusing companion, especially when he talked about other labor leaders and the early days of the CIO and the motion-picture industry and the peculiarities of various politicians. Gammage tried to remember whether they had ever talked about the contract that Cubbin's union had with his industry and decided that they hadn't, probably because neither of them was really interested in it and probably because both of them were equally bored with their jobs.

So after one of those lunches during which Cubbin had been particularly amusing, Gammage had felt that he would like to do something for him. Gammage seldom had been impulsively generous and he had rather enjoyed the feeling it gave him. He had asked Cubbin if he would like to become a member of the Federalists Club and Cubbin had made a small joke about it and Gammage had said that he would submit his name. He had, a week or so later, and he had been surprised and even a little mortified when Cubbin had been blackballed. He had been even more surprised by the letter that Cubbin had written him, that awful, begging letter that almost made Gammage squirm as he read it. With reluctance, Gammage had resubmitted Cubbin's name after a suitable interval and after Cubbin had been accepted, Gammage had avoided the Federalists Club whenever he was in Washington.

"Well, that's the story," said the man who now sat across from Gammage's desk.

"Cubbin's letter is still in our files?" Gammage said.

"Yes."

"How did Jake Jobbins get it?"

"I don't know. It's probably still in Cubbin's file, too."

"I see."

The man who sat across from A. Richard Gammage was Nelson Hardisty, the company's public relations director. Gammage looked at him and wondered whether Hardisty really thought that they were talking about something important. To Hardisty he said, "Well, what do we do?"

"It depends upon how the press reacts."

"They will react, you think?"

"It's a pretty hot story."

"I fail to see how it could possibly interest anyone."

"Politics," Hardisty said, using the most knowing tone he could produce. "Union politics."

"And you think I should have a statement prepared?"

"Well, that's why I called you this morning—"

"Yes, at seven."

"I thought it was important, Mr. Gammage."

"I'm sure you did."

"I could draft a statement for you, if you like."

"No, I think I'll dictate it."

"Yes, well, it might be good if you got to it right away."

"I'll dictate it to you now."

"Well, if you want to make sure the wording's—"

"It's only two words," Gammage said. " 'No comment.' Can you remember that?"

Hardisty flushed. "Yes, I can remember that."

"One more thing."

"Yes."

"I would like a carefully reasoned memo on my desk

by five o'clock tomorrow on why our public relations department should be abolished."

"Are you serious?"

"Yes. Completely."

"Well, I really don't think that I'm the one—"

"By five o'clock tomorrow, Hardisty."

"Am I being fired?"

"It depends on how good a job you do with that memo."

"I don't think—"

"That's all, Hardisty."

After he had gone, Gammage swung his chair around and looked out over the dying lake. I wonder why I did that, he thought. It must have been because I enjoyed it.

Four men who desperately wanted Donald Cubbin to be either defeated or reelected had gathered by chance at National Airport in Washington that Friday morning and by the same chance, they were all going to Chicago on the same United flight. Three of the men were white and one was black. The whites were Walter Penry and his principal associates, Peter Majury and Ted Lawson. The black was Marvin Harmes. The whites wanted Donald Cubbin reelected; the black wanted him defeated and none of them had too many scruples about how it should be done, although Harmes was still not quite sure just how an election is best stolen.

Still, Harmes thought, stealing an election's probably just like stealing anything else, the main thing being, like always, don't get caught. There had been a lot of elections stolen in Chicago, Harmes told himself, and you've phoned for an appointment with the man who's probably stolen more of them than anybody else and who's agreed to see you this afternoon at three o'clock. So at three o'clock, Brother Harmes, you're going to be calling on the nation's top election stealer. You're going to be calling on Indigo Boone.

The only one of the three whites to recognize Harmes was Peter Majury who, dressed as usual in his Afrika Korps trench coat, was slinking around the airport, trying to spot someone or something that should be noted and filed for possible future use. Majury always did this at airports just as he always tried to familiarize himself with anyone who someday might become an adversary or opponent. It was a task that kept him constantly busy, but he was diligent and he already had a comprehensive file on Marvin Harmes, both mental and on paper, which included such items as Harmes's skill as a poker player (semipro, Majury had noted, but steadily improving).

Majury thought that it wasn't particularly noteworthy that Harmes was flying to Chicago because that was his base and home. However, it might be interesting to learn what Harmes had been doing in Washington.

In the living room of the hotel suite that offered a view of Lafayette Park and, beyond that, of the White House, Coin Kensington was enjoying what he had described to his visitor as an "old-timey Kansas farm breakfast." The breakfast consisted of steak and eggs and potatoes, but the steak was a three-inch-thick filet drenched with Béarnaise sauce, the four eggs were Benedict, and the potatoes were what the hotel chef called *pommes de terre dauphinoise* which meant that they were cooked in cream and butter and drenched with Gruyère. The toast was just ordinary toast and Kensington had ordered a "quart of coffee" to wash it all down. He had also asked his visitor to share the coffee, but nothing else.

Kensington's visitor was a thirty-one-year-old man, conservatively dressed in one of the six look-alike suits that he had recently bought from Arthur Adler's. He had a wide pale forehead, dark wavy hair, cunningly styled to look long, but not too long; a sharp nose, pink at its tip; a red, small mouth that somehow looked mean, but which may have been only firm; a bony chin that managed to appear ambitious; and dark, flickering eyes that seldom gave away anything he thought or felt except his impatience with those whom he regarded as slower witted than himself. He was flashing his impatient look at Old Man Kensington now and, of course, he was making a mistake. The thirty-one-year-old man's name was Alfred Etheridge and not too many people called him Al because, first of all, he didn't like it and secondly, he worked at the White House where he thought a certain amount of formality should be maintained. Old Man Kensington, not too much on formality and largely indifferent to White House protocol, had been calling him Al for the last ten minutes.

"Sure you won't have some coffee, Al?" Kensington said.

"No, thank you, sir," Etheridge said. He called everyone "sir" if they were over thirty-five and above him in the pecking order because he believed that it made them feel uncomfortably old. Etheridge's ambition made him use a lot of little tricks like that.

"I didn't know you folks over there were quite so concerned about old Don Cubbin's reelection," Kensington said around a mouthful of steak.

"I thought it was made quite clear how interested we were when you met with us last week."

"Well, it's too bad you don't want him defeated."

"Why?"

"Be easier, that's why. All you'd have to do is have the President come out for him and he'd be bound to lose. Bound to." Kensington almost choked on his own mirth.

"The *President,*" Etheridge said, bearing down hard on the word because it usually worked magic for him, "personally asked me to find out what your assessment of the situation is now."

"You mean he called you into his office and asked you that?"

"I spoke to him over the phone," Etheridge said, lying very well.

"And he wants my assessment?"

"Yes, sir, he does."

"Well, that makes him more of a damn fool than I thought he was."

"I take exception to that remark, sir," Etheridge said and couldn't help but feel that he sounded stuffy.

"I don't mind," Kensington said. "You sure you don't want any coffee?"

"All I want is your assessment of Donald Cubbin's chances."

"Okay. Not good."

"Why?"

"One, he's drinking. Two, he made an ass out of himself on a Chicago TV program last night. You hear about that?"

"No, sir."

"Well, you will. Let's just say that it gave Sammy Hanks some pretty good ammunition, if he uses it right, and of course he will."

"But your own assignment—"

"Assignment?" Kensington said, letting pure wonder creep into his tone.

"At the meeting that was held last week, you were given—"

"I wasn't *given* anything, sonny. I wasn't *told* to do anything. I *mentioned* that I might stir around and *see* if there were some folks who might be interested in helping Cubbin get reelected. Well, I've stirred around some."

"I see," Etheridge said.

"No you don't."

"Well, perhaps you could explain then."

"Now, Al, I'd think it might be better if you didn't know just what I've done."

"I wonder if I might be the judge of that, sir."

"You?"

"Yes, sir. Me."

"Huh," Kensington grunted.

"May I tell the President that you refused to give me your assessment of—"

"Don't throw your weight around so much. Al. Using the President's name like that don't impress me any. What I'm trying to say is that if I tell you what I've done and you tell the President, and then later some smart-assed reporter asks him if he knows what I've done, and the President lies and says, no, he doesn't know anything about it, but then they go and find out that he did know, well, he's going to be embarrassed and I sure don't want to do anything to embarrass the President of the United States, do you, Al?"

"I still think that perhaps I should be the judge of

84

whether the information is given to the President, Mr. Kensington."

"You do, huh?"

"Yes, sir, I do."

"Since you work in the White House and all?"

"Yes, sir, I think it's part of my job."

"All right, sonny, suppose—let's just suppose now—suppose I was to tell you that I rounded up about a dozen of the top executives of the companies that Cubbin's union has a contract with—the contract that's coming up for final negotiation next month—I mean it expires next month—and these company executives don't want a strike and they don't want to pay no thirty-percent increase in wages over the next three years plus a lot of fringe benefits that we don't need to go into right here and now. You following me?"

"Yes, sir."

"Well, suppose I was to tell you that because they don't want a strike and because they don't want to pay any thirty-percent increase they agreed to get up a kitty for Don Cubbin—a $750,000 kitty to help him get reelected because they're pretty sure that if he is reelected, they won't have any strike or pay anywhere near a thirty-percent wage increase either. You're a lawyer, aren't you, Al?"

"Yes, sir."

"Well, I'd have to—"

"Would you think that's legal?"

"You'd have to look up the law?"

"Yes."

"Well, let me ask you this, do you think it's ethical—or would you have to look that up, too?"

"No. sir, I don't think it's ethical."

"Well, let me go on. Let me tell you how I'd spend that $750,000, supposing I got it."

"You?"

"That's right, Al. Me. Nobody else. Supposing those company boys give me the money. Well, for all they'd know I could put it in my pocket and they'd never be any wiser."

"I see."

85

"I bet you do. Well, supposing I went and hired the sneakiest, lowdown, most unscrupulous bunch of operators you've ever heard of and told them that I'd pay them a hundred thousand dollars and give them another six hundred and fifty thousand to play around with if they'd do just one thing, and I wasn't particular about how they did it, but all they had to do was get Cubbin reelected. Now supposing that before I hired this bunch—and I might even give you their name, because you seem to want to know everything—well, supposing that before I hired them, Cubbin's chances against being elected were about sixty-forty. Now they're about fifty-fifty. So that's my assessment and report, Al, and now I'd like to ask this, what're you going to do with it?"

Etheridge's eyes blinked rapidly and his mind raced. "Well, I—"

Kensington decided to give him a little time. "Oh, yeah, I forgot to tell you the name of that bunch of sharpies I just might have hired. It's Walter Penry and Associates, Incorporated. Seeing as how you now know who they are, you might even say that they're sort of working under White House instructions."

He's boxed me, Etheridge thought. If I tell them what he's told me, they'll be on my back for telling them something that they don't think that the man needs to know. But if I don't tell them, and something happens later, and they're not set or prepared for it, then they're going to want to know why I didn't tell them. I'm going to lose either way. I want to get away from here, he decided. I want to get away from this slick, fat old man who's so much smarter than I am, so goddamned much smarter.

Etheridge rose and said, "Well, thank you, Mr. Kensington, for seeing me."

"What're you gonna tell them, son?" the old man said softly, smiling only a little.

"I'll make a report."

"About what?"

"I'll have to consider the various—"

"You're gonna lose, whatever you tell them, you know that, don't you?"

"Yes."

Kensington nodded. "Well, that's good—I mean it's good that you know it. But there's one thing I like about you, Al."

Etheridge was moving toward the door now. "What?"

"You didn't make me any little speech about how the White House couldn't get itself involved in something nasty like I just told you about."

"No."

"You know why I like that?"

"Why?" Etheridge said, his hand on the doorknob.

"Because I've just had myself a mighty fine breakfast and I didn't want to have to throw it up all over the floor."

12

If Truman Goff had been drafted into the army and if the army had sent him to Vietnam and if he had spent a little time there killing Viet Cong and North and even South Vietnamese, he most likely would never have ended up in the assassination business.

But by the time Truman Goff was nineteen he already had a wife and a child so the draft didn't touch him. And by the time he was twenty-four he had left Southwest Virginia where he and his wife had been born and was working for Safeway in Baltimore. He was working as a checker then and living downtown in a row house and sometimes hanging out at a neighborhood bar called The Screaming Eagle.

Another regular customer at The Screaming Eagle was Bruce Cloke who had been forty-three when Goff had first met him nearly five years ago now. They had bought each other a few beers and talked about the Orioles and the Colts and about Cloke's success with women. Cloke was a salesman and wasn't too particular about what he sold as long as he could sell it to housewives. Sometimes he sold vacuum cleaners and sometimes aluminum siding and sometimes encyclopedias and even, upon occasion, magazine subscriptions. He was a big, ignorant, good-looking man with an immense amount of surface charm and if he had wished, he could have had his own sales crew working for him. But Cloke was also a passionate fisherman and hunter and whenever the notion hit him, he liked to drop everything and spend two weeks or ten days going after bass or ducks or deer.

It had been November when Truman Goff had dropped into The Screaming Eagle for a beer. It was also the middle of the afternoon and the only other customer in the place had been Bruce Cloke.

"How come you're not working?" Cloke asked, after buying Goff a beer.

"I got a week off. It's my vacation."

"How come you didn't take it last summer?"

Goff shrugged. "I don't much like vacations. I took a week in July but I didn't have enough money then to go anywhere so I'm taking the other week now. If I don't take it before the first of the year, I'll lose it."

"Well, I'm taking myself a little vacation this week, too. Right down to Virginia." Cloke aimed an imaginary rifle at some imaginary target and went pow-pow a couple of times.

Truman Goff got interested. "Deer, huh?"

"That's right, buddy."

"Where you going? I'm from Virginia, you know."

"Down around Lynchburg."

"Yeah? I'm from down around there."

Three beers later Truman Goff had agreed to go deer hunting with Bruce Cloke. They left the next morning and by nine that night they were settled into the Idledale Motel on the outskirts of Lynchburg. They were also about halfway through the first of two fifths of Old Cabin Still that Cloke had brought along.

"You know something, buddy?" Cloke said.

"What?"

"I been a fisherman all my born days, but guess where I first got interested in hunting?"

"Where at?"

"Italy, that's where."

"What the fuck were you doing in Italy?"

"I was hunting the real thing, that's what I was doing in Italy. I was hunting krauts."

"Oh, yeah, in the army."

"That's right, in the army. In the goddamned infantry is what. In the Forty-fifth Division."

"Yeah, well, I guess that's something all right."

"You *guess* it's something?"

"That's what I said."

"Well, let me ask you something. You ever been in the army?"

"No, you know I ain't ever been in the army."

"Then you ain't never hunted the real thing; you ain't never hunted men."

"Maybe I ain't never hunted men but I've hunted more deer and more possum and more quail and more bobcat than you ever hoped to hunt."

"But you never hunted no man, did you?"

"Well, I reckon I could, if I put my mind to it. Wouldn't be no more trouble than hunting bobcat."

"You think you could kill a man? I mean you think you could get a fellow human bean right in your sights and then squeeeeeze that trigger ever so easy without getting the shakes? You think you could do that, Truman?"

"Shit yes, I could do it," Goff said and poured himself another drink.

Cloke looked at him for several moments, grinning. "I'll be willing to bet you fifty bucks that you can't."

"What kind of a fuckin bet is that?" Goff said.

"Just what I said."

"Shit, I ain't going to no electric chair for fifty bucks."

"You don't have to worry about no electric chair."

"You just said that you was willing to bet me fifty bucks that I couldn't get somebody in my sights and then pull the trigger and I said I bet I could, but I wasn't going

89

to no electric chair just to prove it." The whisky was making Goff confused. "Well, shit, it's a dumb bet anyhow."

"Tell you what, Truman."

"What?"

"What if we fixed it up so that there wasn't no chance, I mean no chance at all, of you going to no electric chair. I mean it."

"How you gonna do that?"

"Never you mind how I'm gonna do it. Is it a bet?"

"Well, shit, I ain't about to—"

"What's a matter, you chicken?"

"Now don't try to get me riled by calling me chicken, Bruce. You could call me chicken all night and it wouldn't bother me none. I been called worsen that. So you can just keep on calling me chicken, but I ain't gonna make no bet until I know what I'm betting on."

So Bruce Cloke explained how Truman Goff could get a man in his rifle sights, pull the trigger, collect fifty dollars, and not go to the electric chair. When Cloke had finished, Goff said, "Well, shit, you didn't tell me that it was gonna be a nigger."

"Well, it's still a man."

"Yeah, but shooting a nigger. Hell, that'd be easy."

"I'm willing to bet you fifty bucks you can't do it."

"All right, smart ass, I'll just bet you fifty I can. Let's go."

Cloke and Goff drove the seventy-four miles to Richmond in a little less than three hours, arriving on the outskirts of the city just after midnight. They had finished the first fifth of Cabin Still and had opened the second. It the back seat of Cloke's 1965 Pontiac was Goff's old .30-.30 Marlin. It was loaded.

"Where the hell you going now?" Goff asked as Cloke drove in an apparently aimless fashion through the Richmond streets.

"What the hell do you care? You ain't gonna do nothing anyhow."

"You just have your fifty bucks ready, smart ass."

"I got my fifty bucks ready. Don't you worry about that. You just worry about what you gotta do. You only

90

get one chance. Just like deer hunting. Ain't nobody gonna stand around and wait for you to make up your mind."

"Just tell me when," Goff said. "That's all you gotta do. Just tell me when."

"Now!" Cloke said and braked the car to a stop. It was a residential street lined with gray, wooden houses. A few lights burned. Cars, most of them several years old, were parked closely together on both sides of the street. It was dark, but three street lamps provided yellow patches of light along a broken cement sidewalk. The houses had small yards and most of them offered nothing but hard-packed dirt although a few had spots of Bermuda grass that were turning an autumn brown.

"Where?" Goff said.

"On your right. Just coming out of that house—about fifty yards down."

Goff looked and then saw what Cloke meant. A man was coming down the steps of a two-story frame house that had its porch light on. He was wearing a dark overcoat. He walked from the porch to the sidewalk and turned left, toward Goff and Cloke who sat double-parked in the Pontiac, its lights off.

"You wanta pay me now, chicken?" Cloke said.

"I'll pay you shit," Goff muttered, turned in his seat, and reached for the rifle. He opened the door.

"Remember, you gotta squeeeeeeze the trigger," Cloke whispered.

Truman Goff got out of the Pontiac, went around the end of a car that was parked next to the curb, and knelt by its rear right fender. He brought the rifle butt up to his shoulder and stared through the sights at the man who was walking toward him. The man was now no more than 120 feet away. In a few seconds he would be directly under one of the block's three street lamps. Goff waited. When the man came under the street lamp Goff saw that he had on a dark tan topcoat, a white shirt, and a dark tie. He also had a black face. Goff squeezed the trigger, the rifle cracked, and the man stumbled. "Shit," Goff thought, "this ain't nothing." He worked the bolt on the Marlin and fired again. This time the man went down, sprawled on

91

the sidewalk and bathed in yellow light. He lay on his left side, his face toward Goff. The man's mouth was open and Goff thought that his teeth were awfully white.

Goff ran toward the already moving Pontiac and scrambled in. "You crazy son of a bitch!" Cloke shouted at him and stamped on the accelerator. The Pontiac shot down the street, past the sprawled body of the man on the sidewalk. They passed by close enough for Truman Goff to get a good look. The dead man appeared to be in his early twenties and Goff noticed that he had some gold teeth among all those white ones.

"Young nigger buck," he said to Cloke.

"Jesus Christ, you're a crazy son of a bitch!"

"Where's my fifty?"

"I don't want nothing to do with you," Cloke yelled. "You're crazy."

"You owe me fifty bucks, fella," Goff said in a cold voice.

"All right," Cloke said, digging his wallet out and fumbling in it while continuing to drive too fast, twisting and turning the car through the streets of Richmond. "All right, here's your fifty goddamned dollars." He flung the bills at Goff.

"What're you so antsy about?" Goff said, folding the bills carefully after he counted them.

Cloke turned to stare at Goff and Goff noted that the older man's features were distorted. His face is all stretched out of shape, Goff thought. The son of a bitch is scared. The big blowhard bastard is scared shitless.

That discovery was so interesting that Goff decided to examine his own feelings. I don't feel no different than if it was a deer, he decided. I don't feel near nothing like the time I got that bobcat. Christ, there really ain't nothing to it, shooting down some poor nigger who can't shoot back or run or nothing. He felt a little sorry for the nigger for a moment, just as he always felt a little sorry for deer. But it was only for a moment.

"I don't want nothing to do with you ever," Cloke was saying. "I don't want to talk to you. I don't want to see you. I don't want to be around you. You're crazy. You know that? You're plumb crazy."

"What the fuck's bothering you?" Goff said, lifting up the fifth and taking a long swallow. "Hell, there wasn't nothing to it. All that crap you gave me about hunting men. Shit! It ain't near as hard as getting yourself a good deer. Not near."

"I ain't never gonna talk to you anymore, hear?" Cloke said. "I mean never."

"All right, see if I give a good goddamn."

When Truman Goff awakened the next morning in the Lynchburg motel room he was alone. He went looking for Cloke in the coffee shop and when he didn't find him, Goff ordered breakfast, a big one, because he knew that it would help his slight hangover. He ordered coffee, three fried eggs, ham, grits, and biscuits. After he ate he went to the motel office and asked about Cloke.

"He checked out early," the man in the motel office said. "He checked out and said you'd pay."

Goff paid and asked the man to call him a cab. He went back to his room and packed his bag and slipped the canvas case over his rifle. I'll clean it when I get home, he thought, and then went back to the motel office to wait for the cab.

Truman Goff caught a Trailways bus to Richmond and then took a nonstop Greyhound to Washington where he caught another Greyhound to Baltimore. In Richmond he had bought *The Times-Dispatch* and read it carefully, but he saw nothing about a black man being shot to death. It probably happened too late for a morning paper, he told himself. And besides that, he was a nigger. Truman Goff never did find out the name of the man that he had killed in Richmond.

In Baltimore that night, Goff's wife wanted to know why he had returned so early. "The guy I went with got sick so I came back."

"Well, what're you gonna do the rest of your vacation?"

"I don't know. Just hang around, I guess."

The next afternoon Truman Goff wandered down to The Screaming Eagle. He went up to the bar and ordered a beer. He took the first swallow and then looked around. In the back booth was Bruce Cloke and another man. Goff didn't recognize the man but he looked out of place in The Screaming Eagle. Too well dressed, Goff decided. The man wore a neat dark suit, a button-down blue shirt, a dark striped tie, and dark shoes. He seemed to be in his late thirties or early forties with a long, narrow face that was decorated with a thick moustache. He wore his hair fairly long and it swirled around his temples in gentle gray waves.

When Goff spotted Cloke he started to wave at him, but Cloke looked at him and then past him or through him without the slightest sign of recognition. To hell with him, Goff thought and started to turn back around toward the bar. But it was then that Cloke leaned toward the gray-haired man, said something, and shook his head slightly as if in warning, but the gray-haired man shrugged and looked up at Goff. He spent nearly a minute staring at Goff with his dark, serious eyes. Goff had stared back, thinking that he was damned if he'd let any pal of Cloke's stare him down. When the minute was over the man had smiled slightly and turned back to Cloke.

Goff faced around to the bar and started thinking, but he didn't much like his thoughts because they made him a little afraid so he ordered another beer. He drank that and started to leave but looked back again at Cloke and the gray-haired man. Cloke still wouldn't look at him, but the gray-haired man turned once more and gave him another careful look, as if inspecting something that he wasn't yet sure that he could afford to buy.

When Truman Goff got home, he switched on the television set, took his rifle out of its case and began cleaning it. When his wife came into the living room he said, "I'm gonna need the car all day tomorrow."

"Where you going?" she said, not because she expected much of an answer, but because she considered it her duty to ask.

"I gotta see a couple of guys," Goff said and rammed the cleaning rod down the rifle barrel.

The next morning at nine Truman Goff waited in his car for Bruce Cloke to come out of his East Baltimore apartment. Cloke always parked on the street and Goff had driven around until he spotted the Pontiac and then found a place to park about half a block from it. Truman Goff was driving a five-year-old Chevrolet Impala then. On its back seat under a blanket lay the Marlin .30-.30.

When Cloke pulled away from the curb, Goff followed. Cloke headed for South Baltimore and thirty minutes later pulled up in front of a yellow brick house that had an FHA-approved look about it. Cloke got out of his car, went around to its trunk, opened it, and took out a large brown leather salesman's case. He closed the trunk and went up to the front door of the yellow house and rang the bell. A moment later he disappeared inside.

Truman Goff waited forty-nine minutes for Cloke to come out. He's probably tearing off a piece in there, Goff thought. He watched the house, not taking his eyes from it except to glance at his watch. When Cloke finally came out of the house, he paused at the door to talk to whoever was inside. Goff got out of his car on the left-hand side, reached back for the Marlin, and moved around to the rear of his car.

When Cloke was through talking he turned and walked down the sidewalk toward his car. He was a little over two hundred feet away when Truman Goff stepped out from behind his own car, lifted the rifle, aimed, and shot Bruce Cloke three times, twice before he even hit the ground. Then Goff got in his car, made a U-turn, and sped back toward East Baltimore.

When he arrived home, he turned on the TV set and started to clean his rifle.

"That didn't take long," his wife said. "I thought you was gonna be gone all day."

"One of the guys I was supposed to see couldn't make it," Goff said.

"I thought you cleaned that thing yesterday," his wife said.

"I didn't do too good a job."

"Well, can I use the car this afternoon? I gotta go shopping."

"Sure, go ahead and use it."

When the telephone rang at three-seventeen that afternoon, there was no one in the apartment but Goff who

95

was sprawled in a living-room chair reading a Max Brand western. After Goff picked up the phone and said hello, a man's voice said, "This is Bill."

"Bill who?"

"Just Bill."

"I don't know any Bill."

"Too bad about old Bruce Cloke and how he got shot up and killed his morning, isn't it?"

"Yeah?" Goff said. "I'm sorry to hear that."

"I guess you're sorry about that nigger down in Richmond, too."

I shoulda killed that son of a bitch down in Virginia before he could talk to anybody, Goff thought. I should'na waited. I shoulda killed him the same night I shot the nigger.

"Whaddya want?"

"Well, Truman, I think you and me can do a little business."

"I ain't got any money, if that's what you're thinking."

"Oh, I don't want any money from you. I wanta give you some."

"For doing what?"

"For doing the same thing you did out on Saracen Street this morning—and what you did down in Richmond day before yesterday."

"I ain't interested."

"Well, the Richmond cops would be mighty interested in you. But not as much as the Baltimore cops. All you did was shoot a nigger down in Richmond. But still, they'd be mighty interested."

"You said something about money."

"That's right, I did."

"How much money you talking about?"

"Thirty-five hundred to begin with. Interested?"

"Go on."

"Well, that's all. You'll get the money in the mail along with a name. All you gotta do then is take care of the name just like you took care of that nigger and old Bruce. You also might have to do a little traveling."

"How many times I gotta do this?"

96

"Oh, I don't know. Maybe once a year. Maybe twice."

"What's the catch?"

"There's no catch. All you gotta do is make sure the job is done within two months after you get the letter with the money and name. That's all."

"There must be some kind of catch."

"Well, if you don't do it, there will be. You understand what I mean."

"Yeah, I understand."

"Well?"

"Well, what the hell do you want me to say? I ain't got any choice, do I?"

"No, Truman, you don't. You don't have any choice at all. You'll be getting a letter in the next couple of weeks or so."

"Can I ask you one question?"

"Sure," the man who called himself Just Bill said.

"Have you got a moustache and gray hair that's sorta wavy on the side?"

The man who said his name was Just Bill didn't answer. He hung up instead.

13

Kelly Cubbin had been born in 1945, three months after V-J Day, and one of his earliest memories was of the CIO convention that he had attended in 1951 and of going with his father to the hotel room of a man with wavy, dull, red hair and twinkling eyes who had given him some orange juice. Kelly remembered the orange juice because the man had squeezed it himself from some oranges that he had bought from a supermarket that was close to the convention hotel. Kelly also remembered that the man had kept squeezing a black rubber ball in his left hand over and over again. Years later, whenever he saw the redheaded man on television, Kelly remembered the orange juice and how much he had admired the man for having had his own oranges in his hotel room.

Kelly was born in Pittsburgh, but he had grown up in Washington after his father's union moved its headquarters there in 1951. He had lived in Northwest Washington in a house that Donald Cubbin had bought at a bargain from a defeated U.S. senator from Washington state. The house was almost new at the time and was in Chevy Chase and Kelly's mother had died in it in 1965 when Kelly was in his senior year at the University of Wisconsin.

Kelly didn't see too much of his father when he was growing up and attending Lafayette School on Broad Branch Road and Alice Deal Junior High and Woodrow Wilson Senior High, graduating from the last when he was still sixteen years old. Kelly remembered his mother as a quiet, shy woman who looked after his clothes, and smiled at his report cards, and gave him books, and tried to spoil him a little, and cooked wonderful dinners, mostly for the two of them because his father was seldom home until late. She had died as quietly as she had lived, in bed alone, except for a copy of the poems of Rupert Brooke.

His father, not knowing too much about children, had always treated Kelly more as a contemporary than as a child, usually assuming that Kelly had the judgment and resources of a grown man. In that way Donald Cubbin escaped much of the responsibilities that go with fatherhood and his son grew up regarding his father as an elder and often errant brother. It was a relationship that made Kelly mature a bit more quickly than most children but it had also helped prevent Donald Cubbin from ever growing up—at least all the way.

When he graduated from Wisconsin in 1965 with a degree in English literature, Kelly, not much wanting to go to Vietnam, had joined the war on poverty's domestic Peace Corps, a draft haven whose overly precious acronym was VISTA, for Volunteers in Service to America. VISTA assigned him and three other volunteers, two white youths and a black girl, to a small unincorporated Negro community just outside of Anniston, Alabama. The community was what the professional experts on poor folks at the Office of Economic Opportunity referred to as a rural poverty pocket. Three months after the VISTA volunteers arrived, wh' ver natural leadership the community might have had abdicated in favor of the young people and Kelly found himself serving as the black community's unofficial mayor. That lasted until the Ku Klux Klan, or a would-be affiliate, came riding by one night and shotgunned the shack that he was living in.

At the time of the shotgunning Kelly had been in the bed of a twenty-six-year-old divorcée whom he had picked up in Anniston. Three days later Washington transferred Kelly to a Navajo reservation in Arizona where he spent the remainder of his year in service to America by getting Indians who had been arrested as drunk out of jail on their own recognizance. Often he would lend them a dollar so that they could buy a jug to keep the shakes away.

In 1966, with the draft still hanging over him, Kelly joined the army. But he wasn't sent to Vietnam. Instead, he spent a cushy two years in Hoechst, just outside of Frankfurt, as an enlisted staff announcer and news reader for the American Forces Network. The deep, polished baritone that he had inherited from his father made him a natural for the job.

Kelly was still only twenty-two when he arrived in New Hampshire fresh from the army in February of 1968 to do what he could for the poet-politician from Minnesota. He became disillusioned with the McCarthy campaign in April of 1968, not because of the senator himself, but because of the people that he had around him. Kelly threw his support to Bobby Kennedy and later explained to his father that "my support consisted of one vote and an expert familiarity with damned near any Xerox or mimeograph machine."

He was in Chicago, of course, for the 1968 Democrat convention and he got slugged once and gassed once and he left Chicago early with a black eye and the resigned conviction that he, alone or in concert, would never do much about steering his country off of its detour to hell.

Kelly thought of himself as a kind of social-democrat about halfway between the Americans for Democratic Action Left and the Trotskyite Right. He also nursed the bitter, but perfectly normal conviction that he would always be in the minority.

Kelly had once tried to explain some, but not all of this to his father. It was nearly two years after Chicago and Kelly had a night off from his job as the midnight-to-dawn disc jockey on a Baltimore radio station. By chance he had picked a good night to talk to his father who was home alone, roaming through the large, empty house, nursing a beer. Sadie was in Los Angeles getting her teeth capped and even the ubiquitous Fred Mure was off somewhere.

Father and son had sent out for a Flying Chicken dinner and after they had eaten they settled down in the living room with a bottle of Martell between them.

"What I've been trying to say, chief, is that I'm a typical product of the upper middle class. We've never been hungry enough. There's nothing that we ever really wanted way deep down—except somebody to love us and that's not much of a base is it?"

Donald Cubbin wasn't much good at talk like that. He decided that the kid probably got it from his mother who'd always had her nose in a book. Cubbin thought of falling back on the current lib-lab line, which he knew by heart, but he also knew that his son wouldn't wear it. So instead he stalled, "You're not a kid anymore, Kelly, and what's more you never gave me and your mother or me and Sadie any problems."

"You mean I've never been busted?"

"Well, hell, you went to college and got your degree. That's more'n I ever did. You served your country in that VISTA outfit and went overseas and came back without getting your ass shot off. You got interested in politics and did something about it. You're not on drugs, at least as far as I know, and you're not a boozer like me so, what the hell, you're normal or nearly so and I'm goddamned glad of it." Cubbin took a sip of his brandy and added, "Also you've got a pretty good job and I guess that's important. Christ, I've made my career out of jobs."

"But I've never been interested in the union."

"Christ, kid, that's no disappointment to me. No, sir. Most of the time it bores me stiff; you know that—or you should know it by now. But it's what I do and I've worked hard at it, well, at least I worked hard some of the time, and what the hell else could I do at sixty? It's too late for me to go out to the Coast like I should've gone back in thirty-two."

"You would have liked that, wouldn't you?"

Cubbin gave his son a rare smile, rare because there was much genuine shyness in it. "Yeah, I've got just enough ham in me to have liked it, really liked it. I might even have made a pretty good living out of it, playing second leads in what they used to call B pictures. Shit, Kelly, I'd have eaten it up."

"Maybe that's what I'm trying to explain. You knew what you wanted; I'm not sure that I do."

"I didn't do anything about it," Cubbin said.

"But you did something else. You achieved a kind of fame and prominence and all that crap."

"Is that what you want?"

"I don't think so, although that might be a damned lie. What I really mean is that I don't want to pay the price that you have."

"You mean look where it got me?"

"No, I don't mean that either. Let me put it another way. What would happen to me if you were to die tomorrow?"

"Well, Christ, you'd get along. You'd make out all right."

"That's not it, chief. You're forgetting something."

"What?"

"I'd be a rich man with half of that insurance that you and the union carry on you."

"You need some money?" Cubbin asked, not really wanting to talk about anything as unpleasant as his own death.

Kelly sighed. "No, I don't need any money, I think

maybe that's what's wrong. I've never *needed* any money because I could always touch you for some."

"Let me tell you something, kid, there's no virtue in poverty."

"I've lived poor," Kelly said. "Down in Alabama that time I lived just like the blacks, ate what they did, and I saw what it could do. But there was one big difference. I wasn't black and I didn't *have* to do it so that wiped out whatever lesson there might have been in it."

Cubbin was silent for a moment. Finally, he said, "Yeah, it does something to you, being poor. I mean really poor. It gives you a twist that you never really get over. Fear, I guess. It makes you afraid."

"How much money did you have when my granddad died?"

"You mean my old man?"

"Yes."

Cubbin smiled again, this time the wry smile of a man who remembers something whose once dreadful importance has been partially erased by time. "When your grandmother and I got back to Pittsburgh from his funeral, we had twenty-one dollars and thirty-five cents between us. That'd be worth about a hundred dollars today, maybe two hundred, I don't know."

"And money was important then?"

"Dear God, yes, money was important."

"And that's really why you didn't go to Hollywood?"

"Yeah, I suppose that was it—that and a lot of other things."

"Well, I can go to Hollywood, chief."

Cubbin brightened, but only for a moment. "I thought there for a second—but, yeah, I see what you mean. You mean you don't really want to go to Hollywood, but if there was something like that you wanted, you could go ahead and do it."

"That's right."

"Well, have you got something in mind?"

"Maybe. I think so."

"I'll back you in anything you want to do."

"Sure, chief."

"I don't know, I guess I haven't been a very good

102

father," Cubbin said, lapsing into a small bid for sympathy, the kind that had always worked very well with his late wife.

He didn't get any sympathy from his son. "No," Kelly said, "I suppose you haven't."

"What kind of lousy crack is that?"

"I don't know. Maybe it's just that somewhere along the line somebody like you should have said hey, look, sonny, you're going to be a biochemist whether you like it or not so you'd better hop to it. Maybe I'd have liked somebody saying that to me. Maybe anybody would."

"Well, you didn't get it."

"No."

"And you're sure as shit not going to get it now."

"No."

Cubbin decided to retreat a little. "You've got a pretty good job with the station."

"I've got that."

"I listen to you whenever I can. You got a hell of a voice."

"I got that from you."

"So what d'you think you're going to do?"

"I know what I'm *not* going to do. I'm never going to make any money. I might have some after you die, but I'm never going to make any."

To Cubbin that was still a kind of economic heresy, but he shrugged it away. "That's not so important."

"And I don't want power. I don't mean I wouldn't take it if it were offered. Hell, who wouldn't. But I haven't got the drive or the hunger or whatever it is to go after it."

Cubbin nodded. He knew about power and what was done to get it. "Well, if you don't crave it, you almost never get it."

Kelly looked at his father. "This is going to sound corny but I found out something about myself. I like to help people, I mean individuals."

"Well, you probably got that from me."

"You bet, chief."

"You sure as hell don't make any money helping people. You usually get kicked in the teeth for it."

"Well, I like it and I've even figured out why. You see,

103

I'm smarter than most people. I'm not bragging, it's just something that happened to me like the fact that I've got black hair and blue eyes. So I know how to do things for people—or get things done for them and I get a kick out of that. I get a kick out of being the one they come to when they have a problem."

"Maybe you oughta be a lawyer. Like you say, you're smart enough. You got that from your mother, I guess," Cubbin said, this time in a mild bid for a little praise.

"I got it from you, too, chief, but I don't want to be a lawyer. You see what I really want to be is the town wise man. I'd like that. I really would like that."

Cubbin looked at his son, at the intense young stranger who sat across from him. I think I know what he means, Cubbin told himself. He wants to be "it." Hell, he might call it a wise man, but he wants to be the one who messes around in other people's lives. He wants to do what the old-time ward heelers who could fix things used to do. That's power of a kind and that's one way to get more of it, doing favors for people. And once you've tasted it, you want a little more and then a little more until one day you wake up and find out that you want it all.

He doesn't understand, Kelly thought, staring back at his father. He thinks that there's really more to it than I've told him, that there's something devious about what I want to do that I don't really understand. Or am not aware of. He doesn't understand that it's partly guilt and partly my need to be respected and liked and loved by a few people, but not too many, because I don't think I could handle that. And wait'll I tell him how I'm going to do it.

"So what do you think you might do, son, go into one of the—what do they call them—the helping professions? Social work, teaching, something like that?"

"No, I'm not wild about kids and I've known a few social workers. A lot of them get bitter after a while and they get all mixed up with their jargon."

"Well, what have you decided on?"

Kelly took a deep breath and then let it out slowly. "I'm going to become a cop, chief."

Cubbin sat bolt upright in his chair and grabbed at the

104

brandy bottle. "Good Jesus Godalmighty, you don't mean it?"

"Yes," Kelly said. "I'm pretty sure I do."

"Jesus. My son, the fuzz."

"Your son, the pig."

Cubbin looked at Kelly carefully. "This isn't just some childhood ambition that you've decided to realize a little late, is it?"

Kelly shook his head. "My attitude toward cops is typically American." He touched his left eye. "Another inch or so up and I'd have lost this at Chicago."

Cubbin nodded and then said, "It's the hard way to do what you want to do, isn't it, become the village wise man?"

"You've got it, chief," Kelly said, "it's probably the hardest way there is."

Two months later Kelly Cubbin joined the Metropolitan Police force in Washington, D. C., at the peak of its recruiting drive for college graduates, a drive that petered out a little less than two years later when Washington decided that it really didn't need any more smart kid cops.

But when Kelly joined they put his picture in the paper and after training assigned him to a beat that was just back of the Hilton and took in most of Columbia Road. It had once been a toney enough white neighborhood, but by the time Kelly arrived the fancy grocery stores had closed, a once-popular nightclub had folded, and one of the movie houses had been torn down and the other ran Mexican films and called itself a teatro instead of a theater. And everybody began putting special locks on their doors and heavy metal screens over their windows.

Kelly tried. He taught himself Spanish and because he was nearly as good a mimic as his father he was speaking it quickly, hamming it up at first on purpose, getting a few giggles from the youngsters that he talked to on the street and patient instruction from the older people.

It took him longer to get an in with the blacks. But after his partner discovered that Kelly wasn't interested in splitting what little juice the neighborhood provided, things got better. His partner was Private R. V. Emerson, a black, sad, tough cop with five kids who passed the word that Kelly was about half human and nobody had better mess with him.

The people in the neighborhood never trusted Kelly completely, but they slowly accepted him, and some of them even liked him—as much as they could ever like any cop. And after a while they began to turn to him with some of their problems because they found that his advice was usually sound and it was always free. And finally he became the neighborhood's unofficial ombudsman, which was as close as he ever got to becoming what he wanted to be, the village wise man.

He liked it. He even liked being pure cop but not well enough, at least not well enough to satisfy the annual review and evaluation board, one of whose members asked him: "You know what they call you, Cubbin?"

"Who?"

"The guys you work with. They call you Mother Cubbin. Now what do you think of that?"

"Not much."

"It don't bother you?"

"No," Kelly said, "it doesn't bother me."

"Do you really like being a cop, Cubbin? I mean really like it?"

"I like it very much. Why?"

"Because you sure don't act like a cop."

Three days later he was placed on what they called administrative leave. Only a few of the residents of the neighborhood back of the Hilton ever asked Private R. V. Emerson what had happened to his ex-partner, "You know, that white kid cop who was always sticking his nose in other folks's business."

It was eleven o'clock in the morning and Kelly Cubbin sat in a chair and drank coffee and watched his father sleep. He had been watching him for nearly a quarter of an hour and thinking: at least you don't hate him. Whether you love him or just pity him probably isn't too important. You've come to know his posturing and his playacting and what they cover up. My father, my elder

106

brother who fell in love with the sound of applause at an early age and spent the rest of his life looking for it in all the wrong places. I didn't fly up here to be consoled by you because the only way you can offer that is from the depths of your checkbook. I flew up here because the village got rid of its wise man who wasn't quite smart enough to hold on to his job. Do you need a wise man, chief?

Donald Cubbin rolled over in his bed and groaned. He was awake and wishing that he weren't. He had to make it to the bathroom and vomit, but it seemed too far away. A mile too far.

"You awake, chief?" Kelly said.

"Kelly?"

"Right here."

Cubbin groaned again. "I'm dying, son."

"Let me help you up."

Kelly helped his father to sit up on the edge of the bed. "Little queasy?"

Cubbin nodded, not trusting himself to speak. "Can you make it to the john?" Kelly said.

Cubbin pushed himself up from the bed. He weaved toward the bathroom almost staggering. He made it to the toilet just as it came up, great wet gobs of it. Cubbin hated the mess that his stomach rejected but he forced himself to look at it because he knew that the sight of it would make more come up and the quicker that happened, the better he would feel.

When he came out of the bathroom a few minutes later he was pale and shaky but the nausea seemed to have gone.

"I've got a little medicine for you, chief," Kelly said and handed his father a tall glass that contained a thick, white liquid. Cubbin took the glass with both hands and raised it to his mouth where its rim clattered against his teeth before he got the first swallow down.

The drink was part cream, part brandy, part crème de menthe, two raw eggs, and a jigger of vodka. It was Fred Mure's invention and after he drank half of it, Cubbin eased himself down into a chair and leaned back, waiting for the alcohol to make it stop hurting.

After a few moments he took another cautious swallow and sighed. That was better. The shakes were going. The queasiness had departed. He looked at his son. "What are you doing here?"

"I came in last night."

"Did I—uh—"

"We talked a little and you went to bed."

Cubbin nodded. "I don't remember."

"You'd had a few."

"I remember that goddamned TV program though."

"I heard about that this morning."

Cubbin finished the rest of his drink. "Where's the other one?" he said. "I need two."

Kelly crossed to the dresser, picked up the other drink that Fred Mure had provided, and handed it to his father. "It's none of my business, but you're hitting it a little hard these days, aren't you?"

"Well, you saw me last night. And this morning. There's no reason to lie to you."

"I just thought I'd mention it."

Cubbin shrugged. He was feeling better. Much better. "I'd be an ass to say that I can handle it so I'll just say that I can make it. Just barely. It's not this bad every day. Not quite. Not yet anyhow."

"It's your liver."

"That's right, kid, it's *my* liver. What're you doing here anyway?"

"I got fired."

Cubbin looked at his son. Be careful now, he told himself. Don't say it wrong. "You did, huh?"

"Yes."

"Does it bother you?"

"A little."

"You want it back?"

"My job?"

"Yes."

"I don't think so."

"What happened?"

"They didn't much care for my attitude. My arrest record wasn't too good. Little things like that." Kelly grinned. "It's not important."

"Do you think you did a good job?"

"I think so, but they don't, and that's what matters."

"No it doesn't, kid. If you think you did a good job, that's all that matters. Take it from me."

"Sure, chief."

"Got any plans?"

"No. Not really."

Cubbin's mind worked swiftly. It could still do that for about twenty minutes a day when the alcohol had dulled the pain but not the mind. He sometimes told himself that twenty minutes were all anybody needed. Most people don't think for even five minutes a day, so if you really make use of the time, you're a quarter of an hour ahead of almost everybody else.

"I got an idea, kid."

"What?"

"Well, this election's going to be just a little bit—uh—shitty, you know?"

"I think so."

"I could use you."

"To do what?"

"Oh, sort of follow me around and remember what's said and what's not said."

"I thought Fred did that."

"Fred's not smart enough for some of these deals. That's one. Two is they won't let him sit in on some of them. But nobody can object to my son and something tells me that I might need a witness."

"You're in trouble?"

Cubbin finished the second drink before he answered. Do it just right, he told himself. Underplay it. He nodded at his son and said, "That's right; I'm in a little trouble."

"Do you really need me, chief, or are you just bullshitting me?"

"What do you think?"

"I think you're bullshitting me," Kelly said, "but I'll do it anyway."

14

Indigo Boone, the man who knew how to steal elections, lived in a third-story, six-room apartment in Sixtieth Street just across the Midway from the University of Chicago. It was still called the Midway because that's what it had been when they had held the World's Columbian Exposition there back in 1893. Later the city had turned it into a park of sorts with a bridle path and for a time they had even flooded sections of it in winter to form ice-skating rinks.

But all that had been a long time ago when the neighborhood had been one of the choicer places to live in Chicago, much favored by intellectuals who liked the university atmosphere. Now it was just another black neighborhood that was not quite yet a slum.

But Indigo Boone kept his place up nice because he owned the building and he thought he should set an example for other landlords. Boone had bought the building in 1946 with money that he had made in the Manila black market. He had bought it through a white attorney because the people who had owned it then would have refused to sell to a black. But all that was more than a quarter of a century ago and Boone had been living in his own apartment in his own building for nearly fifteen years now.

He was not a man who liked to move much. He had been born in New Orleans in 1921 and had grown up in the French Quarter on Dauphine Street where he had had to hustle if he wanted to survive without resorting to steady work. He most probably would still be in New Orleans if he hadn't been drafted in early 1942 and assigned to a black quartermaster outfit that ended the war in Manila with Boone as its top sergeant.

He had made money, a lot of it, on the Manila black market just after the war ended and before the records could get straightened out, selling truckloads of cigarettes, blankets, powdered eggs, Spam, and sometimes even the trucks themselves.

When he had returned to the States he had headed for Chicago because he had it on what he considered to be good authority that the economic, political, and social climate there would be to the liking of a man of his taste and ability. Chicago hadn't disappointed Indigo Boone any more than it had ever disappointed any of the hard, fast, smart hustlers who flocked to it.

Boone had started small in Chicago, first investing a fair amount of capital in several white-occupied apartment buildings, including the one on Sixtieth Street, and then buying into a small construction company. Boone knew little or nothing about the construction business, but he knew almost all there was to know about payoffs and bribes and kickbacks and so his business began to flourish with the collective blessing of various city employees who bought new cars or had their kids' teeth straightened thanks to Boone's generosity.

Indigo Boone also went into politics, starting small and mildly meek at the precinct level and gradually working his way up the Democratic party ladder, largely by doing those onerous chores that nobody else wanted to fool with, until he was now something of a minor power with excellent connections downtown.

Prior to 1960 Boone had helped steal a few elections, but it had been mostly minor stuff that had involved no more than sending some extra Democratic state legislators down to Springfield. But on the night of the election of 1960 the word came down to Boone that they would need a few additional Kennedy votes. Boone had found them here and there, doing what he regarded as no more than his usual workmanlike job. But as the night wore on, additional word came down that more and more Kennedy votes were needed, that in fact a whole raft of them was needed, that indeed a deluge of Chicago Kennedy votes was desperately needed to offset the downstate trend.

Boone found them. At least he found a lot of them and some said most. He invented new ways to filch precincts right out from under the noses of the Republican poll watchers. He improvised foolproof means of inflating the actual Democratic vote. He fell back on time-honored methods and voted the lame, the sick, the halt and the dead. He even, some said, managed to corrupt the voting machines themselves. He sped from polling place to polling place that night and early morning in a squad car, its siren moaning hoarsely, its top light flashing, giving counsel, advice, and instructions to the party faithful and buying what was needed from those who were not so faithful, peeling off fifty- and one-hundred-dollar bills from a roll that one prejudiced observer later claimed was "as big as a big cantaloupe."

Afterward, there were those partisans who claimed that Boone's efforts had saved the nation from Richard Nixon, at least for a while. Illinois went Democratic by 8,858 votes out of the 4,746,834 that were cast for the two major parties. "Well," Indigo Boone had said later, "when they called up and told me they needed some more Kennedy votes, why I just scurried around and got them some more, about nine thousand more, if I recollect right."

Boone's stock shot up enormously downtown after the election and three weeks later he even got a letter from John Kennedy that warmly thanked him for "your invaluable efforts on my behalf." Boone had the letter framed and hung it on his living-room wall and never failed to point it out to visitors when they came calling, even if they had already seen it a dozen times.

Marvin Harmes had never seen the Kennedy letter because he had never been in Indigo Boone's home before. So after the two had formally shaken hands, and the letter had been pointed out to Harmes, he had read it carefully, every word, because he felt that Boone might test him on it. While he read it Harmes felt Boone's eyes on him as they took in his ivory silk double-breasted suit with its twelve imitation black pearl buttons, his Sea

112

Island cotton shirt with its tiny black and white checks, his knit black silk tie, and his ankle-high black calf boots that were so highly polished that they gleamed like patent leather.

Machine written and machine signed, Harmes thought as he read the letter for the third time, but I'm sure as hell not going to tell Mr. Indigo Boone that. Instead, he turned slowly from the letter and said, "Now that's really something. You must be mighty proud of that, Mr. Boone."

Boone knew that the letter had been written by one machine and signed by another, but it served its purpose. It made some people think that he was a bit naïve, even simple, and that sometimes made them a little careless in their dealings with him and if they were, it usually could be worked to his advantage.

"Well, when I was just a raggedy-ass kid growin up in New Orleans, I sure didn't think I'd ever get a letter from the President of the United States of America."

Harmes nodded understandingly, but thought, Don't try to tom me, man. You wouldn't really give a shit if that letter was signed by Jesus Christ himself, unless you could figure on making a quarter out of it. "I met his brother a couple of times," Harmes said as casually as he could, thus establishing his own connection with the nation's departed royalty.

"He was a good man."

"A good man," Harmes agreed solemnly.

"Well, let's make ourselves comfortable," Boone said, indicating a chair after deciding that Brother Harmes sure as hell don't give nothing away for free. He moved over to a closed mahogany cabinet and turned to look back at Harmes. "I'm going to have a little refreshment. You care for something sociable?"

Before Harmes could answer, Boone pressed a button and the top of the cabinet moved up and folded itself back revealing a wet bar with a sink, a small refrigerator, a couple of dozen bottles, and a variety of glasses.

Nice trick, Harmes thought. I'm impressed just like I oughta be. "Scotch on the rocks," he said.

"That's my drink, too," Boone said although he preferred bourbon.

While Boone mixed the two drinks, Harmes took in the room. It was worth a look, he decided, because a vast sum and much time had been spent in an attempt to give it a look of rich, quiet elegance. The room had been done in black and soft shades of brown that ranged from creamed coffee to cinnamon to dark amber. The ceiling was painted a light tan and the walls were covered with a faint brown material that was patterned in raised, dark brown fleurs-de-lis that looked like plush, brown plush, if there is such a thing, Harmes thought. Two black leather couches of an indeterminate, but comfortable design flanked the fireplace whose ornate mantel had been carved out of brown marble. Or maybe it's just painted wood, Harmes thought. If he got hold of the right Italians, they can do things to wood that would make you swear it was marble.

The three windows that faced out over the Midway were draped in dark brown velvet and the windows themselves had fringed, pale tan shades that were drawn half-way down. Above the fireplace was a large sepia sketch of a New Orleans street scene in the French Quarter. There were some other chairs covered in tobacco browns that were carefully placed so as to make conversation easy. Against one wall was a dark walnut table that Harmes thought was probably an antique. It held a copper vase that contained some thoughtfully arranged chrysanthemums whose shade almost exactly matched the vase that held them.

And in one corner, all by itself, next to the door that led to the rest of the apartment, was the Kennedy letter in its plain black frame. That letter's the only white thing in the room, Harmes thought. I do think Mr. Indigo Boone is trying to tell me something.

As Boone came toward him with the drinks, Harmes could see why his parents had named him Indigo. He's sure one black nigger, Harmes thought, and if black is beautiful, he must be the most gorgeous thing in town.

Boone was black, as black as ebony and just as smooth except for his short, kinky hair that had turned dove gray on top and nicely white at the sides. He was a big man who was a little surprised to find himself gray and running to fat now that he was just past fifty. But he covered his stomach up with double-breasted vests and Harmes, who knew a lot about clothes, estimated that the beautifully cut gray worsted suit that Boone wore could have cost no less than $400. I'm gonna have to ask him who did it for him, Harmes decided. I might not ask him anything else, but I'm sure gonna ask him that.

"I was just thinking," Boone said as he handed Harmes his glass, "I was just thinking that it's funny we never ran into each other before."

"We don't socialize much," Harmes said. "Whenever I'm not traveling the wife and I sort of like to stay home."

Boone nodded his understanding. "Well, the older you get the less you mix and mingle, I spect. Of course, if you're into politics, then you almost have to get out and move amongst 'em. And I do believe you wanted to see me about something that's got to do with politics?"

Well, he led into it smooth enough, Harmes thought as he nodded yes and then took a swallow of his drink, automatically noting that the Scotch probably cost twelve dollars a fifth, at least that.

Boone smiled; it was big, white, and warm, the professional kind that goes with an expert salesman or politician and Boone was both. "Well, I can say that I'm just a little disappointed," he said.

"Why?"

"I was sort of hoping that you'd dropped by to see me about a life-insurance policy with your mind all made up and convinced so that all I'd have to do is just provide the pen."

He's not only smooth, Harmes decided, he's slick. "Well," he said, "now that you mention it, it is a kind of insurance that I'm interested in."

Boone nodded and smiled again. "You know something, I didn't pay much attention to life insurance until I was about your age."

"Well, what I'm really interested in is both insurance and politics. What I mean is that I'd like to find out if I can take out some insurance on an election."

115

"Uh-huh," Boone said, his voice flat and totally empty of anything.

"I've heard you're the man."

"Uh-huh." This time Harmes thought it sounded even more empty, if that were possible. Well, you'd better sweeten the pot, he told himself.

"Of course, I'm prepared to pay for advice and counsel."

The two men stared at each other. Neither was in the least awed by what he saw, but neither particularly wanted the other as an enemy. I bet that boy's come a long way to be sitting where he is now in that ice-cream suit of his, Boone thought, and because he was an essentially curious man, he asked, "Where you from?"

"Alabama. Little town called Sylacauga."

"That's a pretty name."

"Nothing pretty about the town."

"Uh-huh," Boone said. "What's Sylacauga, Indian?"

"Must be."

"Know what it means?"

Harmes split his dark, hard face with a white, hard grin. "I never bothered to ask."

Boone grinned back, this time using his real one, not the professional kind that he put on for show. "Well, now, how much, Mr. Harmes, do you think my advice and counsel might be worth?"

Harmes studied his drink for a moment and then looked up. "We might manage the going rate."

"The going rate's five thousand."

"I'm sure that a rich candidate with a whole tree of money would pay that and gladly, Mr. Boone, but I'm representing a poor candidate who's got to depend on the one-dollar bills and four-bit pieces that he collects from working stiffs. We got hard times now and we can't possibly go any higher than twenty-five hundred."

Not bad, Boone thought. He knows what he's doing. "Well, I'm a reasonable man and I'm sure that your candidate's cause is more than just, Mr. Harmes, or you wouldn't be associated with it, so I'm prepared to reduce my fee to four thousand."

Well, by God, that's white of you, Indigo, Harmes

116

hought, but without bitterness. "We got men out of work, amilies going hungry, and to tell the truth, there's just not any money around. If we scraped up every last cent we got, it wouldn't be no more than three thousand dollars."

"We got hard times, Mr. Harmes, I do agree because I feel it myself, every day. In fact, things are getting so bad that I'm willing to risk my professional standing and make you my last offer of thirty-five hundred providing you swear you won't tell nobody."

"Make it thirty-two fifty and your secret's safe as churches," Harmes said.

Boone decided that Harmes had learned a trick or two from that union of his. He squeezes for the last dollar and I bet he gets close most of the time, Boone thought as he stuck out his hand, his professional smile back in place. "You got yourself a deal," he said.

Harmes accepted the hand and then both men smiled at each other, Harmes because he had expected to pay at least $4,000 and Boone because he had anticipated a fee no higher than $3,000.

"Now then," Boone said, "I believe you've got an election coming up in that union of yours."

"That's right."

"And you'd sorta like to insure its outcome, huh?"

"That's the idea."

"Well, maybe you'd better tell me about it."

"Where you want me to start?"

"Tell me when, where, and how you do the voting. After that, you can tell me who's running and who you want to win and maybe I can tell you what you're gonna have to do to make sure that he does."

15

While Marvin Harmes was learning how to steal an election in Chicago, the man that he wanted to steal it for was giving a press conference in Washington. It was only the second press conference that Sammy Hanks had called since his campaign began, the first being the inevitable one to announce his candidacy.

This time he was suggesting, urging, and even demanding that Donald Cubbin resign the presidency of the union and quit the race for reelection.

Hanks didn't really expect to get anywhere with his suggestion except onto the three network news programs that evening and perhaps onto page six or seven of those newspapers who thought that he had enough members among their readers to make the printing of his demand worthwhile.

The basis for Hanks's demands on Cubbin were the revelations contained in the previous night's television program, "Jake's Night," a transcript of which had been furnished the gathered press along with a prepared statement that Hanks was now reading for the benefit of the TV cameras. Hanks was virtually accusing Cubbin of having sold out the union in exchange for membership in the Federalists Club whose other members were all right-wing, big-business types who hated blacks just like Cubbin did.

Sammy Hanks didn't say it quite like that, but it was still strong stuff carefully written in an awful, florid style to make sure that it would be both broadcast and printed.

"In summary," Hanks read, "I must reluctantly call for

118

the resignation of Donald Cubbin as president of this union because of the shocking facts revealed in the television program that I discussed earlier. I charge Donald Cubbin not only with racial bigotry but also with industrial sycophancy—"

"That's a good word," the Associated Press man muttered to a reporter from *The Wall Street Journal*. "The membership will think that old Don's come down with a new kind of clap."

"—which endangers the collective bargaining effectiveness of this union. If Donald Cubbin is half the labor statesman that he claims to be, he will resign—for the good of the union, for the good of the country, and for the good of himself. The evidence is perfectly plain—"

"If he'd said 'crystal clear,' I'd have given him four points," the AP man said. " 'Perfectly plain's' only a two-point cliché."

"Why don't you get a job with Sammy?" *The Wall Street Journal* reporter said. "I hear he pays well."

"I already work for a nut," the AP man said.

"—perfectly plain," Hanks went on, "that Donald Cubbin intends to drag this great organization of ours down the path to country-club unionism with all the vicious racist overtones which that term implies. This must not happen. This will not happen."

Sammy Hanks sat down to the scattered applause of a few of his own sycophants who didn't know any better than to clap at a press conference.

"Who writes this crap for Sammy?" the AP man asked *The Wall Street Journal* reporter.

"Mickey Della, I guess."

"I thought so."

"Why?"

"Only a real pro could make it so bad."

After answering a few perfunctory questions, the press conference ended and Sammy Hanks left the large hotel room on Fourteenth and K Streets and headed down the hall followed by a heavy, stooped, shambling gray-haired man whose bright blue eyes flittered balefully from behind bifocal glasses with bent steel frames. The man had his usual equipment consisting of a Pall Mall cigarette parked in the corner of his mouth underneath a stained, scraggly gray mustache and a newspaper tucked under his arm. He was never seen without either a cigarette in his mouth or a newspaper under his arm because he was addicted to both. He smoked four packs of Pall Malls a day and bought every edition of every paper published in whatever city or town he happened to be in. If asked about his addiction to newspapers—he could never pass a stand or a street seller without buying one—the man always said, "What the hell, it only costs a dime and where else can you buy that much bullshit for a dime?"

The man was Mickey Della and if you bought him a new suit and got the nicotine stains out of his moustache and had it trimmed and took the cigarette from the corner of his mouth, you could have passed him off as at least a lieutenant of industry; or the beloved president of a small liberal-arts college, or even a United States senator with a trace of common sense.

But Mickey Della was none of these. He was a professional political press agent, or public relations adviser, or flack, or whatever anyone wanted to call him, he didn't mind, and he was without doubt the most vicious one around and just possibly the best and he felt right at home working for Sammy Hanks.

He had been at it for more than forty years and for him it contained no more surprises, but he was hooked now, as addicted to politics as any mainliner is to heroin. Mickey Della needed politics to live and he lunched on its intrigue and dined on its gossip. Its heartbreak provided him with breakfast.

Della had lost count of the campaigns that he had handled since breaking with the New Deal in 1937 over a matter of pay, not principle. Della didn't allow himself too many principles, but he always claimed that, "I've never worked for a Communist and I never worked for a Fascist, at least none who'd ever admit it, but I've worked for damn near everything in between."

He had run campaigns in New York with a staff of more than a hundred under him and he had run them in Wyoming where there had been no one but himself and

120

the candidate battling the snowdrifts by car between Sheridan and Laramie.

Causes were another Della speciality and he had done professional battle for at least twoscore of them over the years and most of these were so long lost that even their battle cries had been made meaningless by time, cries such as Save Leland Olds! and MVA Now! They hadn't been popular causes even then because not many people really cared whether Leland Olds was reappointed to such a vague governing body as the Federal Power Commission, whatever that was, or whether the Missouri Valley was developed along the lines of the Tennessee Valley Authority although some people thought it might be nice.

Lumping causes and candidates together, Della estimated that he was hitting around .650 and this kept up the demand for his services, which didn't come cheap. He had learned to use radio in the thirties and television in the fifties and he used them skillfully in a nasty, clever way that assured maximum impact plus the added bonus of the newspaper stories and outraged editorials that his commercials invariably inspired.

But Della remained essentially a newspaperman, a muckraker, an exposer of vice and wrongdoing, a viewer with alarm who had never quite got over the feeling that almost any evil could be cured by ninety-point headlines. And that was the principal reason that he was working for Sammy Hanks, because it was going to be a print campaign, as dirty, nasty, vicious, and lowdown as one could hope for and since it might possibly be the last such campaign ever held, Mickey Della would almost have paid to be in on it. Instead, he had lowered his usual fee of $66,789 to $61,802. Della always quoted his fee in precise amounts because he figured that exactitude served as a balm to the people who had to pay the bill.

As Hanks and Della strode down the hall followed by the usual bunch of hangers-on Hanks turned his ugly head and asked, "How'd I do?"

"You were peachy."

"Jesus, you sure know how to boost a guy's morale."

"You're not paying me to hold your hand."

"Well, what about your professional assessment? I'm sure as hell paying for that."

"Let's sit down first. All this standing around and walking's killing my feet."

Exercise was Mickey Della's only bane. The prospect of a six-block walk could send him into a deep depression. He had been known to take a cab to cross the street, but it had been Constitution Avenue, which is a wide street, and besides it had been raining.

At the door to his hotel-room office Hanks stopped and turned to look at the group that was following him. "Why don't you guys go find something useful to do? The circus is over."

"You were really great, Sammy," one of the men said.

"You sure laid into 'em," another said.

"Old Don's gonna be stewing tonight."

The only one in the six-man group who didn't say anything was Howard Fleer, a tall, thin man in his early forties with brown eyes so sad that they seemed to hurt. He stood a little away from the others as though the slight distance would lend him an identity of his own and disassociate him from their claquish sounds. Fleer was a painfully shy man whose chief concern was that no one would ever notice him doing anything unseemly. Consequently most people didn't notice him at all and that was precisely why Sammy Hanks had picked him as his running mate for secretary-treasurer.

"You said you needed to see Howard?" Hanks said to Della.

"For just a moment."

"Howard, you come on in with us. The rest of you guys go drink some booze or something."

Once inside the room Hanks sat behind his desk, Della sprawled on the couch, and Fleer stood hesitantly by the door as if poised to flee should someone say an unkind word. He was a candidate for secretary-treasurer because the union's constitution required that Sammy Hanks have one and Hanks had carefully picked the one man who would never threaten him as he was now threatening Donald Cubbin. Whenever anyone objected to Fleer's candidacy on the grounds that he had never worked with his hands in a plant, Hanks would answer, "Why the fuck should a bookkeeper get his hands dirty?"

"What'd you wanta see Howard about?" Hanks asked Della.

"I need five hundred bucks for that little girl in Cleveland."

"I thought you already paid her."

"Out of my own pocket, Sammy."

"Give him five hundred, Howard."

Fleer nodded and took a fat wallet from his inside coat pocket. He counted out five one-hundred-dollar bills and handed them to Mickey Della who stuffed them in his trouser pocket. Fleer replaced the wallet and took out a small notebook and started to write something down.

"What the Christ are you doing?" Hanks said.

"Just making a note of it."

"Of what?"

"Of the five hundred I gave Mr. Della."

"Mickey," Della said. "It's not hard to call me Mickey and I don't like being called Mr. Della by the bagman. It makes me uncomfortable."

"What kind of note are you gonna make by the five hundred dollars?" Hanks said. "Are you gonna write down: Mickey Della, five hundred dollars for bribes?"

"For reimbursable expenses," Fleer said.

"You know what Mickey spent that five hundred on?"

"I think so."

"What?"

"On information about the Cubbin letter to A. Richard Gammage," Fleer said.

"Don't fancy it up, Howard. Mickey spent five hundred dollars to bribe a file clerk in Gammage International to Xerox a copy of that Cubbin letter and hand it over to us and us means me, Mickey, and you. Now that's where that five hundred went and I don't want any note made about it."

"Yes, well, we have to have some records, Sammy."

"We sure as hell don't have to have any records about how much we paid out in bribes."

"It was merely for my own information," Fleer said.

"He knows what he's doing," Della said. "He's the head chef when it comes to cooking the books so you'd better just let him cook them his way."

"Well, we might as well have a little talk about money right here and now," Hanks said. "Sit down someplace, Howard."

Fleer moved from the door to one of the folding chairs. He perched on it stiffly, his hands in his lap, and looked apprehensively at Hanks. It's his negotiating look, Hanks decided. He looks like that when we're negotiating and the companies think they have a real dummy and then he starts reeling off the facts and figures that cuts their balls off and he sounds and looks like he's apologizing for the dullness of the knife. "So how do we stand?" Hanks said.

"Overall?" Fleer said.

"Yeah."

"Well, nearly all of the bank money has been channeled to the twenty Rank and File Committees that we set up. The committees are sending the money to us in bits and pieces as we advised. The total so far is approximately three hundred and twenty-five thousand dollars."

"How much more is due?"

"Fifty thousand from the bank in Los Angeles."

"What's their hang-up?"

"None really. It's just that I had to supply them with the names of fifty people that their—uh—intermediary could distribute the money to and who would then send it to various committees as individual contributions."

"And you found them?"

"Yes."

"What else is due?"

"About one hundred thousand from those who've received loans from the pension fund."

"Is that certain?"

"Quite certain."

"Anything else?"

"We've collected approximately twenty-seven thousand, five hundred from locals and individual members. I don't think we're going to get much more."

"What do you mean we're not gonna get much more?"

Fleer looked embarrassed. He clasped his hands tightly and made his body go rigid so that he wouldn't squirm. I hate personal conflict, he thought. I hate it when people are rude and impolite and yell at each other. I hate these two men here because they thrive on conflict and I don't understand why. God, I wish I were dead. Fleer usually wished for death at least a dozen times a day. "There isn't going to be much more in the way of contributions from locals and individuals," he said, "because, well, because they simply don't seem interested."

"In me?" said Hanks who always had to relate everything to himself as quickly as possible.

"In the election," Fleer said. "From what I hear, Cubbin's having the same trouble."

"We're going to have to stir them up," Mickey Della said. "You get a good, nasty fight going and they'll get interested."

"Maybe," Fleer said, which was as close as he could ever come to dissent.

"Well, how much money can we count on from all sources?" Hanks said.

"A little over five hundred thousand," Fleer said.

"And that's it?"

Fleer nodded. "That is the absolute maximum."

Hanks looked at Della. "Is that enough for what you're going to do?"

Mickey Della studied the ceiling for a few moments as he puffed on his cigarette. "If that's all you can raise," he said, "then that's all I'll spend."

16

Truman Goff used a two-wheeled dolly to roll a crate of Golden Bantam corn up to where the vegetables and fruit were displayed along the left-hand wall of the Safeway store, thus making fresh produce the first item to confront customers after they picked up their carts.

Goff was a conscientious employee, a firm believer in the tenet that if you took a man's dollar, you by God worked for him because work was not only some vaguely Christian kind of duty, it also was good for you in another equally mysterious way. Goff never really thought about whether he liked his job although he knew he got a kind of a pleasure out of handling the berries and turnips and spinach and lettuce and tomatoes and plums. "There's variety in it," he had once told his wife on a rare occasion when they had discussed his job for all of three minutes. "You know, there's always new stuff coming in and you gotta plan for it and all."

Goff took the crate of corn from the dolly and put it on the floor. He shifted the few remaining ears of corn already on display so that he could put them on top of the new batch and then started taking each car out of the crate. He used a sharp knife to cut an X through each shuck. This was so a customer could easily lift up one of the triangular flaps created by the X and inspect the condition of the kernels underneath. Goff didn't have to do this. He did it because it was a service he had thought up. It was also one of the reasons that he had been promoted to produce manager.

After he had arranged the corn, he trundled the dolly over to the wood-and-glass enclosure that served as the store manager's office. He opened the door and said, "I'm gonna be a little late getting back from lunch, Virgil."

Virgil looked up from his desk and said, "How late?"

"About fifteen minutes."

"Okay."

"I gotta pick up my ticket to Miami," Goff said.

"Some guys have all the luck," Virgil said and went back to his paper work.

Goff wheeled the dolly back to the receiving and storage room, took off his white smock, put on his jacket and went out to his Toronado. He drove seven blocks and then circled until he found an empty meter. He parked his car and went into the United Airlines office.

"You got a one-way ticket to Chicago on Sunday for Harold F. Lawrence?" Goff said to the girl behind the counter.

"Just a moment, Mr. Lawrence."

In a few moments she produced an already made-out ticket. "Will that be cash or credit card, Mr. Lawrence?"

"Cash," Goff said.

"That will be fifty-one dollars," the girl said.

Goff handed her a worn hundred-dollar bill and she handed him the ticket along with his change plus a merry enough, "And thank you for flying United."

Goff said, "You're welcome," and went out to his Toronado. He drove another twelve blocks and started circling again until he found another open metered space. He didn't like to put his car in parking lots because, first of all, it cost too much, and second, he was convinced that the car jockeys liked to bang up anything over a Ford or a Plymouth.

After locking his car Goff went into a sporting-goods store and bought a box of .30-.30 caliber Winchester softnosed cartridges. Then he went back to his car and unlocked its trunk and put the sack containing the box of cartridges in the trunk along with the airline ticket to Chicago. His wife never looked in the trunk.

There was a diner across the street so Goff crossed over and had two cheeseburgers and a chocolate malt for lunch. The diner also had an enclosed phone booth and when he was through with his lunch, Goff got some change from the cashier, entered the booth, and dropped a dime in the slot. He dialed O and when the operator came on, Goff said, "I want to call Washington person to person." Then he told her that he wanted to speak to Mr. Donald Cubbin, but that he didn't have the number and that Mr. Cubbin was probably at work and that she'd have to get the number of his union.

Finally, a woman's voice said, "Mr. Cubbin's office," and the operator said, "I have a long-distance call for Mr. Donald Cubbin."

"May I ask who's calling?"

"Mr. Jack Wilson," Goff said.

"Mr. Cubbin is out of town, operator, but if Mr. Wilson will leave his number I'll have Mr. Cubbin return his call."

"It's important that I talk to him today," Goff said.

"Is there another number where Mr. Cubbin may be reached?" the operator said.

The woman said yes, that Mr. Cubbin was staying at the Sheraton-Blackstone in Chicago and that he could be reached there for the next few days. She then gave the operator the number.

"Would you like me to try that number?" the operator asked Goff.

"No," he said, "I'll place the call later."

Goff waited until he got his dime back and then left the diner and crossed the street to his car. That story he had read in *The New York Times* had been right, Goff told himself, but it was still a good thing to check because you could never believe what you read in the papers. Now he knew for certain that Donald Cubbin would be in Chicago on Sunday and Monday. He would fly up there Sunday and then Monday afternoon or evening he would buy a ticket and fly on down to Miami. Truman Goff had been to Chicago before but he had never been to Miami and he found himself looking forward to it.

17

Donald Cubbin's hand began to shake a little that Friday as he and Kelly rode the elevator up to Walter Penry's suite in the Chicago Hilton. Cubbin jammed his hands deep into his coat pockets and when the elevator stopped on the fourteenth floor he said to his son, "Why don't you wait here? I need to go back down and get a cigar."

"Come on, chief," Kelly said.

"Look, kid," Cubbin said as he stepped from the elevator, "I'd really like a cigar."

Kelly looked up and down the corridor and then produced a half-pint bottle of Ancient Age and handed it to his father. "Compliments of filthy Fred Mure," he told him. "He said you'd be needing it."

Cubbin took the half-pint, trying to conceal his eagerness, and glanced around. There was no one in sight. He looked at his son. "You know what this is?"

"It's whiskey."

"It's goddamned embarrassing, that's what." He raised the bottle and drank three large gulps.

"That'll put the bloom back in your cheeks," Kelly said, reaching for the bottle.

"Now what kind of a father would do that in front of his own son?" Cubbin said.

"The kind who needs a drink."

Walter Penry opened the door to Cubbin's knock and beamed at both father and son. "How are you, Don?" he said, grasping Cubbin's right hand in both of his.

"Fine, Walter. I don't think you've met my son, Kelly."

129

"No, but I've sure heard a lot about him—and all of it good." Kelly and Penry shook hands and sized each other up. The kid looks brighter than his old man, Penry thought, which could mean trouble. I don't like this slick sonofabitch, Kelly decided as he offered Penry a carefully selected smile, the kind that gave away nothing but a view of his teeth.

Cubbin shook hands with the boys, as Penry always referred to them, thirty-seven-year-old Peter Majury and forty-five-year-old Ted Lawson. Penry then introduced them to Kelly who decided that he didn't like them any better than he liked Penry and thought: the old man's got himself into speedy company. If that sneaky-looking one got a haircut, he could play the mad SS major in some World War Two movie. And that big one, who must wear that smile of his to sleep, could be the gunfighter who can't get enough of his job. Kelly always cast people whom he met and didn't like into film roles. For some reason it helped him to remember their faces and names. As for you, he thought as Penry handed him a drink, you look like that dolt on the FBI show who's always talking over the phone to Junior Zimbalist and telling him that the director's taking a personal interest in this one, Lewis.

"I think your dad told me that you're on the force in Washington," Penry said.

"He's resigned," Cubbin said quickly before his son could say anything. Kelly let it go.

He got bounced, you mean, and I'll bet I know why, Penry thought, but said, "Well, Don, I guess that makes you the only one in the room who's not an ex-cop of some kind. I spent eleven years with the FBI and the only thing I took with me when I left was a handshake from Mr. Hoover and a spotless record. Peter here did something or other for the CIA for above five years and Ted was with the Treasury. Seven years wasn't it, Ted?"

"Eight," Lawson said.

"How'd you like being a cop, Kelly?" Penry said.

"I liked it fine."

"And you resigned to give your dad a hand, huh?"

"Something like that."

130

"Well, from what I hear, Don, you're going to need all the help you can get."

Cubbin bristled. "I don't know where you get your information, but it sounds like you're getting it from Sammy."

"Come on, Don. You know we didn't fly all the way up here just to kid around with each other. I understand Sammy's put himself together a pretty good campaign."

"That television program last night," Peter Majury said and clucked his tongue a couple of times. "That was most unfortunate."

"One TV program doesn't make a campaign," Cubbin said.

"Well, that's what we wanted to talk to you about," Penry said. "Your campaign and how we can help. But let's have some lunch first."

They had lunch in the room, but not before Kelly made sure that his father was fortified with another drink, this time a double bourbon that Cubbin sipped as he nibbled at his steak and salad. While they ate, Walter Penry delivered himself of a number of opinions concerning the state of the nation and the world which, Kelly decided, would have had Attila the Hun nodding agreement. Kelly was thinking of needling Penry, of pricking that bloated self-assurance to see what would ooze out, when Penry said to Cubbin, "Now you and I, Don, we've always thought alike and——"

"What?" Cubbin said, looking up from his drink that was now about three-fourths gone.

"I said we've always thought alike."

"Walter, you're a nice guy but you're also full of shit."

Penry decided to retreat. "Of course, everyone has differences, but usually we wind up on the same side."

Cubbin was staring at Penry now. You don't owe him anything, he told himself. He owes you. You don't have to put up with any crap from him. "You know what I've been doing for the last fifteen minutes, Walter, I've been half lisening to that line of bull you've been handing out and wondering how a grown-up man like you can bring

131

himself to say such damn foolishness, let alone believe it."

"Well, Don, we don't have to agree on everything to be friends," Penry said.

"Who said anything about friendship? Some of my best friends are damn fools."

"Which of Walter's points do you especially disagree with, Don?" Majury asked, always eager for details, especially when they promised conflict.

"All of 'em," Cubbin said. "Now nobody's ever accused me of being a liberal, not since fifty-two anyhow after I came out for Eisenhower instead of Stevenson. I doubt if I'd do it today, but I did it then because I thought Ike wanted to be President. It wasn't my fault that he didn't take to the job. Well, that didn't make me popular. And I didn't get any more invitations to the White House after sixty-four when I first started yelling about Vietnam. Now let me tell you why I did that. I'm no foreign-affairs or military expert, but I used to be a pretty fair bookkeeper. So I just looked at the books. Well, I've got a sort of simple philosophy that's probably old hat nowadays. I believe everyone in this country should have enough to eat, plenty to wear, a good home to live in, an education, and a doctor to go to when they're sick. Now this they deserve just like the air they breathe. That's not too hard to understand, is it?"

"You're doing fine, chief," Kelly said.

"Yeah, well, like I said, I took a look at the books just like any bookkeeper would and I decided that we could either have ourselves a war over in Southeast Asia or we could have a fairly decent country, but we couldn't have both. We just didn't have the money. Well, I decided I'd rather have a decent country and I said so and kept saying so and George Meany got so mad he wouldn't even speak to me for six months until he had to because he wanted something. So there I was for about two years all by myself except for the kooks and the nuts until it finally got respectable to be anti-Vietnam. But let me tell you something, Walter, it wasn't any fun suddenly being the fifty-five-year-old darling of every left-wing, long-haired hippie in the country, but by God that's what I was. Christ, I even got a letter from Norman Mailer."

"Although I didn't agree with you at the time, Don," Penry said, "I believe I told you that it was a courageous stand."

Cubbin grinned. "You told me I was making a damn-fool mistake."

"Well, we're all on the same side now," Penry said. "At least about Vietnam."

"Perhaps we had better talk about our own battle," Majury said.

But Cubbin wasn't through. "You know what Sammy Hanks is saying now? He's saying that he was the one who talked me into coming out against Vietnam. Why in 1965 that dumb son of a bitch didn't even know where it was. You know what I did when Old Man Phelps died? I reached way down in the bottom of the bag and picked out the most insignificant, obscure regional director we had and made him secretary-treasurer because I believed all of his talk about loyalty and dedication. Hell, I was the one who took Sammy out of that Schenectady plant and gave him his first union job as an organizer. Just twelve years ago Sammy Hanks was running a set press and making two seventy-six an hour and happy to get it because it was more'n he'd ever made in his life. He barely had a high school education and some kind of college night course and if it hadn't been for me, he'd still be in that plant. I taught that ugly little prick everything he knows and gave him everything he's got and now he wants my job and goes around telling everybody that I've lost touch with the rank and file."

Kelly decided to interrupt before whiskey and anger drowned his father in a pool of self-pity. "You forgot to teach Sammy one thing, chief."

"What?"

"Gratitude."

You're talking too much, Cubbin told himself. Let them talk awhile. "Yeah, you're right," he said. "That's one thing he never learned. Gratitude."

"Well, perhaps you can teach him another equally im-

133

portant lesson, Don," Majury said in his usual hoarse whisper.

"What?"

"How to be graceful in defeat."

Cubbin smiled. "I'd like to do that. Yeah, I'd like that very much."

"I think we can be of some help to you, Don," Penry said.

"It's like I told you, Walter, we don't have any money."

"You let us worry about the money. In fact, I think we might be able to raise some for you."

"Who from?"

"You've got a lot of friends, Don, who you wouldn't want to go to but who'd be more than willing to help out if somebody'd just ask them. Well, that's one of my jobs—asking them."

"Who?" Cubbin said, because it was one of those days when his hangover was still so bad that he knew he didn't have a friend in the world.

"Well, let's just say they're friends who want to keep on being friends. They don't want you to know that you're in their debt."

"Just how much in debt do you think I could be to them?"

"Maybe three or four hundred thousand," Penry said, thinking: at least that's what you'll get. The rest I'll spend in my own way on your behalf.

"Jesus!" Cubbin said. "You sure it's that much?"

"Positive."

"Is it clean money?"

"It's clean. But it's anonymous."

"What do I have to do? I don't believe that shit you gave me about friends for one minute, Walter."

"I'm sorry to hear that, because they are your friends. And they don't want you to do anything—other than what you'd normally do."

"No strings at all?"

"No."

"What's your angle, Walter? I've never known you to be without one."

134

"Your friends will pay me for my services which will be placed entirely at your disposal. We're in for the duration, Don, if you'll have us."

"I've already got a campaign manager and a PR director."

"We know that," Majury said. "We don't want to involve ourselves at that level of your campaign."

"What level are you gentlemen interested in?" Kelly said.

"Play the tape, Ted," Majury told Lawson.

The big man nodded and rose, walking over to a tape-recording machine. "Now?" he said.

"In just a moment," Penry said. "Kelly, you asked at what level we plan to involve ourselves and that's really quite a good question. We're not interested in the execution of the campaign's general strategy. Don's got competent people to do that. What we will do is to provide certain issues that can be exploited. We'll also anticipate the opposition and try to make them commit tactical errors. This is going to be a brief, but dirty campaign. Our job is simply to make sure that our tricks are dirtier than theirs. Now you can play it, Ted."

Ted Lawson pushed a button and for several moments there was only the sound of some kind of a mechanical noise.

"Recognize it?" Penry said.

Cubbin shook his head.

"You should, you've heard it often enough. That's a mimeograph machine. When we first considered taking part in your campaign a few days ago, I told the boys to go out and see if they could dig up anything that would be both useful and, I might as well admit it, impressive. Peter used his talents and discovered that something interesting was going on in a couple of motel rooms just outside of Washington. Then Ted used his talents and managed to record these happenings on tape. I think you're going to find it informative."

For a while there was nothing on the tape but the sound of the mimeograph machine. Then it stopped and a man's voice said, "Well, that's the last thousand."

Another man's voice said, "How many's that make now?"

"Fifty thousand on this batch."

"God, I'd like to see old Don's face when he reads this one."

"Yeah, it's a pretty good one, all right. You got any of that coffee left?"

"Yeah, I think there's some left."

"Well, I think I'll have another cup before I run any more."

"Yeah, I think it's still hot."

"You know what I can't figure out?"

"What?"

"Why Barnett has such a hard on for Cubbin."

"I hear it goes back a long ways. I hear that he tried it once before back in fifty-five or 'six."

"Barnett?"

"Yeah. He tried to dump Cubbin once before."

"What happened?"

"I don't know. I wasn't around then. But he must not have made it because Cubbin's still president."

"That Cubbin's a funny guy. You ever meet him?"

"Yeah, I met him. He's always about half in the bag."

"He looks good though. On television I mean."

"He wears a wig."

"No shit?"

"Yeah, I hear he paid a thousand bucks for it out in Hollywood. He got his the same place all those movie stars get theirs."

"Well, Barnett's sure got it in for him. He's spending money too. He's got me and you here and Hepple and Karpinski out in L.A. and Joe James and Murray Fletcher in Chicago and what's his name in Cleveland—uh—"

"Fields. Stan Fields."

"Yeah. Fields. Is he Jewish?"

"How should I know?"

"Well, what is that, seven guys living like we're living? Hell, it must be costing a thousand bucks a day."

"More."

"Yeah, more. More like two thousand when we start traveling."

"Well, I don't guess there's any law against it."

"Against what?"

"Against one labor-union president trying to knock off another one."

"Even if they ain't in the same union?"

"I don't know of any law against it."

"Yeah. Any more coffee?"

"There's a little bit left. Here."

"Thanks. Well, it's war anyway. What about this guy Hanks?"

"What about him?"

"He any better than Cubbin?"

"Barnett thinks so, I guess, but shit, you get up there and start taking forty and fifty thou a year and you don't give a good goddamn about the members. You just wanna look good. I don't know anything about this guy Hanks except that he must have some kinda deal with Barnett. They gotta have something fixed up or we wouldn't be working for Hanks."

"Well, when they get up that high they all get bigshoti-tis."

"That's for sure."

"I guess we'd better start on this new batch. You wanna run the machine or stack 'em in the boxes?"

"I'll run the machine awhile."

"Okay."

There was the sound of movement and then the sound of the mimeograph machine and then the tape came to an end. Lawson switched it to rewind as the others in the room turned to look at Cubbin. His face was pale and his lips were tightly compressed. "That son of a bitch," he said.

"Barnett tried it once before, didn't he, Don?" Penry said.

"In fifty-five," Cubbin said.

"That's a highly edited tape that you heard, Don," Lawson said. "Most of the rest of the time they were talking about women."

"You got their names?"

137

Lawson nodded. "I got their names and I also got a sample of what they were running off on that mimeograph machine. And I've got pictures of the interior of the two motel rooms and of them entering and leaving it. You've got all the proof you need."

Cubbin turned to look at his son. "Kelly, get on the phone to Audrey over at the hotel and tell her to call Barnett down in Washington. Tell her that I want an appointment with him Tuesday at eleven A.M. Tell her that I won't accept any excuses and that she can lean on Barnett's secretary or whoever she talks to as hard as she wants. She'll know how to do it."

"What if Barnett's going to be out of town Tuesday?" Kelly said.

"Tell Audrey that I said that he'd better have his ass back in town. Don't worry, she'll fix it up."

When Kelly went over to the phone to make the call, Cubbin turned to Penry. "Have you got some kind of a small portable machine that I can carry in a briefcase and just push the button to play that tape? I'm going to make a little speech to Mr. Howard Barnett on Tuesday and I don't want to ruin its effect by having to fumble around with a tape."

Forever the actor, Penry thought, but replied, "We'll send a small one over to your hotel this afternoon, Don, all threaded and ready to go."

"What do you plan to say to Barnett?" asked Majury, whose craving to know was almost physical.

"Say to him?"

"Yes."

Cubbin stood up. "Well, I guess I'll call him a few names first and then I'm going to tell him that if he so much as looks in my direction again I'm going to kick his ass right up to his shoulders."

Kelly came back from the phone. "Audrey's making the call now," he said.

Cubbin nodded and looked at Penry and his associates. "Well, I guess you guys have dealt yourself in. Thanks."

"We're looking forward to it, Don," Penry said.

Cubbin nodded. "I appreciate it. You know while

you're snooping around there's something else that you
might look into for me."

"What?" Penry said.

"It's just a feeling I've got. A hunch."

"What?"

"Here in Chicago."

"What about Chicago?"

"That's where they're going to try to steal it. Wouldn't
you if you were Sammy?"

"Yes," said Walter Penry, nodding slowly, "as a matter
of fact, I would."

18

Sadie Cubbin lay on her side in the rumpled bed in room
918 of the Sheraton and watched Fred Mure as he slept
and snored. He's earned it, she thought. He's given satisfactory service once, twice and sometimes even three
times a day for the past four months now so you can't
object if he snores a little when he sleeps.

She reached for a cigarette and lit it and then turned
back to watch Mure. I think the first few times he did it to
accommodate Don, not me. He fucked me because he
knew that Don couldn't and so it was part of the service,
like arranging for the elevator and putting Don to bed at
night and getting him to places on time. Too drunk to
fuck your wife, boss? Merely another simple problem in
logistics except that Fred wouldn't use a word like that. So
that's all it was at first, just stud service, but now he's
built it into something more and when Don gets through
with this election and things get back to where they were
before, Fred is going to be a problem. Poor, ignorant,
beautiful, cunning, crafty, sexy Fred Mure's in love with

the boss's wife and she lets him be in love with her because she has to have it. He thinks it's going to continue like this when Don gets well again after the election. Don must know. Don't kid yourself, Sadie, of course he knows. That's why he wouldn't let them send Fred away, because he knew his wife had to have her share and she wasn't going to get it from him and she had to get it from somewhere and somehow Fred is no threat to Don. God, what a mess. It was all right before he started drinking this time. No it wasn't all right, but you could live with it. You got fucked twice a week, sometimes three. Now you get it twice a day, sometimes three. Well, there's no use worrying about it now. You can worry afterward, after the election. God, I hope Don loses. Please, God, make him lose.

Fred Mure opened his eyes and looked at Sadie. "I was asleep."

"I know. I was watching you."

"What time is it?"

"A little after three."

"I'd better get going. He should be getting back around three-thirty."

"What's the schedule for tonight?"

"He's got two meetings," Fred said, "one in Calumet and one in Gary."

"We'd better get dressed."

Fred Mure smiled at Sadie, turned, and ran a hand over her body. "We've got a little time."

She trembled and then the tremble turned into a shiver. "We shouldn't, darling," she said as she wiggled toward him.

At four o'clock that afternoon Donald Cubbin finished reading the memorandum that Charles Guyan had handed him. He looked up at Oscar Imber and asked, "You read it?"

"I read it."

"What do you think?"

"I think it's fine," Imber said. "It's just the kind of PR program you need, if you had a million bucks to spend."

Cubbin turned to Guyan who was half sprawled on the couch in the living room of Cubbin's suite. "How much fat's in there?"

"Not much."

"Come on, I never read one of these things yet that didn't have some frills that could be cut out."

"You might be able to get by on eight hundred thousand."

"We haven't got eight hundred thousand," Imber said. "We haven't got nearly that much."

"We do now," Cubbin said.

Imber leaned forward in his chair. "What do you mean, we do now?"

Cubbin smiled. "I raised four hundred thousand this afternoon. I can probably squeeze another two hundred thousand out of them. With what you've raised we've got enough."

Imber stood up. "Where did you raise that much?"

"Friends."

"Come on, Don. Where?"

"Walter Penry."

"Jesus," Imber said and sat back down, slumping in the chair.

"It's clean money," Cubbin said.

"Bullshit," Imber said.

"Is Penry in on this now?" Guyan said.

"He's going to help out a bit," Cubbin said.

"Then you've got my resignation."

"What the hell do you mean I've got your resignation?"

"I don't work with Penry."

"Why not? What's wrong with Walter Penry?"

"He's slimy, that's what's wrong with him. He's the slimiest son of a bitch in the world and I'm not going to take any crap from him or from that creeping Jesus who works for him."

Imber glanced at Guyan. "You mean Peter Majury?"

"Jawohl," Guyan said and made a Nazi salute. "You know Majury?"

Imber nodded. "I know him and I know Penry, too."

"Well," Guyan said as he rose, "it's been real."

"Sit down, Charlie," Imber said. "Let's find out about this first. If it's like you think it is, I'll go with you." Imber looked at Cubbin. "All right, tell us."

"I don't have to tell you a fuckin thing, sonny," Cubbin said, his voice rising. "If you want to quit, then quit. Christ, everybody else has run out on me. I'm sixty-two years old, but by God I can still run a campaign if I want to and I don't need any help from people who quit if they think they're not going to be the big cheese. I don't need you guys; I don't need anybody."

"Calm down, chief," Kelly said from his chair in the corner. "Just tell them what Penry told you."

"You were there, Kelly?" Imber said.

"I was there."

"What do you think?"

"About what?"

"About what we're talking about, for Christ's sake."

"I think you guys are being childish. All of you. Penry's come up with some money. He swears it's clean and no strings attached. He also claims that he doesn't want anything to do with the PR or the management of Dad's campaign. He seems to want to work on the opposition, to come up with a few tricks that'll be dirtier than theirs. Although it's the first time I've met him, I'd say he might be able to do it. I didn't much care for him."

"All right, Don," Imber said, "let's start all over."

"You guys want to quit, go ahead."

"We're all a little edgy, Don. Just tell us about the money first."

"It's just like Kelly said. There're no strings."

"How about later?"

Cubbin shook his head. "No. None then either."

"Who's putting it up?"

"The money?"

"Christ, yes, the money."

"I don't know. Penry said friends of mine."

Imber shook his head. "What do you think? I mean really."

Cubbin sighed. "I'd like a drink."

Imber looked at Kelly who nodded and said, "I'll get it." He rose and went into the adjoining bedroom. Sadie

142

Cubbin was seated in a chair, reading a magazine. "How's it going?" she said.

"All right," Kelly said, mixing a bourbon and water.

"Is your dad okay?"

"He'll make it," Kelly said and went back into the living room and handed his father the drink.

Cubbin took a large swallow. "You want to know what I think, huh?"

"That's right," Imber said.

"Well, I don't have any friends who're going to put up four or five or six hundred thousand to get me reelected. I don't think anybody has friends like that. So that only leaves one source that I can think of."

Imber nodded. "Me, too."

"What?" Guyan said.

"It's company money," Imber said.

Cubbin nodded. "It must be."

"But you're not sure," Imber said.

"What do you mean I'm not sure?" Cubbin said. "I'm damned sure."

"No, as far as you're concerned, it's money from friends." He looked at Guyan. "You don't care where the money comes from, do you?"

Guyan shrugged. "I just spend it, but I don't want Walter Penry or that kneejerk Nazi of his telling me how to spend it."

"You got Peter all wrong," Cubbin said in a mild tone. "He's really quite a liberal guy.'"

"I'm not going to argue with you, Don," Guyan said. "I'm just going to tell you right now that I'm not going to take any orders from either Penry or Majury."

"But you will take money from them?" Imber said.

Guyan shrugged again.

"What about suggestions and ideas, but not orders?" Kelly said to Guyan.

"It it's a good idea or suggestion, I don't care where it comes from," Guyan said.

"Well," Kelly said, "from what I heard and saw during my first meeting with that bunch, you're going to be getting quite a few suggestions and ideas." He turned to his father. "You'd better play them that tape, chief."

Cubbin nodded. "I guess I'd better. After you hear this tape you're going to understand not just why we can use Walter Penry, but why we need him. Why we need him bad. Play it for them, Kelly."

Kelly Cubbin walked over to the small Sony recorder that had arrived by cab shortly after he and his father had returned from the Hilton. He pressed a button and the sound of the mimeograph machine began.

Cubbin watched the grim expressions that appeared on the faces of Guyan and Imber as the voices on the tape began. I don't guess they've ever played this rough before, he thought. It's going to get rougher, a lot rougher because Sammy's out to win and for him that's everything. Christ, when's the last time you wanted something so bad that it made you hurt the way Sammy must be hurting? Well, yeah, there was that time then when you wanted to get on that bus to L.A. You wanted that all right, but since then you haven't wanted much of anything, at least not anything that wasn't easy enough to get. You want to be reelected this last time, but it won't kill you if you're not. You'd probably be better off, you and Sadie. You've got to do something about Sadie. Maybe explain to her how after the election's over it's going to be okay again. Christ, Cubbin, you can really fuck things up.

When the tape ended, the grim expressions on the faces of Guyan and Imber remained. Imber looked at Cubbin who was wearing a cynical smile. "Surprised?" Cubbin said.

Imber nodded. "What're you going to do about it?"

"I'm seeing Barnett Tuesday."

"What're you going to say?"

"You mean after I stuff that tape down his throat?"

"Yes."

"I don't know." Cubbin said, "but whatever it is, I'm going to have a damned good time saying it."

Imber turned to Guyan. "You'd better tell him about it now."

"Tell me what?" Cubbin said.

"The wire services have been after me for your answer to Sammy."

144

"What's Sammy saying?"

"He held a press conference in Washington this afternoon."

"And?"

"He demanded that you resign."

Cubbin snorted. "Christ," he said, "I thought he might have said something important."

19

The auditorium of the Calumet City high school was packed with 2,711 local union members, including wives and girl friends, who had paid a dollar for ten chances on a shiny new fiber-glass Chris-Craft cruiser that retailed for $6,499. The cruiser now rested on a trailer that was parked on stage next to the blue and white state flag that was correctly displayed on the audience's right.

Donald Cubbin arrived at the high school in Fred Mure's black Oldsmobile. He sat in front with Mure and in back were Oscar Imber, Charles Guyan, and Kelly Cubbin. A phone call from Fred Mure had produced a Chicago squad car that used its flashing top light to shepherd Cubbin's car from the Sheraton-Blackstone to Calumet City. A block from the high school the squad car switched on its siren, thus enabling Cubbin to make something of an entrance.

While the officials of the local union were welcoming Cubbin, Fred Mure walked over to the squad car. He held out his hand to the cop behind the wheel and said, "Thanks, you guys."

The cop felt the folded bills and grinned at Mure. "Anytime, Mr. Mure." He glanced down and saw that Mure had slipped him two twenties. "We'll be glad to stick around a little while, if you think you might need us."

"No, we can find our way back all right," Mure said and patted the sill of the car door.

"Well, thanks a lot," the cop said.

"Sure thing," Mure said and turned away, reaching for his notebook. He went back to his own car and used its interior light to write down, "Chicago Police Escort, $75." Then he moved over to join Cubbin and the local union's welcoming committee.

"Well, you're sure looking good, Don," the local union president was telling Cubbin for the fourth time.

"Feeling fine, Harry, really fine. You got a pretty good crowd?"

"Packed," Harry said. "Right up to the roof."

"What's the schedule?"

"Well, you're the big attraction, just like I told you you'd be. No other speakers except me when I introduce you and I'm gonna make that sweet, but short. Of course we're gonna pledge allegiance to the flag and then we got some fella who used to sing with Fred Waring who's gonna lead us in 'The Star-Spangled Banner' and then after I introduce you well, you're on."

"When did he sing with Waring?" Cubbin said.

"I think back in forty or forty-one."

"Huh," Cubbin said. "What's he do now?"

"He teaches music here in the high school and sings around at funerals and weddings and stuff like that. I guess he's over sixty now but he can still carry a tune pretty good."

They led Donald Cubbin through a side door to the high school and down a corridor to the backstage entrance of the auditorium. The group made its way down the corridor, with the local union officials jockeying for advantageous positions close to either Cubbin's right or left elbows.

Inside the auditorium Charles Guyan found that all three networks had already set up their cameras, lights, and sound equipment. The three newsmen were standing together near the stage. Guyan went over to them and said, "Welcome to Calumet City, gentlemen."

146

"We're all atremble," the CBS man said and shook hands with Guyan who then shook hands with the two men from ABC and NBC.

"I thought you were down in Guatemala or some such place," Guyan said to the ABC man.

"I was in some such and now I'm being punished. You got a copy of his speech?"

"Here," Guyan said and gave each of them two copies. "The more brilliant passages are noted in the margin in case you don't want to read the whole thing."

"Who's writing his stuff now?" the NBC man asked.

"Don still writes his own," Guyan said. "He stays up all night and writes on parchment with a quill pen. I thought you knew that."

"I forgot," the NBC man said as he scanned the speech. "Where's he reply to Sammy?"

"It's not in the speech," Guyan said. "He'll probably say something about it in the beginning."

"He say anything else?" the CBS man said.

"He makes a passing reference to what a wonderful job he's done for the union," Guyan said.

"Anything nasty about Sammy?" the ABC man said.

"Page five," Guyan said. "I think he calls him a man with a 'chronic case of the can'ts.'"

Guyan moved off toward the cafeteria table that had been set up in the space just beyond the stage for five men whose professionally bored expressions told Guyan that they were gentlemen of the press. Nobody else in the world, he thought, can look quite that bored.

Backstage in a small dressing room Donald Cubbin was combing his long silver hair. He wore a dark blue suit, a blue and white polka dot tie, and a white shirt. He had slept for two hours that afternoon and after that he had gone down to the hotel barbershop for a shave and a massage. Now he looked rested, pink, and sober, which he almost was. He turned from the mirror and asked his son and Fred Mure, "Do I look okay?"

"Fine," Mure said. "You look great, Don."

"Kelly?"

"Great."

"Where's my speech?"

147

"Here," Kelly said, handing him the ten-page speech that had been typed on a special machine in twenty-four-point capital letters. Cubbin glanced at the first page and then flipped quickly through the rest of it. He glanced up at the ceiling and moved his lips silently. Then he nodded to himself and looked at Fred Mure.

"Well, shit, Fred, I guess I'll have one for the road," Cubbin said and glanced at his son as if to see how Kelly would take the news. Kelly grinned at his father. "You don't have to check with me."

"Well, I don't like to drink in front of you like this," Cubbin said as he reached for the half-pint of Ancient Age that Mure held out to him.

"I'm not my father's keeper," Kelly said.

"Yeah, well, by God, I'm beginning to think he needs one," Cubbin said as he handed the bottle back.

There was a knock at the door and Fred Mure answered it after slipping the half-pint into his coat pocket. It was the local union president, a little nervous, but trying to conceal it.

"I guess we're ready if you are, Don."

"Okay, let's go," Cubbin said.

"Well, you get in here behind me in the middle and then we'll go out and sit down on the stage."

There were twelve men standing around outside the dressing room in dark suits and white shirts and ties, all of which seemed to have too much red in them. They were the officers and board members of the local union.

"Here, you mean?" Cubbin said, indicating a space between two men.

"No, just up there ahead of Dick."

"Here, you mean?"

"Yeah that's fine."

The local union president looked around and decided that they were in as much of a line as they would ever be. "Okay," he said, "let's move on out." The twelve local union officials and their international president, all wearing expressions that were grim enough for such a solemn occasion, expressions that indeed would have been appropriate for a hanging, moved out onto the stage to

148

scattered applause and took their seats in folding chairs that were placed against the green backdrop that bore a large white paper sign that read "WELCOME, PRES. CUBBIN."

"You coming out front?" Kelly asked Fred Mure.

"No, I'll stay back here in case Don needs me."

Kelly nodded and left. By the time he reached his seat in the front row of the auditorium between Guyan and Imber, the young Methodist preacher had finished his prayer for the general welfare of everyone assembled there that night, and especially for their national leaders, and the local union's secretary-treasurer was introducing his twelve-year-old niece who was going to have the privilege of leading the audience in the pledge of allegiance.

After the pledge of allegiance the music teacher who had once sung with Fred Waring was introduced and he led the audience in the first verse of "The Star-Spangled Banner" accompanied by his wife on the piano. Cubbin thought that for an old guy, the music teacher did pretty well on the high notes.

Cubbin got a nice hand as she strode to the podium after his introduction. As the applause died Cubbin stood there, his head bowed, not looking at the audience.

"You ever see him make a speech like this?" Imber whispered to Guyan.

"Not like this," Guyan said.

"He knows what he's doing."

Cubbin stood there for all of a minute, the spotlight gleaming on the silver hair of his bowed head. Slowly he raised his head and looked at the audience, raking it with his eyes until the auditorium was perfectly still.

When he spoke he made it sound like a whisper, but one that reached all the way to the back rows. He put a great deal of feeling into his tone, a mixture of contempt and bitter scorn:

"They say that I should quit my job and run."

He paused and then repeated the line stronger, louder, and with even more scorn:

"They say that I should quit my job and run."

Another dramatic beat, and then the blast:

"Quit, hell! I've just begun to fight!"

It brought some of them to their feet cheering and whistling, and those who didn't rise pounded their hands together as much in anticipation of a good show as in appreciation for Cubbin's declaration.

"I'll be damned," Guyan said. "What is it? Does he do it every time?"

"You tell him, Kelly," Imber said.

"It's a combination," Kelly said. "I don't think he knows he's doing it really. He just knows that it works. Did you get those first two lines?"

Guyan glanced down at some notes he'd made. "Yeah. It's really not much of a line when you read it: 'They say that I should quit my job and run.' "

" 'Till Birnam Wood remove to Dunsinane,' " Kelly said.

"Jesus."

"Five feet to the line, iambic pentameter," Kelly said. "But he doesn't only steal the beat from Shakespeare, he also borrows from the blues. The first line of all real blues songs is usually repeated and if you think about it, they're also iambic pentameter, or try to be."

"Does he do it consciously?" Guyan said.

Kelly shrugged. "He's been doing it as long as I can remember. I tried to analyze it for him one time, but he wasn't interested. He said he just kept thinking up lines until he got one that felt right."

Donald Cubbin spoke for fifteen minutes and was interrupted by applause twenty-one times. He sat down to a standing ovation that came from an audience that not only liked his speech, but that also wanted to thank him for not speaking too long. The audience was in such a good mood that nobody seriously objected when the $6,499 Chris-Craft was won by the brother-in-law of the local union's secretary-treasurer.

20

In Washington's Cleveland Park on September 10, a Sunday, Samuel Morse Hanks was seated in his kitchen, drinking coffee, and reading the comics to his daughter Marylin who had turned six the day before.

Sammy Hanks was reading the comics to his daughter because his father had never read them to him. When his father had died ten years before Hanks had not gone to the funeral. He sometimes thought that he probably would have gone if his father had taken the time to read the comics to him. But his father always had been too concerned with his own private misery to pay much attention to the needs of his son.

Samuel Morse Hanks, Senior, had spent his life teaching European and American history to the sons and daughters of the men who worked in the plants and factories of Schenectady when those plants and factories were open. Shortly after he had arrived in the town he met a girl who was almost as ugly as he and to whom he quickly proposed marriage, mostly because she had a job in a library. Samuel Morse Hanks, Jr., was born in 1933, inheriting his pickle nose and Punch chin from his father and his bad skin from his mother.

His mother had lost her library job as soon as she had married because the library had a policy of not employing married women. She had pretended to be surprised when she had been dismissed, although she had known she would be, but she had also known that nobody other than Samuel Morse Hanks, Senior, would ever ask her to marry.

The earliest emotion that Samuel Morse Hanks, Jr.,

could remember was anger. He had been an angry child because his parents were poor, ugly, and seldom spoke to him, or for that matter, to each other. The only way that he could draw attention to himself was by throwing tantrums. That sometimes won him a little attention, although not enough, so he increased the number of tantrums, but with diminishing results. The more tantrums he threw, the less attention his parents paid him, until they virtually ignored him just as they ignored each other.

Until he was fifteen years old, Sammy's mother maintained what could be called a nodding acquaintance with reality. She cleaned the house sometimes and occasionally cooked meals, although she had a tendency to serve breakfast at 6:30 P.M. and dinner at seven in the morning. She had become completely oblivious to her son's tantrums, although he still produced them, but mostly from habit.

When Sammy came home from school on his fifteenth birthday his mother was sitting in a chair, motionless, staring without comprehension into what may have been the lower depths of some private hell. She was also completely naked.

"What's wrong with you?" Sammy said and when his mother didn't answer, Sammy threw a tantrum, a real beauty that lasted for nearly five minutes. When she didn't even blink at that he took a blanket from his parents' bed and threw it over her and then found her purse and stole all she had, eighty-seven cents, and went downtown to a movie.

When he came back that evening, his mother was still sitting motionless in the chair with the blanket over her. His father was listening to the radio, which was virtually his sole amusement and had been since 1933.

"What's wrong with her?" Sammy said.

"I don't know," his father said.

"Maybe you'd better get a doctor."

"She'll snap out of it."

Sammy shrugged and went to bed after fixing himself a peanut-butter sandwich. When he got up the next morning he found his mother in the same position except that there

152

was now a large pool of urine on the bare floor under her chair.

"She's pissing all over the floor," he told his father.

The senior Hanks had shrugged. "Then she can clean it up."

When Sammy came home that afternoon his mother had gone, but his father was already there. "What happened to her?"

"They took her away."

"Away where?"

"To the insane asylum. She's catatonic. An interesting case, the doctor said."

"When's she coming back?"

"I don't know," his father said. "Perhaps never. Do you mind?"

"No," Sammy said. "Do you?"

"No," his father said, "I don't mind."

Three weeks later Sammy Hanks was awakened shortly after midnight when his father tried to crawl into bed with him.

"What the hell are you doing?"

"Just lie still, I'm not going to hurt you."

"What do you mean lie still?"

"Just turn over and lie still; you'll like it."

Sammy Hanks didn't know what else to do so he threw a tantrum. That didn't prevent his father from finishing what he had started and when it was over he had giggled and told Sammy, "Thank you very much."

By five-thirty that morning Sammy was packed. At five thirty-five he crept into his parents' bedroom and stole his father's wallet which contained nine dollars. He never saw his father and mother again, but if anyone ever mentioned his father, Sammy promptly threw a tantrum. He couldn't help it.

Twenty-four years and four months later Sammy Hanks was sitting in his kitchen with his slender blond wife and his slender blond daughter, determined to do for them what his father had never done for him and his mother.

Sybil Davis Hanks had married Sammy after Donald Cubbin had made him secretary-treasurer of the union because he seemed to worship her, he had a politically acceptable job that paid well, and because it was time for her to get married and Sammy at least didn't bore her. An additional bonus was the way that his dark ugliness provided a splendid setting for her blond beauty. Sammy had married Sybil because she was everything that his mother had never been.

Sammy Hanks put down the second section of *The Washington Post*'s comic strips and tousled his daughter's blond hair. "That's all, honey. Why don't you run out and play in the street?"

"I'm not supposed to play in the street."

"You're not?"

"No."

"Where are you supposed to play?"

"In the yard. You know that, Daddy."

"I guess you're right. Okay, why don't you go out and play in the yard?"

It was an old joke between father and daughter and both of them still liked it. He also liked to watch her play, sometimes with other children in the neighborhood, and sometimes with her imaginary friends. Marylin hadn't minded introducing her father to her imaginary friends because she knew that he would treat them with grave respect.

"We oughta get her a dog, a big one," he said as his daughter wandered out into the backyard.

"A St. Bernard or a Great Dane?" Sybil said.

"I mean a big one. One of those Irish wolfhounds."

"Who do you want it for, you or Marylin?"

Sammy Hanks smiled his charming smile at his wife. "For me, I guess."

"You never had a dog?"

The smile vanished. "No," he said. "I never had a dog or a cat either."

Sybil recognized the danger signals and quickly shifted the topic because Sammy's childhood was something they had spoken of only twice and both times he had gone into raging tantrums. The first time she had asked casually about his parents. The second time she had done so purposely, to see what would happen, and when she found out she had never mentioned his parents again. Instead, she mothered Sammy a lot because he seemed to like it.

"When do you have to leave?"

"I have to be out at Dulles by three so I'd better leave here around one forty-five."

"Who's going with you?"

"Just Mickey Della."

"Is he as good as you thought he'd be?"

"Uh-huh. He's better than what Cubbin's got."

"I should call her, you know."

"Who?"

"Sadie."

"What the Christ you wanta call her for?"

"Because she's a good friend."

"She *was* a good friend."

"Just because you and Don are in a fight is no reason that Sadie and I have to be."

"What're you going to do, call her up and say isn't it just terrible how the boys are behaving? For Christ's sake, Sybil, I'm going to have to teach you how to hate."

"I don't hate Sadie."

"Well, learn."

"And you don't hate Don."

"I don't?"

"No."

"Well, I'm going to take his job away from him so I might as well hate him. It'll make it easier."

"We used to have some fun together."

"Who, you and Sadie?"

"The four of us."

"I don't remember any good times."

"Well, I do."

"Cubbin was always sloshed."

"Not always."

"Well, I hear he is now."

"Poor Sadie."

"Poor Sadie, my ass."

"What's he going to do?"

"Who?"

"Don."

155

"When?"

"When it's over."

"Get drunk and stay that way probably."

"I don't know, but it just doesn't seem fair."

"What doesn't?"

"He's dedicated his whole life to the union and—"

"Jesus, you sound like his campaign stuff. He hasn't dedicated his life to the union, he's worked all his life for the union. There's a big difference. Christ, most of the time it's bored him silly. It still bores him. I don't think he even really cares if he's reelected or not. He's just going through the motions."

"Then what are you worried about?"

"Because no matter what else I might say about him, Mr. Donald Cubbin's a damned good actor and if he just goes through the motions of trying to get reelected, he'll put on a campaign that's a hundred percent better than anybody else around."

"But you can beat him," Sybil said, making it a statement rather than a question because she knew that her husband would prefer it that way.

"I can beat him because I want it. I want it so bad that—" Hanks broke off. "Hell, I sometimes ache when I think about it."

Sybil put her hand on his arm. "That's just tension, honey."

"Yeah, I guess so."

They were silent a moment and then Sybil said, "What if he wanted it as bad as you do?"

"Don?"

"Yes."

Hanks thought about it for a moment. "If he wanted it even half as much," he said, "I wouldn't stand a chance in hell."

21

Sunday was feast day for Mickey Della. It was the day that he rose at seven to devour *The New York Times, The Washington Post, The Sunday Star, The Baltimore Sun,* and the New York *Daily News* in approximately that order.

Della lived in the same large one-bedroom apartment on Sixteenth Street N.W. that he had lived in since 1948. It was an apartment from which two wives had departed and whose goings Della had scarcely noticed. Now he lived alone, surrounded by hundreds of books, some mismatched but comfortable enough furniture, and six green, five-drawer filing cabinets that were crammed with articles and features that Della had ripped from newspapers and tucked away for future possible reference.

The apartment was cluttered, but not messy. The ashtrays were all clean, except for the one that Della used as he read his twenty-five pounds or so of newspapers. Only one coffee cup was visible. An old wooden desk with an equally old typewriter in its well had no litter on its surface. Della had cooked his own breakfast at seven-fifteen that morning, but there was no evidence of it in the kitchen. His bed was made and his pajamas were hung neatly behind the door of the bathroom whose tub was innocent of a ring. It was the apartment of someone who had lived alone long enough to learn that it was easier to be neat than not.

At noon Della crossed to the phone and dialed the home number of the man he bought his liquor from. "Mickey Della, Sid. . . . I'm fine. Sorry to bother you on Sunday but I want to place a standing order with you and

I'll be out of town for a few days. . . . Yeah. What I want is a fifth of real cheap bourbon, I don't care what kind, to be delivered personally and gift wrapped to the same guy every day for the next month. And I want the same card to go with it each time. Now he's going to be out of town most of the time so you're going to have to arrange it with American Express or Western Union or whoever you work through. . . . Yeah, it's kind of a joke. I want it to start today, if possible. He's in Chicago. Okay. Now I want the card to read, 'Courage, a Friend.' That's all. Hell, I don't remember whether they sell booze in Chicago on Sunday. It's not famous for its blue laws. . . . Yeah, well, the guy I want you to send it to every day for the next month is Donald Cubbin. Today and tomorrow he'll be at the Sheraton-Blackstone in Chicago. Thanks, Sid."

Della chuckled as he went back to his newspapers. Later there would be other needling harassments that would be far better and much more vicious. But it was okay for a start and just right to set the tone for another Mickey Della campaign.

At Baltimore's Friendship Airport Truman Goff pulled his Oldsmobile Toronado up to the entrance and turned to his wife. "I'll be back in about a week," he said.

"Well, have a good time."

"Yeah, thanks. You need any money?"

"No, you already gave me plenty."

"Well, I guess I'll go on in now."

"Give your daddy a kiss, honey," Goff's wife said to their daughter who leaned forward from the back seat and pecked at her father's cheek.

"You want me to pick you up when you come back?"

Goff shook his head. "No, I'll just take an airport bus on in."

"Well, all right, hon. Have a good time in Miami."

She leaned over and gave Goff a dry kiss on the cheek.

"You all take care," he said as he got out of the car and lifted his suitcase from the rear seat. "Bye, now."

"Bye," his wife and daughter said.

Goff entered the airport and checked his bag through to Chicago. He had thirty minutes to wait so he went over to the paperback-book stand and studied the titles until he found a Louis L'Amour western that he didn't remember reading. He glanced at the first few pages and then at the last two, but he still couldn't remember reading it. It don't matter, he told himself as he handed the cashier a dollar and waited for his change. Sometimes when you read 'em twice they're even better the second time.

In Washington on Sixteenth Street, about a mile south of Mickey Della's apartment, Coin Kensington was pouring coffee for his visitor in the hotel suite that had a view of the White House. Kensington sat on the couch, squashing its cushions with his bulk. In front of him was the coffee service and a large dish that held the contents of a twelve-ounce can of Del Monte cling peaches. After pouring coffee for his guest, Kensington picked up a can of Hershey's chocolate syrup and poured most of it over the peaches.

"I got sort of a sweet tooth," he explained, trying to keep the defensive tone out of his voice, but not succeeding too well.

"So it would seem," his guest said.

Kensington spooned one of the chocolate-drenched peaches into his mouth and smiled at its taste. "Sort of my breakfast dessert, you might say."

"Yes," his guest said.

"Well, I must say you sure remind me of your daddy."

"Thank you," said the president of Gammage International, A. Richard Gammage III.

"He was sort of a maverick, too, you know."

"Yes."

"We did some business together back in the late thirties."

"Yes, I remember Father describing it to me."

"He wasn't too complimentary about me, I guess."

"No, I can't say that he was."

"Well, that's all over now."

159

"Yes."

"We got other fish to fry now."

Gammage looked at the fat old man and nodded. Dear dead Daddy warned you about this terrible old man, Richard the Third, which was how Gammage often addressed himself because he thought it was a bit ironic and he was fond of irony because it was such a rare quality nowadays. Daddy warned you that this old man was bad, brilliant, and a bullshitter. He must be, if he took dear old dead Daddy.

"You must be talking about money," Gammage said.

"Now how did you know that?"

"Because you smiled, Mr. Kensington."

"Well, now, that's an interesting point because some people think that money's nothing to smile at."

"It has never failed to delight me," Gammage said.

"Well, it's been my life study."

"Yes."

"Do you know what money is, Mr. Gammage?"

"Technically?"

"Philosophically."

"Power? Security? Greed? Avarice? War? Treason?"

"Well, you're on the right track except you're a little negative."

"Sorry."

"Money, Mr. Gammage, is love."

"Oh."

"Think about it."

"I shall."

"Money is love. People who say it ain't just don't have enough. But let 'em have to make a choice between principle and a dollar and ninety-nine percent of 'em will go for the dollar. The other one percent are just damn fools."

"Which, I suppose, brings us to your point."

"Well, I thought that since you had to come down here from Cleveland today anyhow, we might get together to see how you're coming."

"It takes a little time," Gammage said with a shrug. "But there's no problem. I think I'll have at least four hundred thousand by Tuesday and the rest by the end of the week."

"Well, that's good because they're getting a might skittish over there," Kensington said, jerking his thumb in the general direction of the White House.

"Mr. Kensington, I have not the slightest interest in what anyone *over there* thinks. I *know* the man who occupies the White House. Unfortunately I've known him for years and I've always found him to be a singularly odious man—vulgar in thought, opportunistic in deed, offensive in manner, and frankly terrible in appearance. God, those suits of his!"

"Well, I didn't vote for him either," Kensington said.

"The only reason that I've agreed to coordinate the fund-raising for Cubbin is because he's the devil I know and he poses less of a threat to my company than this Hanks person. And quite frankly, Cubbin can be pleasant company, if it weren't for his tendency to today. He also drinks too much." Christ, you sound like a prig, Richard the Third, Gammage thought.

"Well, like I said, money is love and it's gonna take a lot of love to get him reelected. But it's also gonna take a little something else."

"I don't think I follow you."

"Well, if you want Cubbin elected, you could help a lot by doing something that's gonna please him."

"What?"

"Well, I think you should head up a committee."

"What committee?"

Kensington smiled. "The Committee for Industrial Stability. Its only business will be to endorse and support the election of Sammy Hanks."

He's not stupid, Kensington thought. It's going to take him about five seconds to make up his mind because that's all he'll need to sort out the ramifications. His old man was like that. Smart. But not quite smart enough. Not always.

"The kiss of death, to counterfeit a phrase," Gammage said.

"Exactly."

"You were right; it will please Cubbin."

"You'll do it then?"

"Of course."

In a second-floor sample room of a Loop hotel in Chicago, Marvin Harmes watched as the room filled up with thirty-one men, seventeen of them black, the rest white. Harmes nodded at each as he came in. They filled the rear rows first, not sitting next to each other until they were forced to by a shortage of folding chairs.

Harmes waited until they stopped coughing and scuffling their feet. He walked to the center of the room and picked up a paper bag. Behind him was a blackboard on an easel. He looked at the men for several moments and let them look at his cream suede jacket, his black and white checked trousers, his faded blue chambray shirt open at the throat, and his polished black ankle boots that still gleamed like patent leather. He had tried for an elegantly casual effect and he was particularly proud of the faded blue work shirt.

"You all know who I am," he began. "But in case maybe you've forgotten, I'm gonna pass out my calling card."

Carrying the brown paper bag in his left hand, Harmes moved down the rows of men, stopping before each one and dipping into the bag. Each time his hand came out it held five one-hundred-dollar bills clipped to a four-by-five-inch sheet of paper which bore the date and the Xeroxed message: "Received $500 from Marvin Harmes for services rendered."

"Just sign your name," Harmes told each man. When he had passed out all the money and collected all of the receipts he moved back to the front of the room and stood once again before the blackboard.

"Now that five hundred bucks you just got is the down payment. We're gonna have about six more sessions up here and you'd better not miss any of them because it's gonna be just like school except there ain't no excuse for being absent. I'm gonna be your principal and your teacher. I'm also gonna give you your final report card and if you pass your final test, then you're gonna get a report card that'll consist of five more pictures of Mr. Benjamin Franklin like you just received. Any questions?"

A large black in the rear held up a bare, hard-muscled arm. "The money's fine, Marv, but who we gonna have to kill to get the rest of it?"

That brought a laugh, but not much of a one. "You're not gonna have to kill anyone."

"Then what we gonna learn how t'do?"

"You," Marvin Harmes said, turning to the blackboard, "are gonna learn how to steal an election. And you're gonna start learning right now."

That Sunday had been a day off for Donald Cubbin. He had gone to bed fairly drunk the night before, but he had slept late that morning and when he awoke he felt better than usual. Not well, but not sick. He had had only two double Bloody Marys before breakfast, a meal that for him had been surprisingly sizable.

Glancing through the *Tribune* he had seen an advertisement for a film he had missed in Washington that starred James Coburn, an actor who Cubbin thought to be seriously underrated. There was a show beginning at five o'clock so Cubbin decided to make it a family outing and invited his wife, his son, and Fred Mure to go along. Fred had already seen the film, but he didn't say anything.

In the theater lobby, Sadie and Kelly Cubbin waited while Fred Mure and Cubbin ducked into the men's room so that Cubbin could have a quick one from a half-pint of Ancient Age. The four of them found good seats together in the theater itself and Cubbin enjoyed himself immensely as he always did at films.

After the motion picture they went to an Italian restaurant for dinner where the proprietor turned out to be a personal friend of Fred Mure's and both the service and the food were exceptionally good. During the dinner, Cubbin drank a little too much red wine, but not enough to really bother him, and he told some amusing stories and anecdotes, some of which even Fred Mure hadn't heard before.

It was a pleasant evening and Cubbin was in fine spirits when they arrived back at the Sheraton and waited in the car for Fred Mure to go in and arrange for the elevator. Mure sent a bellhop out to tell the Cubbins that the elevator was ready and while he waited he scanned the lobby as he always did. They were the usual bunch, he decided. People who're stuck in a hotel on Sunday night, but who don't want to spend it by themselves in their rooms alone so they come down and bunch up together in the lobby. Like sheep. Mure was thinking that they all looked like sheep until he saw the lean, young man with the pinched features and the bitter eyes who sat motionless in one of the chairs, watching the revolving door. He's no sheep, Mure thought, he's the weasel among the sheep, if that's where weasels hang out. The lean, young man seemed to feel Mure's eyes because he glanced that way and for a moment their eyes met and Mure decided that he didn't like what he had seen. He wasn't sure why he didn't like it, but he kept his own eyes on the man as Cubbin swept into the lobby trailed by his wife and son.

Cubbin's glance roved around the lobby, on the prowl for anyone he should speak to. Finding none, he waved at the desk clerk who waved back. Then Cubbin saw the lean young man staring at him, so as he went past, he said, "Hi yah, pal."

"Hi," Truman Goff replied.

22

The building was one of the newer temples of labor in Washington, built in the middle sixties on a prime corner just off Sixteenth Street within easy walking distance of AFL-CIO headquarters and the White House, and only a seventy-five-cent cab ride from the Department of Labor.

The building was not named after the union that it headquartered, but after the man who had been its president since 1940 and who was now only sixty-one years old, but who some of the more venerable officials of other unions still thought of as "the kid."

He had been a genuine boy wonder in the labor movement, first elected president of his union when he was only twenty-eight. He had remained a boy wonder for nearly twenty years after that and even now his face was strangely unlined and his hair was still a wavy, coppery brown except for two handsome gray streaks at the temples. His body was trim, his movements quick, and his teeth were his own. Even his pale gray-blue eyes, chilly and remote and intelligent, were unaided by glasses except for a plain-lensed pair of the Ben Franklin type that he sometimes wore down on the end of his nose for effect.

Because of his looks, some of his colleagues referred to Jack Barnett as the Ronnie Reagan of the labor movement, which didn't bother Barnett because he found his appearance to be a useful political tool, especially since nearly half of the members in his union were women. Most of his detractors, and there was no lack of them, claimed that he had screwed his way into his job, but that had never lost him any votes either.

He had a few fetishes. He lived on fruits and nuts and raw vegetables and refused to eat meat. He did sixty-five push-ups every morning followed by one hundred sit-ups. When in Washington, he ran two miles to his office in a gray track suit. He had quit smoking and drinking on his fortieth birthday, although he had never done very much of either. He would not ride in a car manufactured by the Ford Motor Company. He bought all of his clothes from Sears, sometimes ordering them from the catalog by phone at three o'clock in the morning. He believed that someone was trying to kill him and always traveled with a bodyguard, even on his morning runs. He was a convinced socialist and a bitter anti-Communist. He liked children and had nine of his own although he wasn't a

165

Catholic. And he hated Donald Cubbin and sometimes wished that he would get hit by a truck.

They had been friends once back in the early days of the CIO when they had both been young, handsome, and still a little awed by how far they had come so fast. There was no one incident that had caused the rift. As they both had acquired power and prestige, they gradually grew suspicious of each other's maneuverings and jealous of each other's triumphs. They were simply natural rivals for some never defined prize.

On September 12, a Tuesday, at three minutes till eleven, Donald Cubbin, accompanied by his son and chauffeured by Fred Mure, arrived in a black Cadillac limousine at the front entrance of the Barnett Building.

Cubbin got out first followed by Kelly. "You got everything?" he asked.

"It's all in here," Kelly said, indicating the attaché case that he was carrying.

"I mean everything."

"I've got that, too."

"Okay, Fred, you wait for us."

"You sure you don't want me to come with you?"

"No, I don't want you to come with me; I want you to wait right here."

"Okay, Don, okay," Mure said.

In the lobby of the Barnett Building was a mural that portrayed some hard-hatted workers doing something or other with cables and wires and gigantic wrenches, although one couldn't be sure whether they were building a bridge or stringing a highline. There were some women in the mural, too, and about the only thing that distinguished them from the men was that they wore no hard hats. Kelly thought the mural was awful; his father didn't even notice it.

After making their way past a tough-looking blond female receptionist with a deep, stern voice, father and son rode the elevator up through the layers of union bureaucracy, past the floor where the computerized membership records were kept, past the department of reseach and economics, past the education department and the public relations section, past the bookkeeping division

166

where they counted the dues money, past the publications section and the department of organization, past personnel, pensions and welfare, past the legal department, and past all the sections where the union's hard work was done and up to the twelfth floor, as high as the building went, where all the decisions were made.

It's just like a business, Kelly thought, except all that they have to sell is labor and if they don't get enough for their product, then they take it off the market for a while until the price goes up, and there you go oversimplifying again.

The twelfth-floor corridor was carpeted and the walls were paneled in some imitation plastic that looked a little like walnut, but not much. Another receptionist, this time pretty enough to have had a job with some trendy ad agency, smiled pleasantly at them and asked how she could be of help.

"Where's the men's room?" Cubbin said.

"Do you have an appointment?" the pretty girl asked.

"Not with the men's room, sweetie," Cubbin said. "With Barnett, but if I don't find the men's room, I might pee all over that fancy rug of his."

"It's just down there to your left."

"Let's go, kid," Cubbin said as he turned and headed down the hall.

Kelly grinned at the girl. "Just think, that man's my dad."

"Lucky you."

"Come on, Kelly," Cubbin called.

"Next week he starts going all by himself," Kelly said as he turned toward Cubbin.

Inside the men's room, Cubbin put a finger to his lips and then knelt down to peer under the doors of the stalls. By the time he rose, Kelly had the half-pint open. "Here you go, chief," he said, "a drop of the best."

Cubbin drank, sighed, and handed the bottle back. "Well, since we're here we might as well use it. Go when you can, they say."

As father and son stood in front of the urinals, Cubbin

167

said, "This reminds me of something about Barnett I'd almost forgotten."

"What?"

"He's piss-shy."

"So?"

"You can never trust a guy who's piss-shy."

"Why not?"

"Because most of them are nances."

"I never heard of one with nine kids," Kelly said.

Jack Barnett looked up from something that he was writing when Cubbin and Kelly were shown into his office. Then he looked back down and said, "What do you want? Hello, Kelly."

"Hello, Jack," Kelly said.

"Well, take a seat someplace," Barnett said as he continued with his writing. Kelly took one of the chairs in front of Barnett's desk. Cubbin selected one farther away so that Barnett would have to turn his head to see him.

Kelly had been in Barnett's home countless times because three of the Barnett children were about his age and they had all spent nearly as much time in each other's homes as they had in their own. Even when the feud had reached its most bitter point in the mid-fifties after Barnett had helped finance Cubbin's opposition, neither of the fathers had ever objected to their children's choice of friends.

But Kelly had never been in Barnett's office before and he decided that it was just the thing for either the president of a large labor union or the chief executive of a prosperous dog-biscuit company. None of them can escape that "Hey, gang, just look at me now" appearance, Kelly thought. Barnett's office had a thick brown carpet, walls paneled with real walnut, a big, neat desk, a console telephone, a brown leather couch, some comfortably upholstered chairs, a coffee table, and about two dozen framed and autographed photographs on the wall of prominent politicians from throughout what Barnett still referred to as the free world.

Cubbin said nothing until Barnett stopped writing and turned to look at him. "Well?" Barnett said.

"I want you to keep your fuckin nose out of my union," Cubbin said, making his tone a calm growl.

"Aw, shit," Barnett said and flung his ball-point pen on his desk. He turned to Kelly. "Is he drunk again? I know he's your old man and it's only eleven o'clock in the morning, but I've seen him drunk before eleven."

"He's not drunk, Jack," Kelly said.

"If you don't get your fuckin nose out of my union, and keep it out, I'm going to have your ass," Cubbin said, putting just a little more growly menace into his tone and enjoying every second of it because for once he was certain that he was absolutely in the right.

"I don't know what the hell you're talking about."

"You're a goddamn liar."

"Who you calling a liar?"

"You, you greasy little prick," Cubbin roared, hugely enjoying himself.

Barnett was up now, leaning over his desk at Cubbin, pointing to the door with his left hand, leaning on the phone with his right. "Out!" he yelled. "You got just ten seconds."

"Play it, Kelly," Cubbin said, just like Bogart and then smiled nastily at Barnett. "You're gonna love it."

"Out!" Barnett screamed. "Get your ass outa my office!"

"You'd better hear it, Jack," Kelly said as he took the Sony tape recorder from the attaché case and placed it on the desk.

"Hear what?" Barnett said.

"Just listen," Cubbin said.

Kelly punched the play button and the tape recording started. Barnett was standing when the tape began. By the time it was over he was sitting in his chair, his hands folded on the desk, his eyes straight ahead. "It's a fake," he said.

"Show him the rest, Kelly," Cubbin said.

Kelly placed on the desk pictures that had been taken by Ted Lawson of the interior of the motel room and of the two men leaving it. He also put before Barnett three samples of what the mimeograph machines had run off. Barnett looked at the pictures without touching them. He picked up a letter opener and used it to shove them to one side and to move the mimeograph sheets over so that he could see them better.

"You don't want to hear this again, do you?" Kelly said, indicating the tape recorder.

Barnett shook his head. Kelly put the tape recorder back in the attaché case. "You can keep the pictures and that other crap," Cubbin said.

Barnett picked up the pictures and the mimeographed sheets and dropped them into his wastebasket. After that he turned slowly toward Cubbin and said, "So?"

"So call 'em off."

Barnett seemed to think about Cubbin's demand for a moment. Then he shrugged and smiled. It was the smile of a man who has just thought of something vicious to say and who knows that he will enjoy saying it. "They don't matter now," he said. "You're already whipped."

"That's your ass talking, pal," Cubbin growled. "Your face knows better."

"In three weeks you're gonna be a has-been. You're gonna be ex-President Cubbin."

"Let me catch you just one more time," Cubbin said, his voice rising, "and I'll have you up on charges."

"You're done, Cubbin. You're finished! Through!" Barnett's last word was a shout. He had risen and was leaning over his desk toward Cubbin who now was also up.

"If I go down, I'll take you with me!" Cubbin shouted.

"Don't threaten me, you son of a bitch!"

"I'm not threatening you, you little cocksucker!" Cubbin said, roaring the words, "I'm telling you!"

Barnett moved rather well for sixty-one. He was around his desk and the right that he aimed at Cubbin almost connected. Cubbin retreated, the back of his knees caught the edge of his chair, and he sat down hard, not hurt, but surprised and angry.

"Well, goddamn you!" he yelled.

"Get up, you old shit, and I'll knock you down again!"

Cubbin bounced up off the chair and with his eyes closed swung his right fist in the general direction of

Barnett's chin. Cubbin opened his eyes in surprise when his fist collided with something hard that turned out to be Barnett's left cheek. Barnett staggered back a step.

"Attaway go, chief," Kelly called to his father, moving his chair around for a better view.

Both men now had their fists up in what each hoped was a rough approximation of the boxer's stance. Barnett was in far better shape and danced around on his toes as Cubbin, flatfooted, circled to meet him.

"What's a matter, fuckhead?" Cubbin panted. "You leave your fight in the gym?"

Barnett led with a right again and Cubbin tried to duck, but it landed on his forehead. He roared some wordless cry and jumped at Barnett who blocked a right but forgot about Cubbin's wildly swinging left that landed with a wet smack on his nose. Blood spurted from Barnett's nose onto Cubbin's white shirt. At the sight of blood, both men paused in their fight.

"You broke my fucking nose!" Barnett screamed and looped a right that caught Cubbin on the shoulder. Cubbin staggered back and then both men moved in swinging wildly, their eyes tightly closed, all pretense of any knowledge of boxing discarded.

"Keep your left up, chief," Kelly called to his father whose right eye had just run into Barnett's left fist. Cubbin was nearly exhausted, but he put everything he had into one final blow, a hard left that was something of an accidental hook. It caught Barnett flush on the chin and broke the third finger on Cubbin's left hand. Barnett stumbled back, tripped over his own feet, and sat down hard on his carpet, blood still streaming from his nose.

"Oh Jesus God, my hand!" Cubbin yelled as the door of Barnett's office burst open and two men moved in quickly, but not before Kelly was up and out of his chair.

"Throw that son of a bitch out!" Barnett yelled, still on the floor, but now mopping at his nose with a handkerchief.

"Don't try it," Kelly said, positioning himself between his father who was sucking on his broken finger and the two men who had started toward Cubbin. "We're just leaving," Kelly said. "Come on, chief."

The two men stopped for a moment to assess Kelly. They were both young, in their early thirties, and they had that calm, slightly preoccupied look that most bodyguards have.

"What the hell's going on?" one of them said.

"My old man just beat the shit out of your boss," Kelly said.

The bodyguard who had spoken stared at Cubbin. "He don't look so good himself," he said.

"Your boss is on the floor," Kelly said and moved over to Barnett. "Come on, Jack, I'll help you up."

"Lucky punch," Barnett muttered as he got up from the floor, his handkerchief still at his nose.

Cubbin took his finger out of his mouth long enough to say, "Like I told you, buster, lay off."

"Aw, you're already dead," Barnett said. "You just forgot to roll over."

"Come on, champ," Kelly said, taking his father's arm.

As they went past the two bodyguards, one of them asked Kelly, "What the hell were they fighting about?"

"A woman," Kelly said and winked.

23

After Sadie Cubbin slipped the dress on over her head she turned to Fred Mure and said, "You should have been with him."

Mure stretched and yawned in the sex-rumpled bed. "He wouldn't let me. I asked, but he wouldn't let me."

"It's a wonder they didn't kill each other."

172

"Two old goats like that?"

"Well, Don broke his finger."

"It'll teach him a lesson."

"You're supposed to look after him."

"Look, I told you how it happened."

"You should have gone with him."

"Kelly was with him."

"Well, I shouldn't have left him," Sadie said as she lit a cigarette.

"You said he was asleep."

"He might wake up and wonder where I am."

"Kelly's there."

"I think Kelly's beginning to wonder."

"What about?" Fred Mure asked.

"About Don and me."

"Not about us?"

"He'll get around to that, if we keep this up."

"Kelly's a good kid."

"That's why I don't want him to find out."

Mure yawned again and swung his feet over the side of the bed. "You've only been gone an hour."

"Look at me, Fred."

Mure turned his head. "You look fine."

"This is important."

"What?"

"What I'm going to tell you."

"All right, I'm listening."

"This is the last time. It's over."

Fred Mure rose quickly and walked slowly over to Sadie. He was naked and conscious of the effect that it usually had on her. He shook his head slowly as he walked toward her.

"It's not over," he said. "It's just starting."

"No."

"I told you why I never got married."

"It's over."

"I never got married because I never met anyone that was like you. You're it, Sadie. You might as well face it."

"Goddamnit, Fred, I'm trying to tell you that we're through. No more. Never."

Fred Mure shook his head again. "We're gonna get married, Sadie."

"And what do I do with Don?"

"You divorce him, just like we talked about."

"We never talked about my divorcing him. All we ever talked about was why I couldn't."

"Well, you can now. You got plenty of grounds."

"I'm not going to divorce him, Fred."

"Sure you will."

"Fred, you're a nice guy. I like going to bed with you. I like it better than anything I've ever done. But I'm not going to divorce Don. I like Don. I like being his wife. Who knows, maybe I even love him."

"He's no good anymore."

"He'll be all right after the election. He'll stop drinking and it'll be all right then."

"Sadie, you know he's not going to quit drinking."

"He's quit before."

"But he won't this time."

"I'm not going to argue about it. I'm just telling you we're through."

"You've told me that before."

"This time I mean it."

Fred Mure put his arms around Sadie, but she broke away from him. "No," she said. "No more motel romance. No more chances."

"That's when you liked it best," Fred said, grinning. "You liked it best when he was right in the next bed snoring away. That's when you really liked it."

Sadie crossed over to the dresser and picked up her purse. She turned and looked at Mure. "Fred, I want you to listen to me. I want you to listen carefully."

"I'm listening."

"I'm not going to divorce Don. I'm not going to marry you. I'm not going to bed with you anymore. Now do you understand?"

Mure grinned. "I'll give you two days to change your mind. I'll bet you don't even hold out two days."

"No. Not this time. It's over. Really over."

"All right, then let me ask you something."

"What?"

"Why?"

"Why is it over?"

"Yes."

"Because it's too dangerous. Too dangerous for you, for me, and especially for Don. They could use us on him."

"Ah, Christ, Sadie. They don't care about anything like that."

"I'm not going to take the chance."

"Let me ask you something else then."

"Just as long as you understand that we're through."

"Okay. Okay. I understand. But what if Don divorced you, what if he found out about us and divorced you, would you marry me then?"

"You're not threatening me, are you, Fred?"

"No. I'm just asking you a question. Would you marry me if Don divorced you?"

Sadie shrugged. "Maybe, but he won't."

"How do you know? If he finds out, he might."

Sadie moved over to Fred and touched his cheek. "Fred, you're really not very bright, are you?"

"I'm not so dumb."

"No, if you were bright, you'd understand."

"Understand what?"

"Don's never going to divorce me."

"If he found out about us he would."

Sadie shook her head slowly. "No, darling not even then."

"Why?"

"Because he already knows about us."

24

It was the last week of the campaign, the week of October 8, and the shifts changed at seven o'clock in the morning and by six forty-five they had Donald Cubbin stationed at gate number five and the cameras of three television networks were aimed at him as he steadily pumped the hands of the plant workers who streamed in and out.

Clustered around Cubbin were Charles Guyan, the public relations man; Oscar Imber, the campaign manager; Fred Mure, the general factotum, and Kelly Cubbin, son, who stood about twenty feet away, safely out of camera range.

Officials of the local union were scattered about, hustling the members to "step over and shake hands with President Cubbin." They said it over and over, until they found the phrase meaningless, but they still said it because they felt they had to participate somehow.

Everyone but the television crews seemed faintly embarrassed. The union members were embarrassed to see their international president out soliciting their votes at the ungodly hour of seven in the morning. Cubbin was embarrassed because he felt that the members thought him a fool. Oscar Imber was embarrassed because he kept overhearing the members say, "Who the fuck was that?" after they shook hands with Cubbin. Charles Guyan was embarrassed because the scene was too static to make a good television segment. Kelly Cubbin was embarrassed because his father was making an ass of himself at a manufactured event. And Fred Mure was embarrassed because he couldn't figure out why everyone else was and he didn't want to ask.

Cubbin's line was, "Hi yah, pal, good to see you." He was too good an actor to say it mechanically and each time it came out as a completely personal greeting.

"You gonna vote for him?" Melvin Gomes, a dip stage assembler who earned $10,357 the previous year, asked his car-pool driver, Victor Wurl, molder, who last year earned $12,391.

"Who?"

"What's-his-face, Cubbin."

"I don't know, maybe."

"I think I might vote for that other guy, Hanks?"

"Yeah. Hanks."

"I might vote for him."

"Why?"

"I don't know. Why're you gonna vote for Cubbin?"

"I don't know. I guess it don't make a damn who we vote for. It's still gonna be the same old shit."

"Well, at least that's something we can count on."

At ten minutes past seven the television crews began packing up their equipment. Cubbin turned to Oscar Imber and said, "Let's get the hell out of here; I'm freezing."

"We're on our way," Imber said.

"What else this morning?" Cubbin asked Charles Guyan.

"You've got that radio program at eleven."

"What radio program?"

" 'Here's Phyllis.' "

"Jesus, who listens to that?"

Guyan shrugged. "I don't know. Maybe the guys who're sick."

A little over two thousand miles away in Washington, D.C., it was ten o'clock in the morning as Mickey Della walked into Sammy Hanks's campaign office and slammed an 8½″ x 11″ leaflet down on his desk.

"Now where in the hell did they get that?" Della snapped.

Hanks picked up the leaflet. "Jesus Christ," he said.

Most of the leaflet was taken up by a large picture of Sammy Hanks, nattily attired in tennis whites, a racket in his hand, a foolish smile on his face, as he stood by a sun umbrella. In the background were tennis courts and a large, rambling structure that looked like exactly what it was, a country club. The headline on the leaflet read:

Tennis Anyone?
What's All This About Country
Club Unionism, Sammy?

The text embroidered the theme that while Sammy Hanks tried to tag his political opponent with practicing country-club unionism, the union members just might be interested in what posh clubs Hanks hung out at. The copy was pithy, not quite cute, and in Mickey Della's opinion, deadly.

"Where'd they get that picture?" he said.

"My wife took it. It was about five years ago when she was trying to teach me tennis."

"At a country club?"

"That's right, damn it, at a country club. It's up in Connecticut."

"Where's the picture now?"

"In her scrapbook."

"Is she home?"

"She's home."

"Call her. Ask her if it's still there."

"Look, you're not trying to say that my wife gave it to those bastards?"

"I just want to see if it's still there."

Hanks held the phone while his wife went to look for the scrapbook. When she came back and told him what she had found, he said, "Thanks, honey, I'll call you later," and hung up the phone. "It's still there," he told Della.

"They copied it then," Della said, not bothering to keep the admiration out of his voice. "They broke into your house, swiped the picture, copied it, and broke in again to put it back. Slick. Very slick."

Hanks felt the anger building in him and fought it back. "You mean I got burgled?"

"You did indeed."

"And they're getting this thing around?" he asked, touching the leaflet gingerly.

"I imagine they've printed a million of them. I know I would."

"Well, what're you going to do?"

Mickey Della smiled slyly. "Don't worry, Sammy. I've still got a couple of tricks left."

"What kind?"

Della smiled again. "Dirty ones, of course. Are there any other kind?"

It had been a dirty, mean campaign and now that it was in its final week it promised to get even dirtier. A syndicated editorial service that operated just outside Washington in Virginia had supplied its normally conservative clients, who were often too lazy or too ignorant to write their own editorials, with a stinging attack on Sammy Hanks for having introduced gutter politics into a trade-union campaign. The editorial was dutifully printed in twenty-nine newspapers and all it had cost Ted Lawson of Walter Penry and Associates was $5,000. The man who owned the editorial service had once been nominated for a Pulitzer Prize for his writing ability. He now wrote for the highest bidder whenever he could and if Sammy Hanks had been first in line with $5,000, the man would have cheerfully written an editorial slamming Donald Cubbin.

Except for reports and appearances on TV news programs, it had been a print campaign with Mickey Della setting the tone in his first leaflet that had used a photograph of Cubbin as he followed through with a two wood on some unidentified golf course. The leaflet had a black border around it, another Della trademark, and a caption that read: ....

At the Next Hole Will This Man Sell You
Out to His Big Business Buddies?

The text, written in Della's florid, but extremely readable style, described Cubbin's efforts to get into the exclusive Federalists Club and then went on to warn darkly that

Cubbin might sell out his members to satisfy his social ambitions.

Della had liked that leaflet, but he liked his second one even better. It showed the face of a handsome black wearing a hard hat tipped at a rakish angle. The caption asked:

Why Isn't This Man Good
Enough for Donald Cubbin?

This time, Della's text raked over Cubbin's refusal to resign from the Federalists Club after the black government official had been blackballed. Mickey Della had liked both of his leaflets so much that he had had a million of each printed.

At first, Charles Guyan had tried to ignore Della's attacks. Guyan put out an eight-page tabloid newspaper that was mailed to each of the union's 990,000 members. The tabloid dutifully recorded Cubbin's past achievements. It was a sprightly-looking paper with big type and lots of pictures, but praise is never as interesting as slander, and Guyan had the feeling that nobody read it.

Guyan felt lost without television. With a minute spot he could destroy an opponent's entire campaign. He needed only twenty seconds to show why his own candidate should be elected. He was accustomed to thinking in sharply defined scenes that lasted sometimes no more than a second or two, but which could have devastating impact. It was two o'clock in the morning after Mickey Della's last leaflet appeared when Guyan came to his decision. He picked up the phone and placed a person-to-person call to Peter Majury of Walter Penry and Associates.

"I think we'd better meet," Guyan said after Majury whispered his hello.

"Yes, I think that would be decidedly advantageous. Where are you now?"

"In Pittsburgh. At the Hilton."

"Ted Lawson and I will be there at ten. Would you mind ordering breakfast for us both?"

The meeting lasted only an hour, but to Guyan it was

worth five years of personal experience in practical politics, the ward-heeling kind that he had never known. The first thing that Peter Majury did was to casually hand Guyan the picture of Sammy Hanks dressed in his tennis whites.

"We thought you might be able to use this," Majury said.

"Jesus," Guyan said. "Where'd you get it?"

"Ted found it someplace, I think."

"Ah, hell, tell him," Ted Lawson said. "He's gotta learn sometime."

Majury smiled slightly and smoothed his hair. "Ted paid a burglar he knows five hundred dollars to steal the picture. He paid him another five hundred to put it back—after we made a copy."

"You might get a kick out of this, too," Lawson said. "We didn't print too many of them, but I've got it fixed so that every time Sammy rides in a car he'll see this bumper sticker around and he'll think there're millions of them."

He handed Guyan a bumper sticker printed in bright yellow and scarlet Da-Glo that read: "SAMMY HANKS SUCKS."

"Jesus," Guyan said.

"Merely a minor irritant to Sammy, but we thought you'd find it amusing," Majury said.

"We've got some more stuff, too," Ted Lawson said.

"One item in particular might be useful. It's a compilation of remarks that Hanks has made about Cubbin over the years." Majury scanned a sheet of paper that he had taken from a large manila envelope. "Yes, this is it. On October twenty-first, 1969, in Philadelphia, Hanks called Cubbin—and I quote—'The greatest man in the American labor movement.' On February twentieth, 1967, in Los Angeles, he described Cubbin as the man who 'has earned my respect, my love, and most important, my undying loyalty.' It goes on like that. Do you think you can use it?"

"Christ, yes," Guyan said, "except you're making me feel a bit simple."

"There's lots more in there," Lawson said, indicating the manila envelope.

"You shouldn't feel simple, Charles," Majury said. "If this were a regular campaign and you had full use of your own medium, which is, of course, television, then you would be perfectly matched against someone like Mickey Della. But in a print campaign such as this there is virtually no one who can match Mickey for sheer viciousness unless, of course, it's Ted and I. I think we've given you enough ammunition to finish the campaign, but if you run into any problem, just give us a call."

"I'll do that," Guyan said, deciding that if he must deal in slime, he might as well trade with the guys who owned the pit.

By four that afternoon, Ted Lawson and Peter Majury were sitting in Walter Penry's office, giving him a report.

"I think that Guyan will work out rather well after all," Majury said. "Once he found that he was out of his depth, he called for help. That shows a certain amount of resourcefulness."

"Good," Penry said. "Can you think of anything else that we should do?"

"Nothing except in Chicago," Majury said. "I'm having a very difficult time finding out just how they intend to steal it there."

"Keep working on it," Penry said.

"Oh, I intend to, but it will cost."

"How much have we spent so far?"

"Nearly a hundred and fifty thousand," Lawson said.

"And we gave Cubbin?"

"About four hundred and fifty thousand."

"So we've got about fifty thousand dollars left?" Penry said.

"Yes."

"Is that enough?"

"I—uh—think so," Majury said. "That reporter wants ten thousand."

"For one question?"

"Well, it's going to be a rather big question."

"All right, pay him. When are they going to announce it?"

"Tomorrow. This is Friday so that will give them a day over two weeks to build up the publicity."

"You're sure Hanks will accept?"

"Oh, yes," Majury said. "He's been yelling for a debate with Cubbin."

"But it won't be a debate?" Penry said.

Majury shook his head. "No."

"Okay," Penry said. "On Sunday, October fifteenth, Cubbin and Hanks appear on—Christ, I can never remember the name of the damn thing—"

" 'The Whole World Is Watching,' " Majury said.

"No wonder I can't remember it. All right, they appear on that, side by side, to be interviewed by a panel of distinguished newsmen, so-called. Both sides and the network will give it a big buildup because it'll be the only appearance of the two candidates together. And this program will make or break Cubbin's campaign."

"Unless they manage to steal it from him in Chicago," Lawson said.

"Yes," Penry said, looking at Majury, "unless they steal it from him in Chicago."

Majury smiled and again smoothed his hair. "For some reason," he said, "I don't think they will."

25

There were several reasons why the television program "The Whole World Is Watching" had proved to be surprisingly popular, the principal one being that it was scheduled one hour before the network's Sunday pro football game.

But the program had other features. It chose its controversies carefully and it always procured the two chief spokesmen for the opposing sides. Then, too, its panel of four newsmen had been selected for their overall nastiness, and the program often disintegrated into a yelling match that delighted its pregame audience who got the comfortable feeling they were keeping up with public affairs without sacrificing entertainment.

The program's moderator, although "provocateur" would be a more accurate description, was Neal James, the syndicated political columnist who specialized in political muckraking and whose backlog of libel suits seldom totaled less than twenty million dollars. The more heated the discussion, the better James liked it, and if the program's pace flagged, James was always ready with an insultingly provocative question or observation that more than once had sent a guest into bitter ranting. On three occasions, fists had been used and this, of course, had served as a delightful appetizer for the nearly forty million fans who were settling down for a long afternoon of fairly mindless violence.

At ten o'clock the morning of October 13 in his suite in the Madison Hotel in Washington, Donald Cubbin was being subjected to a merciless interrogation by a team of experts led by Peter Majury. Others included Charles Guyan, Oscar Imber, two union economists, and the union's highly paid legal counsel, who at the last moment had decided to abandon his neutrality and back Cubbin.

For two hours they fired questions at him and when they didn't like his answers, they told him what he should have said. They went into the Federalists Club affair, into his drinking, his personal political philosophy, his home life, his religion, his stewardship of the union, past, present, and future, and finally, why should an old man like you who's past sixty still want to clutch at power? They were bitter, cynical, extremely knowledgeable questions, and Cubbin answered most of them surprisingly well.

Over in Sammy Hanks's campaign headquarters at 14th and K Streets, Mickey Della was subjecting Hanks to a similar inquisition, except that the questions that Della and his crew asked were even nastier than those put to Cubbin. After two hours of it, Della signaled a halt, turned to Hanks and said, "You'll do." Mickey Della never liked to praise anyone too much.

At a quarter to one, Coin Kensington was waddling back and forth in his hotel suite between the kitchenette and the coffee table, laying out the snack that he planned to munch on during the interview program and the game that followed.

It was going to be a long afternoon and Kensington didn't want hunger to make him miss anything exciting so he had decided to set out an ample supply. Arranged on the coffee table were half a pound of kosher salami, a pound box of Sunshine soda crackers, three half-pound chunks of Swiss, cheddar, and Monterey Jack cheese, two containers of Sara Lee Brownies, a pint of stuffed olives, an immense bowl of potato chips, a can of Planter's mixed nuts, half a loaf of sliced pumpernickel, a plate of fried chicken, and a quart container of potato salad. Kensington's final trip to the refrigerator was to get a quart of buttermilk and a jar of dill pickles.

At ten minutes to one Kensington went to answer a knock at his door. Standing there in a blue, double-breasted cashmere jacket, dove-gray trousers, and figured silk shirt was Walter Penry who, Kensington decided before he said hello, had sure come a hell of a long way from the FBI.

"Come on in," Kensington said, "I was beginning to wonder if you'd be late."

"Not a chance," Penry said.

"Got a little something to eat here, if you get hungry," Kensington said, making a vague wave toward the laden coffee table.

"No, thanks."

"Got beer in the icebox."

"I'll take a beer," Penry said.

"You mind getting it? I been up on my feet all day."

"Sure," Penry said and took a can of beer from the refrigerator, deciding against a glass because he knew Old

Man Kensington would like to see him drink it from the can.

He took a swallow of the beer and watched Kensington lower his immense bulk onto the sofa within handy reach of the coffee table. "If you'll just turn up the sound, we'll be ready to go," Kensington said.

Penry walked over, turned up the sound on the 24-inch color television set, and then settled into a comfortable club chair.

"So you think it's gonna be an interesting program?" Kensington said.

"It had better be," Penry said. "We spent ten thousand bucks to make it one."

In his Baltimore living room, Truman Goff switched on the television set and went back to an article in *The New York Times* that was a wrapup of the battle between Cubbin and Hanks and ended with a paragraph describing how each candidate would cast his vote on Tuesday, Cubbin in Pittsburgh at Local Number 1 where he still maintained his membership, and Hanks in Washington at the Headquarters Local. Goff tore the article out and put it in his wallet.

His wife came in from the kitchen carrying two cans of beer. She handed one to Goff and said, "You gonna watch that talky program?"

"I thought I might."

"All they do is scream at each other."

"It gets pretty hairy all right sometimes."

"What time you leaving tomorrow?"

"I don't know." Goff said. "About ten."

"Well, be sure to tell your mother hello for me when you get down to Lynchburg."

"Okay. You need some more money?"

"No," his wife said, "you already gave me plenty."

Donald Cubbin used the union-supplied limousine to drive out to the network studio in northwest Washington. Fred Mure drove with Kelly beside him. In the rear with Cubbin were Oscar Imber and Charles Guyan. On the jump seats were Peter Majury and Ted Lawson.

Mickey Della drove Sammy Hanks out to the studio in Della's five-year-old Ford Galaxie. "You're going to make Cubbin feel like a shit if you don't bring along a big crowd," Della said.

Hanks and Cubbin met face to face for the first time in two months on the steps of the studio. They looked at one another warily, each suspicious of the hidden knife, until Cubbin growled, "Hello, Sammy."

"How are you, Don?"

"Who you betting on?"

Hanks looked slightly surprised, but grinned hastily and said, "Me, of course."

"I meant the ball game, stupid," Cubbin said and brushed on past.

Mickey Della fell into step with Pete Majury. "I'm surprised that you decided to crawl out of the woodwork where the light can get at you," Della said.

"Ah, Michael, it's good to see you up and about," Majury whispered. "I'd heard you were in a rest home."

Neal James met his two guests, shook hands with them, and then sent them off to makeup. The girl who worked on Cubbin told him that he looked like an actor. After he caught the one who was assigned to him biting her lip, Sammy Hanks said, "What do you say we try a paper bag?"

After Cubbin came out of makeup, Charles Guyan drew him aside. "Just one word of advice, Don. Keep your answers short and don't let them needle you."

"What about making a little joke when I'm introduced? You know, something about since I've been accused of spending most of my time at country clubs, maybe I should have brought along my golf clubs."

Guyan couldn't keep the pained expression from his face. "No, Don, please. No jokes. Just be dignified."

"You don't think it's funny?"

"No, I don't think it's funny. Sorry."

"Yeah, sure," Cubbin said and decided to make the joke anyway if he got the chance. It would help ease the tension, he thought.

Peter Majury sidled up to Cubbin and tugged him away

from Guyan. "Be kind to Sammy, Don," he whispered. "Don't be too hard on him."

"What do you mean don't be too hard on him? I'll be as hard as I can on the son of a bitch."

Majury smiled sadly. "Just remember what I said, Don, please. Be kind. Compassionate."

"What the hell are you talking about?"

Majury shrugged and again smiled sadly. "Just remember what I said."

After Cubbin was ushered onto the set, Ted Lawson moved over to Peter Majury. "You give him the word?" Lawson said.

"I told him as much as I could."

"It's sure as hell an iffy thing."

"It'll work," Majury whispered, as though trying to convince himself. "I just know it'll work."

Kelly Cubbin sat next to Fred Mure, watching on a monitor as the guests and the reporters were seated on the studio set.

"Old Don looks great on TV, don't he, Kelly?" Mure said.

"Fine."

"And he's only had two drinks today, too. I offered him one just before he went in there, but he didn't even want it."

"You're nothing but kindness, Fred."

Mure nodded comfortably. "I try to look after him."

On the set four reporters, nicknamed "The Cutthroats," sat behind a curved table on a raised dais, looking down on the guests, or victims, as Neal James sometimes called them. The two guests sat in plain, straight, armless chairs that gave them no place to rest their hands other than in their laps, which made them look frightened. However, Cubbin knew what to do with his hand. He sat straight in his chair, his chin up, his legs crossed, his right arm casually resting on his crossed left leg, his left hand loosely grasping his right wrist. He looked attentive, casual, relaxed, and above all, dignified, and he knew it.

Sammy Hanks used the only weapon he had, his delightful smile. He turned it on and kept it on except when

188

he thought it would be better to look serious and concerned. As for his hands, he forced them to hang straight down at his sides and Mickey Della thought it made him look like a man waiting to be strapped into the electric chair.

Neal James sat on a raised podium behind a small desk between his two guests. He had a round, almost cherubic face that made him look younger than forty-six. He also smiled frequently and the smile was at its sweetest just after he had asked a particularly nasty question.

James had chosen his panel of reporters more for their abrasive personalities than for either their looks or their journalistic abilities. Before they had started appearing regularly on the program, they had been small-time Washington correspondents with cubbyholes in the National Press Building who worked for various newspapers in states such as Louisiana, Texas, Idaho, and Nebraska. Now two of them, Ray Sallman and Roger Krim, had their own syndicated columns and the other two, Frank Felix and Arnold Timmons, were getting requests for articles from such magazines as *Playboy* and *Esquire*, although Timmons didn't think he was getting his share.

They all realized that their new prestige and popularity depended on their continuing appearance on "The Whole World Is Watching," and they also knew that Neal James would go on paying each of them $500 an appearance only as long as they continued to be nasty. And so nasty they were, even vicious, and each week they competed among themselves to see who could produce the most sordidly embarrassing questions.

The program actually had turned them into much better reporters because to come up with the right questions they had to do an immense amount of spadework, something that none of them had ever bothered with before. But they also found that as their prestige rose so did the level of their sources and the four of them were now considered to be among the best informed reporters in Washington.

After the introductions, the questioning was started by Neal James. His first question, a slam-bang one, went to Sammy Hanks.

"Mr. Hanks, how long have you known that your opponent here, Mr. Cubbin, was an alcoholic?"

"For several years," Hanks said and thought, God, I didn't know it was going to be like this. Della warned me, but I didn't think it would start off this bad.

"And that's why you decided to run against him, because you thought that you could beat a sick man?"

For twenty-two minutes the questions came much like that, first to Hanks and then to Cubbin. At the end of ten minutes, Hanks was yelling his answers. Cubbin, using every bit of his acting ability, managed to answer most of the questions crisply although once he snarled at Neal James: "I'm not going to answer that."

"Why not?"

"Because it's a damn-fool question."

"Well, perhaps your opponent, Mr. Hanks, will answer it for you."

"Sure," Sammy said, grinning happily, "I'll be glad to."

At twenty-two minutes past one Arnold Timmons took a deep breath, thought once more of the $10,000 that had been paid him in cash by Peter Majury, and said, "My next question is for Mr. Hanks." Timmons paused and Hanks looked at him curiously before he smiled and said, "Go ahead. It can't be any tougher than the ones I've already answered."

"Your father was a graduate of Princeton, Mr. Hanks," Timmons said, "yet you barely finished high school—"

Nobody ever did find out what the last of Timmons' questions was because at the mention of his father, Sammy Hanks shot to his feet. "You!" he screamed, pointing at Timmons. "You're the worst man I've ever met. You're rotten! Oh, God, you're rotten!"

Hanks had now moved between Neal James and the four reporters and still aimed an accusing finger at Timmons as he screamed, "I'm going to get you! I'm going to get you! You'll be sorry!"

In the control room the program's director was talking happily to his number-three cameraman, "Oh, beautiful, beautiful! Keep it right on him, baby, all the way even if he flies out the window."

In the studio Sammy Hanks had sunk to his knees and was pounding the floor with his fists, screaming the word that sounded like "cawg!" over and over again. Then he looked up at Timmons and some forty million persons got a good close-up view of Hanks's face, now made incredibly ugly by the lips that were drawn back in a dog's snarl, by the tongue that flicked in and out of his mouth, and by the spittle that trickled down his chin. Sammy Hanks crawled across the floor toward Timmons, pounding the floor and screaming as he went and the camera followed him all the way.

Well, shit, Donald Cubbin thought, nobody deserves this, not even Sammy. He rose and walked over to Hanks and stood there for a moment, a tall, dignified man with silver hair, wearing an expression of infinite compassion, which was only half put on.

In the control room, the director was still yelling his instructions, "Three on Cubbin, close and hold, now two on Hanks, hold, and back three to Cubbin and cry for us a little, Sammy, baby, oh God, that's beautiful."

Hanks was still crawling slowly, screaming his one-word scream, when Cubbin bent down and said, "Come on, Sammy, let's get out of here."

Hanks looked up at Cubbin and also up into the number three camera. "Cawg!" he screamed and the tears ran down his cheeks to mingle with the spit on his chin.

Cubbin helped Hanks to his feet, turned, and started to lead him away when Neal James said, "How many votes do you think that'll win you, Mr. Cubbin?"

Cubbin turned slowly and glared at James. He put a lot into the look: scorn, contempt, a little hurt, and the camera caught it all nicely and the microphone faithfully carried the deep baritone when it softly said, "I'm not thinking about votes; I'm thinking about another human being."

On a monitor Mickey Della watched Cubbin lead the weeping Hanks out of camera range. Della took the cigarette from his mouth, ground it into the studio carpet, turned and walked down a hall and out of the building to his car. Mickey Della had no use for crybabies.

In his hotel suite Coin Kensington crammed a heaping

spoonful of potato salad into his mouth, his eyes fixed on the television screen. "Oh, my God, that's awful, that's just awful," he said from around the potato salad.

"That's what we paid ten thousand bucks for," Walter Penry said.

"Yeah, I know but it's just God-awful."

"It still won't win Cubbin the election."

Old Man Kensington tore his eyes from the screen long enough to glare at Penry. "Well, it sure as shit ain't gonna lose it for him."

When Cubbin led the still weeping Hanks out into the corridor, he looked around and asked, "Isn't there anybody around who can take care of him? I'm not his goddamn nurse."

"Della walked out," Majury said.

Kelly Cubbin stepped up to his father. "Let me have him, chief."

"Well, somebody take him."

"Come on, Sammy," Kelly said. "I'll take you home. Give me the keys, Fred."

"How're we going to get home then?" his father asked.

"It'll come to you," Kelly said and led Sammy Hanks off down the hall.

"That was a damned fine thing you did, Don," Oscar Imber told him. "Damned fine."

"It didn't lose any votes either," Charles Guyan told him.

"You think I handled it all right, huh?" Cubbin said.

"You were perfect, Don," Guyan said, "perfect, and God you should have seen it on the monitor. Great TV. Simply great."

"Maybe we can get a tape and run it sometime," Cubbin said.

"Jesus, you were good," Ted Lawson told Cubbin and clapped him on the back.

"Very nice, very nice indeed," Peter Majury said.

Cubbin winked at him. "Was I compassionate enough for you, Pete?"

"Nicely so, very nicely indeed."

Considerably buoyed not only by Sammy Hanks's misfortune, but also by his own noble reaction to it, Cubbin turned to look for Fred Mure. "Let's go find the can, Fred."

"Sure, Don."

Inside the men's room, Cubbin first checked the stalls to make sure that they weren't occupied. He then took the half-pint from Mure, drank deeply, and closed his eyes and sighed.

"I thought you looked great, Don, real great."

Cubbin opened his eyes and looked at Mure. "Fred," he said.

"Yeah?"

"I want you to do me a favor."

"Sure, Don, what?"

"Stop fucking my wife."

26

On the day of the election, October 17, a Tuesday, the two cops came for Marvin Harmes at seven o'clock in the morning. They were from the Chicago detective bureau and one was a lieutenant and the other was a sergeant.

The lieutenant, who identified himself as Clyde Bauer, was bald and having trouble with his weight. His partner, the detective-sergeant, was a thirty-eight-year-old redhead whom everyone called Brick. His real name was Theodore Rostkowski.

Lieutenant Bauer first informed Harmes that he was under arrest and then he told him about his rights and even let him look at the two warrants, one for his arrest and the other for the search of his home.

"What're you expecting to find?" Harmes said.

Bauer shrugged. "A little pot, maybe even a little heroin."

"Go ahead and search."

"We already have," Bauer said and smiled. "I'm afraid we're gonna have to take you downtown, Mr. Harmes."

"Why the rig?"

Bauer smiled again. It was the tired, resigned smile of a man who was weary of his job, perhaps even weary of life. "Just get dressed, Mr. Harmes."

"Can I make a phone call?"

Bauer looked at Rostkowski who shrugged. "Go ahead."

Harmes turned to his wife who stood, shivering a little in her robe, although it wasn't cold. "Don't worry," he told her. "Just go upstairs and see to the kids. I'll fix it."

He watched her climb the stairs and then crossed to the phone and dialed a number. Harmes wasn't calling his lawyer; he knew that a lawyer wasn't going to do him much good. He was calling Indigo Boone.

When Boone muttered a sleepy hello, Harmes wasted no time. "This is Harmes. There's a couple of cops here who're gonna bust me on a rigged-up dope charge. Man, this is one day I can't afford to be busted."

"Yeah, today is the day, ain't it?"

"It sure as hell is."

"Well, it won't work unless you're there to do the final switching."

"I know. That's why I'm calling."

"I'm glad you called me. Lawyer ain't gonna do you no good today."

"Think you can do something?"

"I'm already doing it," Indigo Boone said and hung up.

Harmes went upstairs, got dressed, told his wife to call his lawyer, and to tell anyone else who called that she didn't know where he was. As he walked out to the plain black Ford with the two detectives, Harmes asked Bauer, "This is costing somebody a bundle. You got any idea how much?"

Something that looked like anger flicked over Bauer's face, but it didn't last. He smiled his tired smile again.

"You may be right, Mr. Harmes, this might have cost somebody a bundle, but I'll tell you something, if you're real interested."

"What?"

"It wasn't a bundle of money."

Indigo Boone put down the phone, and moved over to a window, and stared out over the Midway at the gray buildings of the University of Chicago. It was the third call that he had made since talking to Marvin Harmes and he knew there was no use in making any more of them. Whoever rigged this one, he thought, rigged it all the way from the top, the very tip-top, and there ain't nothing can be done for that boy. He's just gonna have to sit it out till seven o'clock. They'll let him go then, after seven. After the polls close.

In Walter Penry's Washington office the phone rang at eight-thirty and Penry answered it himself on the first ring. After he said hello he nodded across his desk at Peter Majury. Penry listened for a while and then said, "Well, I certainly appreciate your cooperation, Ron. And be sure to tell the boss that I appreciate it, too. And Ron, if you get the chance, tell him I'd like to arrange a little testimonial dinner for him sometime next month, if he's got a free date. Thanks again. I'll be talking to you."

Penry hung up the phone and smiled his rogue smile at Peter Majury. "They picked Harmes up half an hour ago. They'll hold him until seven tonight."

"Well," Majury said, "at least they won't steal it in Chicago, not without Harmes to coordinate it."

Penry nodded. "Can you think of any other mischief we should do?"

"No," Majury said, "I think we've done it all."

Donald Cubbin awakened in the Pittsburgh Hilton the morning of October 15 without a hangover. He even caught himself whistling as he shaved, something that he hadn't done in months. He had had only two drinks the day before and only three on Sunday. Not even his broken finger bothered him. Maybe I'll cut it out altogether, he told himself as he patted shaving lotion onto his face. Maybe I don't need that stuff anymore.

One other reason for Cubbin's unusual sense of wellbeing were the preelection reports that had flowed into his campaign headquarters after his television appearance with Sammy Hanks. They had been encouraging and Cubbin, knotting his tie, stopped halfway through because he had just had a peek into himself and was surprised by what he had found. You really wanted it again, didn't you? he thought. You still wanted it all, the attention, the comfort, the hangers-on, the waiting elevators, all that crap. But there's something else. There's that feeling you sometimes get when they're all sitting there waiting for you to say it, the yes or the no, because you're the man they've chosen to tell them which is right, yes or no. And some of them who're waiting for you to say it are smarter, and a lot of them are richer, but none of them can say it except you and that's really what it's all about. And either you thrive on it or it scares the shit out of you and you try to hide from it in a bottle of booze. Well, Cubbin thought, giving his face a last admiring glance in the mirror, you don't have to hide anymore.

Cubbin enjoyed his thoughts, but he enjoyed the memory of the previous night even more because he had made love to his wife, more or less successfully, at least for him, for the first time in more than seven months and, by God, he was going to lay off the booze today and try it again tonight. That's what had done it, he decided, the booze. There wasn't anything wrong with him. Last night hadn't been bad at all, not for an old crock of sixty-two. Damn near sixty-three, he corrected himself. You might as well start being halfway honest, at least with yourself.

He came out of the bathroom where he had dressed so as not to disturb Sadie, something that had never concerned him before. She was already awake, but still lying in the bed, smiling at him. "Good morning, lover," she said.

"How're you, sweetie?"

"I'm just fine. Just fine. A couple of more nights like last night and I'll feel so wonderful I won't be able to stand myself."

"Well, there's always tonight," Cubbin said and winked.

"Is that a promise?"

"It's a promise."

"Give us a kiss," she said and Cubbin bent over the bed and kissed her for a long moment, enjoying it thoroughly.

"Do you have to go?"

"I have to go vote."

"Oh, that's right. I forgot."

"We'll have lunch together though."

"Good. Bye, darling."

"Bye."

Cubbin entered the living room of his suite where the four men waited for him. He looked at them and thought, well, I'm not going to have them hanging around anymore either. Maybe Kelly, though. Kelly's all right. But not Fred Mure. Fred goes tomorrow. As for Imber and Guyan, they'll just drift off, no matter what happens.

"Now," Cubbin said, smiling brightly and clapping his hands together lightly, "let's go vote for a good man."

"Just wait a couple of minutes, Don," Fred Mure said, "while I go get the elevator."

They left the Hilton and drove south and then west through Pittsburgh's Golden Triangle. Cubbin was in the back between Imber and Guyan. In front was Kelly with Mure at the wheel.

"Right over there where that new building is," Cubbin said after a few blocks, "that's where Old Man Pettigrew's Business School used to be. He's the one who got me the job with the union. 'They do a lot of swearing and dirty talking,' " Cubbin said, in a perfect imitation of the long-dead Pettigrew. "That's why I got the job, because the old man didn't think a girl should be around all that cussin."

They rode for another three blocks in silence until Cubbin said, "And right over there, where that parking lot is, that's where the old Sampson Plant used to be before they tore it down. In the summer of thirty-eight I spent forty-one days in that place and God, it was hot. We lived on hot dogs and beans that they used to send up to us in a bucket that we lowered out of the window with a rope. It was a sit-down and the old man sent me in to sit with them and I never spent a more miserable forty-one days in my life. I remember at first that there were a couple of babes that got in at night and took care of anybody who had a quarter, but after a few days they had to lower their price to fifteen cents. Jesus Christ, they were ugly."

Cubbin lapsed into silence for a few minutes. Then he said, "God, Pittsburgh's changed. This used to be one real tough town."

"We're going where it's still tough, Don," Imber said.

"You mean across the river?"

"Yes."

"Yeah," Cubbin said, "it's still pretty grim over there."

Across the Monongahela, Fred Mure drove the green Oldsmobile through gray, tired-looking streets. At a red light, a woman of about fifty, dressed in a shapeless brown coat and clutching a six-pack of beer, looked casually into the back seat, and then looked again, a smile brightening her already seamed face. She waved at Cubbin and called, "Hi yah, Don."

Cubbin grinned, rolled the window down, leaned over Imber, and called back, "Hi yah, pal."

"I'm votin for you today."

"Good for you, I'll need it."

"Ah, you'll win all right."

"Let's hope so."

The light changed to green and Mure drove on. "Who was that?" Imber asked.

Cubbin grinned happily. "I haven't got the vaguest idea."

Local Number One's hall was on a side street, across from a row of two-story buildings that had shops on the ground floor and apartments above. The union hall, built of red brick, was two stories high, and looked as if as little as possible had been spent on its design.

Outside the hall on the sidewalk, television crews from the three networks were already set up. The elected officials of Local Number One waited on the steps for Cubbin as a fairly steady stream of union members filed in and out from the polling booths. The stream was steady because it was in their contract that they got three hours off with pay to vote in their union's biennial elections.

The cameras followed Cubbin as he left the car and walked up the steps to shake hands with the local union officials. As he turned from them, an old man of about seventy wearing day before yesterday's whiskers and a worn gray topcoat stepped up to Cubbin, threw his arms around him, kissed him wetly on the cheek, and in a choked voice said, "God bless you, Don Cubbin, because you're a good man."

Cubbin couldn't help the tears that came to his eyes. He brushed them away with his left hand and used his right one to shake the old man's hand. "Thanks, pal," he said. "Thanks very much."

"How much did he cost you, Charlie?" the NBC newsman asked Guyan.

"Fifty bucks," Guyan said.

"That's all right, we'll still use it."

Kelly Cubbin and Fred Mure waited outside together for Cubbin while he voted. Oscar Imber and Charles Guyan chatted with the TV newsmen who had decided that they would get some more film of Cubbin as he came back down the steps.

"Can I ask you something, Kelly?" Fred Mure said.

"Sure."

"Is your dad mad at me?"

"Not that I know of. Why?"

"He's been acting sort of funny the past couple of days."

"How funny?"

"Well, he's hardly drinking anything at all."

"Don't you think that's an improvement?"

"Yeah, I guess so, but he don't seem his old self for some reason."

"I haven't noticed."

"Maybe I'm just oversensitive."

Kelly grinned. "Yeah, Fred, maybe you are."

Inside, Cubbin voted without hesitation for himself and his slate, shook some more hands, signed one autograph, and then headed back for the entrance. He paused at the top step to wave at the cameras and then started down them slowly.

The first bullet hit him in the shoulder and a moment later the second went into his stomach, ricocheted off something, and lodged finally in his right lung. He started to fall, but caught himself, and managed to stagger down another step, thinking only: This can't be happening. Not to you.

And then because he knew he had to fall, he thought: Do it right. Do it like Cagney used to do it. Then the pain hit again and he went down, folding up first, then unfolding, then turning, and finally sprawling face-up on the sidewalk, eyes open and staring right up into the turning cameras.

Kelly was the first one to reach him. Cubbin looked up into his son's strained face and he knew that he had to say something, something that the kid could keep, but the only thing that he could think of to say was something that represented nearly forty years of regret, but it was all that he could think of, except for a mild curiosity about how he would look on television that night. So he said it, the two words that made up the name that symbolized the might-have-been world of Donald Cubbin.

"Bernie . . . Ling," Cubbin said and then he died.

There was shouting now, and a little panic, and some shoving, and even a few screams, but Kelly ignored it all as he knelt by his father, weeping, until Oscar Imber took him by the arm and helped him up.

"Is he dead, Kelly?"

"He's dead."

"Did he say something there—right at the last?"

They had the microphones stuck in front of Kelly's face now as the cameras objectively recorded the grief that was his face. "What did your father say—was it a name?" one of the TV newsmen asked, hating himself for doing it.

Kelly nodded. "It was a name."

"Can you tell us what it was?"

"Sure," Kelly said as he tried to choke back the tears. "Rosebud."

27

At the sound of the first shot, Fred Mure whirled around in a crouch. His eyes swept the street, found nothing, but when the second shot came his ears told him where to look and his gaze moved up to the roof of the two-story building across the street.

He thought he saw a blurred, shiny motion on the roof, but it disappeared before he could make sure. He felt that he should do something so he raced across the street, tugging the .38 Chief's Special from its hip pocket holster. A car, coming fast from his right, slammed on its brakes and squealed to a stop, but not before its right bumper grazed Mure's leg. The car's white-faced driver pounded his horn and screamed, "Stupid bastard!" but Mure didn't hear him. He didn't even know that he had been hit.

To the right was a narrow passageway where they kept the garbage cans. It ran between two buildings back to an alley. Mure tore down it, but slowed and then stopped when he reached its end. It was not training, but instinct that made Mure peer cautiously around the corner of the building. In his right hand was the revolver that he had carried for three years, but had fired a mere dozen times, and then only at tin cans. Cubbin had always made fun of him for carrying it and once, when drunk, had even tried to take it away from him. Boy, he wouldn't make fun of me now, Mure thought as he squatted down and peeked around the corner of the building into the alley.

He saw the back of a blue Toronado with Maryland plates. It was parked next to a steel fire escape. The Toronado's engine was running and traces of blue smoke escaped from its exhaust in steady gasps. Its left-hand door was open.

When Mure heard the clatter of leather shoes on the steel steps of the fire escape, he jerked his head back around the corner. You gotta look, he told himself. You got to make yourself look. He edged the right side of his face around the building's corner until one eye could see the man who clattered down the fire escape, taking two and even three steps at a time. The man wore white, transparent plastic gloves and carried a rifle in his left hand.

I seen him before, Mure thought. I seen him and Don somewhere together before. Mure had a phenomenal memory for faces, home numbers, dates, names, and addresses, but he could seldom recall yesterday's weather because, to him, it was totally useless information.

In Chicago, he remembered, at night, in the Sheraton-Blackstone lobby after that $43.85 dinner we had at Gino's. He was the weasel sitting there in the lobby and Don said "hi yah" to him and he said "hi" back.

As Truman Goff raced down the fire-escape steps he rehearsed his next moves in his mind. Rifle in the trunk, slam the lid hard, into the car, straight ahead, turn right, go two blocks, turn left and keep straight on. In five minutes, maybe five and a half he would be on the highway that led to Wheeling, West Virginia.

That first shot had gone high, Goff told himself, remembering how he had forced the second one, willing his finger to squeeze the trigger of the Remington .308 that he had stolen from a parked car in Miami. But the second shot had been all right; it had killed him. Goff wasn't sure how he knew about the second shot but he knew. He always knew.

Goff trotted to the rear of the Toronado and lifted the trunk lid that he had left carefully unlocked. He put the rifle under an old blanket, slammed the lid, and then froze when the voice behind him said, "Hey, you."

He must have a gun, Goff thought. He's gotta have a gun. You can either try for the car or you can try the other. His right hand moved quickly to his belt and pulled

202

the .38 Colt Commander free, but held it hard against his belly.

Now, he thought and whirled quickly, but before he turned all the way around the bullet slammed into his right thigh and knocked him back against the car.

Why don't he fall down? Fred Mure thought as he watched the thin, intense man slowly bring the automatic up. Why don't he fall down? I hit him. When you hit 'em they're supposed to fall down.

Goff didn't recognize the man who stared at him from only ten feet away. He felt the pain in his leg, but it didn't bother him. Truman Goff could ignore pain the way some people ignore Christmas. He brought the automatic up and was squeezing its trigger when Fred Mure's second shot struck Goff's right shoulder, throwing his aim off. Mure fired again and this time Goff crumpled to his knees with a bullet in his left side just below the heart. Goff tried to lift the automatic again, to aim and fire it at the man once more, but it had grown too heavy. All he could do was lift his head and watch the man walk slowly toward him.

Fred Mure and Truman Goff stared at each other for ten seconds of long silence and during that time they exchanged life histories, agreed on at least one major philosophical point, and then with considerable mutual regret on both sides, agreed to part.

So in a back alley in Pittsburgh Truman Goff bowed his head and into it Fred Mure fired two bullets.

28

Three days after it impounded the ballot boxes, the U.S. Department of Labor retained the Honest Ballot Association to count the votes in the election contest between Donald Cubbin and Samuel Morse Hanks.

Nearly 65 percent of the union's members had bothered to vote and on October 23, a Monday, the results were announced by the Secretary of Labor: Cubbin, 316,587; Hanks, 317,132; Void 5,941. The wags around the department agreed that Void would have had a better chance if his campaign hadn't peaked so soon.

The FBI had been called in to investigate the circumstances surrounding Cubbin's death on the grounds that there was some possibility that his civil rights might have been violated. The Pittsburgh police ruled that Truman Goff, deceased, was guilty of murder one and closed the case. Manslaughter charges against Fred Mure were quietly dropped.

The day after the election results were announced, Sammy Hanks moved into Cubbin's vacated office. Hanks's first official action was to appoint Marvin Harmes to the newly created post of "special assistant to the president," which meant that Harmes would now be earning $37,500 a year instead of $30,000.

Now that he was president, Hanks didn't feel that he could afford to inquire too closely into how Marvin Harmes had stolen the election in Chicago, so he didn't, and Harmes could never see any point in telling Hanks that he hadn't.

Hanks's second official act was to call Oscar Imber in

and fire him. The next day Imber went to work for the Teamsters.

Twenty minutes after he fired Imber, Hanks called Fred Mure in and did the same thing to him. Mure could think of no one who needed his talents so he called Sadie Cubbin, but she refused to talk to him.

Charles Guyan, who had already collected the last of his fee a week before Cubbin was killed, loaded his wife onto their Chris-Craft, along with two cases of Scotch, and sailed off down the inland waterway to Florida.

As soon as he heard of Marvin Harmes's new appointment, Indigo Boone sold him a $100,000 life insurance policy over the telephone. Neither of them mentioned the election, but Harmes thought it best to take out the policy anyway.

Two days after Cubbin's death, Walter Penry received a scrawled note on a piece of ruled tablet paper from his immensely wealthy, immensely eccentric client, informing him that his services were no longer required.

A day after it was announced that Hanks had won, Mickey Della sent him a bill for the balance of his fee which amounted to, in Della's estimation, $21,312.57. Hanks threw it in the wastebasket.

A number of editorial writers who had mourned Cubbin's death as the passing of a colorful labor statesman, indeed the passing of an era, now started writing about how Hanks's election signaled the dawn of a tough, new breed of leadership for the nation's hard hats.

And on October 27, a Friday, ten days after his father's death, Kelly Cubbin went calling on Coin Kensington.

The fat old man opened the door to his hotel suite and liked what he saw. He's got his old man's looks, he decided, but he's got something else, too. He's got spunk.

"Come in, son," Kensington said. "I've been expecting you."

"Thank you," Kelly said.

"You like a drink?"

"No thanks."

"I'm having a little refreshment of my own concoction.

You take a Coke, add a jigger or two of chocolate syrup, and a couple of scoops of vanilla cream."

"Sounds good," Kelly said.

"You like one?"

"Sure."

Kensington calculated how much ice cream he had left, decided that there was enough, and bustled over to the kitchenette. "Find yourself a seat, son. Walter Penry said you wanted to see me."

"Did he tell you why?"

"He said it was something to do with your dad's death."

"That's right."

Kensington came over from the kitchenette carrying two of his concoctions. "I find this real tasty," he said, handing Kelly one.

Kelly sampled it with a spoon. "Good," he said. "I never had one with chocolate syrup before."

"I gotta confess to you, son, that I'm afraid I'm addicted to chocolate. You know it makes me sympathetic to folks who're hooked on drugs or booze. I've tried to quit and there were times when I thought I had it licked, under control, you know, but then I'd bite down on a little old bar of Baby Ruth and whoosh, I was gone again."

With that Kensington devoted himself to the sticky mixture and Kelly watched him poke it into his mouth. I guess gluttony's what he has left, Kelly thought, that and power and wealth and the desire to meddle in other people's lives. I can understand that because that's what I wanted to do, be the village wise man, and maybe that's what he's been able to do except on a grander scale. Wise man to the nation, not the village.

"I was sorry about your dad, son," Kensington said when he finished his sweet.

"Did you know him?"

"No, not personally, but I'd read after him, as they say. Now I ain't gonna tell you he was a great man, but I think I'd have liked him if I'd known him."

"A lot of people did, I guess."

"Now just what is it you wanted to see me about?"

"I want to find out who killed him."

"Huh," Kensington said and set his mind to racing. Well, now, maybe he knows something and maybe what he knows can be useful and just maybe it'll tie up all those loose ends that are still flopping around all over the place.

"Cops say that Goff fellow killed him," Kensington said.

"He pulled the trigger for a price," Kelly said. "I want to find out who met his price."

"From what Penry tells me they got eleventy-dozen FBI agents tracking that Goff boy back to the year one."

"I know," Kelly said. "I used to be a cop."

"Any good at it?"

"I would have been if I stayed in it long enough to get mean."

"You got a theory, then?"

Kelly nodded. "That's right. I've got a theory."

"And you're gonna tell me because I've got something to do with it?"

"That's right."

"Well, I'm listening, son."

"It'll take a while."

"I got time."

"Goff didn't have a motive. None at all. I've done some checking on him and all he was interested in was his job over in Baltimore and television and paperback westerns. I'm not saying I've done as thorough a job as the FBI'll do, but I'm satisfied that Goff wasn't crazy. So that means that he did it for money."

"So who paid him?"

"I think they're going to find out that Goff was a pro, a free lance. I don't think they're ever going to find out who paid him because I think it was a professional murder broker and those guys just don't get caught."

"How much you think he got paid?"

"You can get a pretty good east-coast murder done for around seven or eight thousand, if it's somebody that's going to stir up a lot of heat. My guess is that whoever signed up to kill my old man probably asked ten or eleven thousand."

"How much would just a run-of-the-mill kind cost?" asked Kensington who always found details fascinating.

"Anywhere from two-fifty up to three thousand."

"Huh. Life's pretty cheap when you get right down to it."

"It is in this country, but it's even cheaper in others."

"Well, I suppose you've got a suspect."

"Two," Kelly said.

"Well?"

"You're one of them."

"That's what I thought. Why?"

"The stock market. The day after my old man got killed, the stock in the companies that the union has contracts with took a nose dive. They kept on diving for three days because they didn't know whether there was going to be a strike or not. Stock in two of them dived so far that they even suspended trading."

"I know that," Kensington said.

"Anybody who knew that my old man was going to be killed, and who knew the market, could have sold short and cleaned up. You sold short, Mr. Kensington."

"How much did I make?"

"Three million dollars, give or take a hundred thousand."

"I made four point two million, boy, but your homework's pretty good."

"How's my theory?"

"It's a pretty good theory, but it just ain't true. I sold short because I back my judgment and I honestly thought that Sammy Hanks would beat your dad. Even after that television fiasco, I still thought Sammy would beat him. Now I didn't have any inside information, but I can spot a trend because that's my trade and the trend in labor unions in the last few years has been to throw the rascals out and your dad, and no offense is intended here, was about the top rascal of them all. So I figured Sammy would win and with all his strike talk, he'd just scare the hell out of the market. Well, there wasn't any reaction after that TV program, because they thought your dad had it won, but when he got killed and there was the chance that fit-throwing nut was gonna be president, well, the smart money panicked and I cleaned up. Now you can believe that or not, son, but that's how she happened."

After a moment, Kelly nodded. "I believe you."

"Good. Now who's your other suspect?"

"Before I tell you, I want to find out if you'll do what I want you to. I don't guess I put that very well. What I'm asking for is your help. I went to Penry, but he said he couldn't do it without your okay."

"Penry works for me. If you need something done and I think it needs doing, then I'll síc him on it."

"I want to check somebody's checking and savings accounts for the last three or four months. I can't get that kind of information."

"Big sums of money, huh?"

"Yes."

"In or out?"

"Out."

"You don't think the FBI's gonna do that?"

"It might take them a while and that might be too late."

"Just give me the name and we'll have what you want in fifteen minutes. Well, hell, maybe thirty."

A half hour later, Coin Kensington walked Kelly to the door. Kelly turned and held out his hand. "Thank you, Mr. Kensington. I'll let you know what happens."

Kensington nodded and then scratched the top of his bald head. He looked almost embarrassed. "Your dad leave you any money, son?"

"Yes, he left me some."

"You wouldn't want to come study it with me, would you?"

"Study it?"

"I mean study what it really is. You can make a lot of it while you're studying, if you want to do that, too."

Kelly looked at the fat old man. He's lonely, too, I

guess. The nation's wise man is lonely just like everybody else. "What is money, Mr. Kensington?"

The old man brightened. "You come back, son. You come back when you're done with all this and I'll tell you."

Kelly grinned. "I may just do that."

Coin Kensington looked at Kelly closely and the bright expression faded from the old man's face. "No, you won't come back."

"Why not?"

"Because, son, to learn about money, you gotta be mean and—" Kensington broke off.

"And what?"

"You're just not mean enough."

At three o'clock that afternoon Kelly knocked on the door of apartment 612 in a three-year-old building in Southwest Washington. The door was opened by a man who hadn't shaved that day, or the day before, or the day before that. He stared at Kelly for a moment before he said, "You should've called."

"I took a chance. You busy?"

The man shook his head. "No, I'm not busy."

"Can I come in?"

"It's not cleaned up."

"That won't bother me."

The man shrugged. "Come on in."

Inside Kelly saw that a coffee table was littered with two empty vodka bottles, a half-full one, four crumpled, empty packs of Lucky Strikes, two brimful ashtrays, three smeared glasses, and a .38 revolver. The man took a chair near the vodka and the pistol.

"You want a drink?" he said, and for the first time Kelly noticed the slight slur in his speech.

"No, thanks."

"You never liked me, did you, Kelly?"

"That's got nothing to do with it."

"You never liked me and your dad never liked me."

"Why did you do it?"

"Why did I do what?"

"Why did you have the chief killed, Fred?"

Fred Mure's hand moved out and closed around the butt of the revolver. He picked it up and rested it in his lap not aiming it at anything.

"I loved him, Kelly," Mure said, his face distorting itself into a parody of grief, although real grief often seems to parody itself. "I loved him like a——"

"Like a son, Fred."

"That ain't nice to say."

"How much did it cost you, Fred, twelve thousand dollars? That's what you took out of your savings account on July twenty-fifth."

"Sadie was gonna marry me. We were gonna get married."

"Sadie never said that."

"She didn't have to say it. I knew. I could tell."

"You mean you took Sadie to bed a few times when the chief couldn't get it up and you thought it was true romance. Hell, the chief knew all about it and Sadie knew that he knew."

"He told me——" Mure said. "He told me—uh—"

"What'd he tell you, Fred?"

Fred Mure's eyes bulged and his mouth twisted. "He told me to stop fucking his wife!" It came out as a long, loud shout.

"After he died, what did Sadie say?"

"She wouldn't see me. She wouldn't even talk to me."

"Jesus," Kelly said and wiped his hands on his trousers as though they were soiled. "Who'd you hire to do it, Fred? Who'd you broker it through?"

"Goff," Mure said. "Truman Goff."

"You got his name out of the papers. Who set it up for you?"

"I killed Goff," Mure said, and there was pride in his tone now. "I killed him after he killed Don. I killed Don's murderer."

"You shit, too," Kelly snapped. "Who'd you broker it through? Who'd you pay the money to?"

"Bill," Mure whispered, clutching the revolver more tightly.

211

"Bill who?"

"Just Bill."

"Where'd you find him?"

"It was a phone number that I got from some guy I met in a bar. I don't know who he was. Just some guy. He said if I ever wanted anything done, all I had to do was call that number in New York at ten sharp on any Wednesday."

"What was the number?"

"382-1094," Mure said. "Area code 212."

"Pay phone," Kelly said. He got up. "Come on, Fred, I'm taking you down."

"You're not a cop. You're not a cop anymore."

"Let's go."

Mure seemed to remember the gun he held in his hand. He aimed it at Kelly. "You're not taking me nowhere, Kelly. You're not a cop."

"Go on, Fred, pull the trigger. Get it over with." Kelly held his breath and then let it out to say, "You want a real fat mess? Then go ahead. Pull the trigger."

Fred Mure looked down at the gun, examining it as if he had never seen it before. "They gave it back to me," he said. "The Pittsburgh cops. They gave it back to me."

"Let's go, Fred."

"Oh, God, I don't want to live!" Fred moaned and then visibly brightened at the thought. He looked slyly at Kelly, darted across the room, down a short hall, and into the bathroom. As Kelly followed he heard the click of the lock on the bathroom door.

Kelly waited. After a moment, Fred Mure called: "You won't have to worry about me no more, Kelly. Nobody will. I'm gonna shoot myself."

Kelly waited some more.

"Tell Sadie. Tell Sadie I still love her."

Kelly kept on waiting.

"I'm no fuckin good!" Mure screamed.

Kelly waited.

"I'm gonna do it now, Kelly."

Kelly said nothing. He only waited.

"I hate this fuckin world!" Fred Mure yelled through the door.

Kelly waited another full minute before the door opened and Mure slowly came out, his eyes downcast, a sheepish, embarrassed look on his face. "I just couldn't do it, Kelly."

"That's what I was afraid of."

29

On October 26, a Saturday, the gray-haired man who sometimes called himself Just Bill came out of his apartment building on West Fifty-seventh and turned left. In his right hand he held a leash that was attached to an aged English pit bull that waddled as it walked and wheezed as it breathed. In his left hand, Just Bill carried a brown, oblong, stamped and addressed manila envelope.

"Come on, Dum-Dum," Just Bill said to the dog and strolled slowly down the block toward the mailbox. Halfway there he stopped and bought a New York *Daily News* because its screamer headline had caught his eye:

CUBBIN'S 'REAL'
KILLER SQUEALS

Just Bill raised his eyebrows as he read the story while waiting at a lamppost for Dum-Dum to relieve himself. As he walked on toward the mailbox, Just Bill ran the facts of the story through his mind to determine whether any of them might implicate him. When he was satisfied that there was no possible way that they could, he smiled slightly, and checked the envelope again to make sure its address was correct:

> Mr. Karl Syftestad
> Room 518
> Benser Building
> Minneapolis, Minnesota 55401

Just Bill read the address twice to make sure it was right, nodded to himself in a satisfied way, and dropped the envelope into the mailbox.

THE PERENNIAL LIBRARY MYSTERY SERIES

Ted Allbeury

THE OTHER SIDE OF SILENCE   P 669, $2.84
"In the best le Carré tradition . . . an ingenious and readable book."
      —*New York Times Book Review*

PALOMINO BLONDE   P 670, $2.84
"Fast-moving, splendidly technocratic intercontinental espionage tale
. . . you'll love it."   —*The Times* (London)

SNOWBALL   P 671, $2.84
"A novel of byzantine intrigue. . . ."—*New York Times Book Review*

Delano Ames

CORPSE DIPLOMATIQUE   P 637, $2.84
"Sprightly and intelligent."
      —*New York Herald Tribune Book Review*

FOR OLD CRIME'S SAKE   P 629, $2.84

MURDER, MAESTRO, PLEASE   P 630, $2.84
"If there is a more engaging couple in modern fiction than Jane and
Dagobert Brown, we have not met them."   —*Scotsman*

SHE SHALL HAVE MURDER   P 638, $2.84
"Combines the merit of both the English and American schools in the
new mystery. It's as breezy as the best of the American ones, and has
the sophistication and wit of any top-notch Britisher."
      —*New York Herald Tribune Book Review*

E. C. Bentley

TRENT'S LAST CASE   P 440, $2.50
"One of the three best detective stories ever written."
      —Agatha Christie

TRENT'S OWN CASE   P 516, $2.25
"I won't waste time saying that the plot is sound and the detection
satisfying. Trent has not altered a scrap and reappears with all his old
humor and charm."   —Dorothy L. Sayers

Andrew Bergman

THE BIG KISS-OFF OF 1944   P 673, $2.84
"It is without doubt the nearest thing to genuine Chandler I've ever come across. . . . Tough, witty—very witty—and a beautiful eye for period detail. . . ."   —Jack Higgins

HOLLYWOOD AND LEVINE   P 674, $2.84
"Fast-paced private-eye fiction."   —San Francisco Chronicle

Gavin Black

A DRAGON FOR CHRISTMAS   P 473, $1.95
"Potent excitement!"   —New York Herald Tribune

THE EYES AROUND ME   P 485, $1.95
"I stayed up until all hours last night reading *The Eyes Around Me*, which is something I do not do very often, but I was so intrigued by the ingeniousness of Mr. Black's plotting and the witty way in which he spins his mystery. I can only say that I enjoyed the book enormously."
                                    —F. van Wyck Mason

YOU WANT TO DIE, JOHNNY?   P 472, $1.95
"Gavin Black doesn't just develop a pressure plot in suspense, he adds uninfected wit, character, charm, and sharp knowledge of the Far East to make rereading as keen as the first race-through."   —Book Week

Nicholas Blake

THE CORPSE IN THE SNOWMAN   P 427, $1.95
"If there is a distinction between the novel and the detective story (which we do not admit), then this book deserves a high place in both categories."   —New York Times

END OF CHAPTER   P 397, $1.95
". . . admirably solid . . . an adroit formal detective puzzle backed up by firm characterization and a knowing picture of London publishing."
                                    —New York Times

HEAD OF A TRAVELER   P 398, $2.25
"Another grade A detective story of the right old jigsaw persuasion."
                           —New York Herald Tribune Book Review

MINUTE FOR MURDER   P 419, $1.95
"An outstanding mystery novel. Mr. Blake's writing is a delight in itself."   —New York Times

THE MORNING AFTER DEATH   P 520, $1.95
"One of Blake's best."   —Rex Warner

A PENKNIFE IN MY HEART   P 521, $2.25
"Style brilliant . . . and suspenseful."   *—San Francisco Chronicle*

THE PRIVATE WOUND   P 531, $2.25
"[Blake's] best novel in a dozen years . . . . An intensely penetrating study of sexual passion. . . . A powerful story of murder and its aftermath."
     —Anthony Boucher, *New York Times*

A QUESTION OF PROOF   P 494, $1.95
"The characters in this story are unusually well drawn, and the suspense is well sustained."   *—New York Times*

THE SAD VARIETY   P 495, $2.25
"It is a stunner. I read it instead of eating, instead of sleeping."
     —Dorothy Salisbury Davis

THERE'S TROUBLE BREWING   P 569, $3.37
"Nigel Strangeways is a puzzling mixture of simplicity and penetration, but all the more real for that."
     —*The Times* (London) *Literary Supplement*

THOU SHELL OF DEATH   P 428, $1.95
"It has all the virtues of culture, intelligence and sensibility that the most exacting connoisseur could ask of detective fiction."
     —*The Times* (London) *Literary Supplement*

THE WIDOW'S CRUISE   P 399, $2.25
"A stirring suspense. . . . The thrilling tale leaves nothing to be desired."
     —*Springfield Republican*

Oliver Bleeck

THE BRASS GO-BETWEEN   P 645, $2.84
"Fiction with a flair, well above the norm for thrillers."
     —*Associated Press*

THE PROCANE CHRONICLE   P 647, $2.84
"Without peer in American suspense."   *—Los Angeles Times*

PROTOCOL FOR A KIDNAPPING   P 646, $2.84
"The zigzags of plot are electric; the characters sharp; but it is the wit and irony and touches of plain fun which make the whole a standout."
     —*Los Angeles Times*

John & Emery Bonett

A BANNER FOR PEGASUS   P 554, $2.40
"A gem! Beautifully plotted and set. . . . Not only is the murder adroit
and deserved, and the detection competent, but the love story is charming."   —Jacques Barzun and Wendell Hertig Taylor

DEAD LION   P 563, $2.40
"A clever plot, authentic background and interesting characters highly
recommended this one."   —*New Republic*

THE SOUND OF MURDER   P 642, $2.84
The suspects are many, the clues few, but the gentle Inspector ferrets out
the truth and pursues the case to its bitter and shocking end.

Christianna Brand

GREEN FOR DANGER   P 551, $2.50
"You have to reach for the greatest of Great Names (Christie, Carr,
Queen . . .) to find Brand's rivals in the devious subtleties of the trade."
                    —Anthony Boucher

TOUR DE FORCE   P 572, $2.40
"Complete with traps for the over-ingenious, a double-reverse surprise
ending and a key clue planted so fairly and obviously that you completely
overlook it. If that's your idea of perfect entertainment, then seize at once
upon *Tour de Force.*"   —Anthony Boucher, *New York Times*

James Byrom

OR BE HE DEAD   P 585, $2.84
"A very original tale . . . Well written and steadily entertaining."
 —Jacques Barzun and Wendell Hertig Taylor, *A Catalogue of Crime*

Henry Calvin

IT'S DIFFERENT ABROAD   P 640, $2.84
"What is remarkable and delightful, Mr. Calvin imparts a flavor of satire
to what he renovates and compels us to take straight."
                    —Jacques Barzun

Marjorie Carleton

VANISHED   P 559, $2.40
"Exceptional . . . a minor triumph."
 —Jacques Barzun and Wendell Hertig Taylor, *A Catalogue of Crime*

George Harmon Coxe

MURDER WITH PICTURES   P 527, $2.25

"[Coxe] has hit the bull's-eye with his first shot."

—New York Times

Edmund Crispin

BURIED FOR PLEASURE   P 506, $2.50

"Absolute and unalloyed delight."

—Anthony Boucher, *New York Times*

Lionel Davidson

THE MENORAH MEN   P 592, $2.84

"Of his fellow thriller writers, only John Le Carré shows the same instinct for the viscera."   *—Chicago Tribune*

NIGHT OF WENCESLAS   P 595, $2.84

"A most ingenious thriller, so enriched with style, wit, and a sense of serious comedy that it all but transcends its kind."

—The New Yorker

THE ROSE OF TIBET   P 593, $2.84

"I hadn't realized how much I missed the genuine Adventure story . . . until I read *The Rose of Tibet*."   —Graham Greene

D. M. Devine

MY BROTHER'S KILLER   P 558, $2.40

"A most enjoyable crime story which I enjoyed reading down to the last moment."   —Agatha Christie

Kenneth Fearing

THE BIG CLOCK   P 500, $1.95

"It will be some time before chill-hungry clients meet again so rare a compound of irony, satire, and icy-fingered narrative. *The Big Clock* is . . . a psychothriller you won't put down."   *—Weekly Book Review*

Andrew Garve

THE ASHES OF LODA   P 430, $1.50

"Garve . . . embellishes a fine fast adventure story with a more credible picture of the U.S.S.R. than is offered in most thrillers."

—New York Times Book Review

THE CUCKOO LINE AFFAIR   P 451, $1.95

". . . an agreeable and ingenious piece of work."   *—The New Yorker*

A HERO FOR LEANDA
P 429, $1.50

"One can trust Mr. Garve to put a fresh twist to any situation, and the ending is really a lovely surprise." —*Manchester Guardian*

MURDER THROUGH THE LOOKING GLASS
P 449, $1.95

". . . refreshingly out-of-the-way and enjoyable . . . highly recommended to all comers." —*Saturday Review*

NO TEARS FOR HILDA
P 441, $1.95

"It starts fine and finishes finer. I got behind on breathing watching Max get not only his man but his woman, too." —Rex Stout

THE RIDDLE OF SAMSON
P 450, $1.95

"The story is an excellent one, the people are quite likable, and the writing is superior." —*Springfield Republican*

Michael Gilbert

BLOOD AND JUDGMENT
P 446, $1.95

"Gilbert readers need scarcely be told that the characters all come alive at first sight, and that his surpassing talent for narration enhances any plot. . . . Don't miss." —*San Francisco Chronicle*

THE BODY OF A GIRL
P 459, $1.95

"Does what a good mystery should do: open up into all kinds of ramifications, with untold menace behind the action. At the end, there is a bang-up climax, and it is a pleasure to see how skilfully Gilbert wraps everything up." —*New York Times Book Review*

FEAR TO TREAD
P 458, $1.95

"Merits serious consideration as a work of art." —*New York Times*

Joe Gores

HAMMETT
P 631, $2.84

"Joe Gores at his very best. Terse, powerful writing—with the master, Dashiell Hammett, as the protagonist in a novel I think he would have been proud to call his own." —Robert Ludlum

C. W. Grafton

BEYOND A REASONABLE DOUBT
P 519, $1.95

"A very ingenious tale of murder . . . a brilliant and gripping narrative." —Jacques Barzun and Wendell Hertig Taylor

THE RAT BEGAN TO GNAW THE ROPE   P 639, $2.84
"Fast, humorous story with flashes of brilliance."

—The New Yorker

Edward Grierson

THE SECOND MAN   P 528, $2.25
"One of the best trial-testimony books to have come along in quite a while." *—The New Yorker*

Bruce Hamilton

TOO MUCH OF WATER   P 635, $2.84
"A superb sea mystery. . . . The prose is excellent."
—Jacques Barzun and Wendell Hertig Taylor, *A Catalogue of Crime*

Cyril Hare

DEATH IS NO SPORTSMAN   P 555, $2.40
"You will be thrilled because it succeeds in placing an ingenious story in a new and refreshing setting. . . . The identity of the murderer is really a surprise." *—Daily Mirror*

DEATH WALKS THE WOODS   P 556, $2.40
"Here is a fine formal detective story, with a technically brilliant solution demanding the attention of all connoisseurs of construction."
—Anthony Boucher, *New York Times Book Review*

AN ENGLISH MURDER   P 455, $2.50
"By a long shot, the best crime story I have read for a long time. Everything is traditional, but originality does not suffer. The setting is perfect. Full marks to Mr. Hare." *—Irish Press*

SUICIDE EXCEPTED   P 636, $2.84
"Adroit in its manipulation . . . and distinguished by a plot-twister which I'll wager Christie wishes she'd thought of." *—New York Times*

TENANT FOR DEATH   P 570, $2.84
"The way in which an air of probability is combined both with clear, terse narrative and with a good deal of subtle suburban atmosphere, proves the extreme skill of the writer." *—The Spectator*

TRAGEDY AT LAW   P 522, $2.25
"An extremely urbane and well-written detective story."

—New York Times

UNTIMELY DEATH   P 514, $2.25
"The English detective story at its quiet best, meticulously underplayed, rich in perceivings of the droll human animal and ready at the last with a neat surprise which has been there all the while had we but wits to see it."   —*New York Herald Tribune Book Review*

THE WIND BLOWS DEATH   P 589, $2.84
"A plot compounded of musical knowledge, a Dickens allusion, and a subtle point in law is related with delightfully unobtrusive wit, warmth, and style."   —*New York Times*

WITH A BARE BODKIN   P 523, $2.25
"One of the best detective stories published for a long time."
                                                       —*The Spectator*

Robert Harling

THE ENORMOUS SHADOW   P 545, $2.50
"In some ways the best spy story of the modern period. . . . The writing is terse and vivid . . . the ending full of action . . . altogether first-rate."
—Jacques Barzun and Wendell Hertig Taylor, *A Catalogue of Crime*

Matthew Head

THE CABINDA AFFAIR   P 541, $2.25
"An absorbing whodunit and a distinguished novel of atmosphere."
                                        —Anthony Boucher, *New York Times*

THE CONGO VENUS   P 597, $2.84
"Terrific. The dialogue is just plain wonderful."   —*Boston Globe*

MURDER AT THE FLEA CLUB   P 542, $2.50
"The true delight is in Head's style, its limpid ease combined with humor and an awesome precision of phrase."   —*San Francisco Chronicle*

M. V. Heberden

ENGAGED TO MURDER   P 533, $2.25
"Smooth plotting."   —*New York Times*

James Hilton

WAS IT MURDER?   P 501, $1.95
"The story is well planned and well written."   —*New York Times*

S. B. Hough

DEAR DAUGHTER DEAD P 661, $2.84
"A highly intelligent and sophisticated story of police detection . . . not to be missed on any account." —Francis Iles, *The Guardian*

SWEET SISTER SEDUCED P 662, $2.84
In the course of a nightlong conversation between the Inspector and the suspect, the complex emotions of a very strange marriage are revealed.

P. M. Hubbard

HIGH TIDE P 571, $2.40
"A smooth elaboration of mounting horror and danger."
—*Library Journal*

Elspeth Huxley

THE AFRICAN POISON MURDERS P 540, $2.25
"Obscure venom, manical mutilations, deadly bush fire, thrilling climax compose major opus.... Top-flight."
—*Saturday Review of Literature*

MURDER ON SAFARI P 587, $2.84
"Right now we'd call Mrs. Huxley a dangerous rival to Agatha Christie." —*Books*

Francis Iles

BEFORE THE FACT P 517, $2.50
"Not many 'serious' novelists have produced character studies to compare with Iles's internally terrifying portrait of the murderer in *Before the Fact,* his masterpiece and a work truly deserving the appellation of unique and beyond price." —Howard Haycraft

MALICE AFORETHOUGHT P 532, $1.95
"It is a long time since I have read anything so good as *Malice Aforethought,* with its cynical humour, acute criminology, plausible detail and rapid movement. It makes you hug yourself with pleasure."
—H. C. Harwood, *Saturday Review*

Michael Innes

APPLEBY ON ARARAT P 648, $2.84
"Superbly plotted and humorously written." —*The New Yorker*

APPLEBY'S END P 649, $2.84
"Most amusing." —*Boston Globe*

THE CASE OF THE JOURNEYING BOY   P 632, $3.12
"I could see no faults in it. There is no one to compare with him."
—*Illustrated London News*

DEATH ON A QUIET DAY   P 677, $2.84
"Delightfully witty."   —*Chicago Sunday Tribune*

DEATH BY WATER   P 574, $2.40
"The amount of ironic social criticism and deft characterization of scenes and people would serve another author for six books."
—Jacques Barzun and Wendell Hertig Taylor

HARE SITTING UP   P 590, $2.84
"There is hardly anyone (in mysteries or mainstream) more exquisitely literate, allusive and Jamesian—and hardly anyone with a firmer sense of melodramatic plot or a more vigorous gift of storytelling."
—Anthony Boucher, *New York Times*

THE LONG FAREWELL   P 575, $2.40
"A model of the deft, classic detective story, told in the most wittily diverting prose."   —*New York Times*

THE MAN FROM THE SEA   P 591, $2.84
"The pace is brisk, the adventures exciting and excitingly told, and above all he keeps to the very end the interesting ambiguity of the man from the sea."   —*New Statesman*

ONE MAN SHOW   P 672, $2.84
"Exciting, amusingly written . . . very good enjoyment it is."
—*The Spectator*

THE SECRET VANGUARD   P 584, $2.84
"Innes . . . has mastered the art of swift, exciting and well-organized narrative."   —*New York Times*

THE WEIGHT OF THE EVIDENCE   P 633, $2.84
"First-class puzzle, deftly solved. University background interesting and amusing."   —*Saturday Review of Literature*

Mary Kelly

THE SPOILT KILL   P 565, $2.40
"Mary Kelly is a new Dorothy Sayers. . . . [An] exciting new novel."
—*Evening News*

Lange Lewis

THE BIRTHDAY MURDER   P 518, $1.95

"Almost perfect in its playlike purity and delightful prose."

—Jacques Barzun and Wendell Hertig Taylor

Allan MacKinnon

HOUSE OF DARKNESS   P 582, $2.84

"His best . . . a perfect compendium."

—Jacques Barzun and Wendell Hertig Taylor, *A Catalogue of Crime*

Frank Parrish

FIRE IN THE BARLEY   P 651, $2.84

"A remarkable and brilliant first novel. . . . entrancing."

—*The Spectator*

SNARE IN THE DARK   P 650, $2.84

The wily English poacher Dan Mallett is framed for murder and has to confront unknown enemies to clear himself.

STING OF THE HONEYBEE   P 652, $2.84

"Terrorism and murder visit a sleepy English village in this witty, offbeat thriller."   —*Chicago Sun-Times*

Austin Ripley

MINUTE MYSTERIES   P 387, $2.50

More than one hundred of the world's shortest detective stories. Only one possible solution to each case!

Thomas Sterling

THE EVIL OF THE DAY   P 529, $2.50

"Prose as witty and subtle as it is sharp and clear. . .characters unconventionally conceived and richly bodied forth . . . . In short, a novel to be treasured."   —Anthony Boucher, *New York Times*

Julian Symons

THE BELTING INHERITANCE   P 468, $1.95

"A superb whodunit in the best tradition of the detective story."

—August Derleth, *Madison Capital Times*

BOGUE'S FORTUNE   P 481, $1.95

"There's a touch of the old sardonic humour, and more than a touch of style."   —*The Spectator*

Julian Symons (cont'd)

THE COLOR OF MURDER   P 461, $1.95
"A singularly unostentatious and memorably brilliant detective story."
—*New York Herald Tribune Book Review*

Dorothy Stockbridge Tillet
(John Stephen Strange)

THE MAN WHO KILLED FORTESCUE   P 536, $2.25
"Better than average."   —*Saturday Review of Literature*

Simon Troy

THE ROAD TO RHUINE   P 583, $2.84
"Unusual and agreeably told."   —*San Francisco Chronicle*

SWIFT TO ITS CLOSE   P 546, $2.40
"A nicely literate British mystery . . . the atmosphere and the plot are
exceptionally well wrought, the dialogue excellent."   —*Best Sellers*

Henry Wade

THE DUKE OF YORK'S STEPS   P 588, $2.84
"A classic of the golden age."
—Jacques Barzun and Wendell Hertig Taylor, *A Catalogue of Crime*

A DYING FALL   P 543, $2.50
"One of those expert British suspense jobs . . . it crackles with undercur-
rents of blackmail, violent passion and murder. Topnotch in its class."
—*Time*

THE HANGING CAPTAIN   P 548, $2.50
"This is a detective story for connoisseurs, for those who value clear
thinking and good writing above mere ingenuity and easy thrills."
—*The Times* (London) *Literary Supplement*

Hillary Waugh

LAST SEEN WEARING . . .   P 552, $2.40
"A brilliant tour de force."   —Julian Symons

THE MISSING MAN   P 553, $2.40
"The quiet detailed police work of Chief Fred C. Fellows, Stockford,
Conn., is at its best in *The Missing Man* . . . one of the Chief's toughest
cases and one of the best handled."

—Anthony Boucher, *New York Times Book Review*

Henry Kitchell Webster

WHO IS THE NEXT?   P 539, $2.25

"A double murder, private-plane piloting, a neat impersonation, and a delicate courtship are adroitly combined by a writer who knows how to use the language."   —Jacques Barzun and Wendell Hertig Taylor

John Welcome

GO FOR BROKE   P 663, $2.84

A rich financier chases Richard Graham half 'round Europe in a desperate attempt to prevent the truth getting out.

RUN FOR COVER   P 664, $2.84

"I can think of few writers in the international intrigue game with such a gift for fast and vivid storytelling."

—New York Times Book Review

STOP AT NOTHING   P 665, $2.84

"Mr. Welcome is lively, vivid and highly readable."

—New York Times Book Review

Anna Mary Wells

MURDERER'S CHOICE   P 534, $2.50

"Good writing, ample action, and excellent character work."

—Saturday Review of Literature

A TALENT FOR MURDER   P 535, $2.25

"The discovery of the villain is a decided shock."   *—Books*

Charles Williams

DEAD CALM   P 655, $2.84

"A brilliant tour de force of inventive plotting, fine manipulation of a small cast and breathtaking sequences of spectacular navigation."

—New York Times Book Review

THE SAILCLOTH SHROUD   P 654, $2.84

"A fine novel of excitement, spirited, fresh and satisfying."

—New York Times

THE WRONG VENUS   P 656, $2.84

Swindler Lawrence Colby and the lovely Martine create a story of romance, larceny, and very blunt homicide.

Edward Young

THE FIFTH PASSENGER P 544, $2.25
"Clever and adroit . . . excellent thriller. . . ." —*Library Journal*

If you enjoyed this book you'll want to know about
THE PERENNIAL LIBRARY MYSTERY SERIES

Buy them at your local bookstore or use this coupon for ordering:

Qty	P number	Price
———	———	———
———	———	———
———	———	———
———	———	———
———	———	———
———	———	———
———	———	———
———	———	———
———	———	———
———	———	———
———	———	———
———	———	———
———	———	———

postage and handling charge $1.00
_____ book(s) @ $0.25

TOTAL

HARPER & ROW, Mail Order Dept. #PMS, 10 East 53rd St., New York, N.Y. 10022.
Please send me the books I have checked above. I am enclosing $_____ which includes a postage and handling charge of $1.00 for the first book and 25¢ for each additional book. Send check or money order. No cash or C.O.D.s please

Name_____

Address_____

City_____ State_____ Zip_____

Please allow 4 weeks for delivery. USA only. This offer expires 12/31/85
Please add applicable sales tax.